TWISTED SCREAMS

Praise for Sheri Lewis Wohl

Scarlet Revenge

"Vampire stories have been written by hundreds of authors, but this is probably one of the few times that you will actually see one who works at the Library of Congress…With the setting of the story, it almost gives the feel of *National Treasure* meets paranormal."—*American Library Association's GLBT Round Table*

Vermilion Justice

"It's probably impossible to read this book and not come across a character who reminds you of someone you actually know. Wohl takes something as fictional as vampires and makes them feel real. Highly recommended."—*American Library Association's GLBT Round Table*

Necromantia

"This is one of the most sensational and thrilling books I have read in a long time. From the stirring opening scenes to the dramatic and exhilarating conclusion, this novel keeps the reader completely engrossed."—*Rainbow Reviews*

By the Author

Crimson Vengeance

Burgundy Betrayal

Scarlet Revenge

Vermilion Justice

Twisted Echoes

Twisted Whispers

Twisted Screams

Necromantia

Visit us at www.boldstrokesbooks.com

TWISTED SCREAMS

by

Sheri Lewis Wohl

2016

TWISTED SCREAMS
© 2016 By Sheri Lewis Wohl. All Rights Reserved.

ISBN 13: 978-1-62639-647-0

This Trade Paperback Original Is Published By
Bold Strokes Books, Inc.
P.O. Box 249
Valley Falls, NY 12185

First Edition: September 2016

Credits
Editor: Shelley Thrasher
Production Design: Stacia Seaman
Cover Design by Sheri (graphicartist2020@hotmail.com)

This book is dedicated to

Linda Emerson,
whose art has always been an inspiration,
and her willingness to share her
talents to teach so many of us
is a testament to the generosity of her soul.

And to Steve Emerson,
whose incredible research
into the history of the Spokane area
has more than once helped
to ignite my imagination.

The weak can never forgive.
Forgiveness is the attribute
of the strong.

—Mahatma Gandhi

Chapter One

Sadie returned to consciousness with a start. Jesus, everything hurt. She pushed up to a sitting position and rubbed her head. When she moved even slightly, little sparks of bright light appeared in front of her eyes, and pain shot through her skull. She was no doctor, but she had to believe that wasn't a good thing.

What the hell had happened to her and where was she? Everything was foggy and unclear, made worse by the pounding in her head. How could she think when lightning bolts blasted across her skull? For at least a full minute she sat still, willing the waves of pain to subside. Tentatively, she tilted her head one direction and then the other. Her stomach didn't roll, and the sparks behind her eyes disappeared.

One more minute of stillness and she began to feel more like herself. She risked an unhurried look around, moving her head slowly so as not to trigger pain. Dim light filtered through windows caked with decades' worth of grime and fell across the dusty floor. A tall ceiling made the room feel massive. Lined up against the walls were rows of old metal bed frames that once had held their now-missing single mattresses. It was a dormitory, but where? She didn't remember the room or even coming into a building.

Think, Sadie, think. How in the world had she ended up in this dusty old building? Blackouts were not her thing, so surely if she tried hard enough she'd remember. Gradually, recollection rolled in and a whisper of relief loosened her shoulders. Unfortunately, it didn't help to make any more sense out of where she sat. She was so certain she hadn't gone into any building and definitely not into this room. She'd remember seeing this place if she had.

Earlier, she'd been out scouting locations for the television series her company would be filming over the next year. First, she'd checked out the old monastery on Mt. Spokane, and then she went to a fascinating homestead cemetery on the north side of town. Both turned out to be incredible and perfect locations for several episodes of the new series that would showcase the area. She'd been really excited by the finds, that much she did remember.

The cemetery was the last place she could clearly recall. Her next stop was to have been the abandoned grounds of the mental hospital west of the city, and if this was the hospital, she had no clue how she got here. She couldn't recall leaving the cemetery or even walking back to her car, for that matter. It was at least thirty miles between the cemetery and the hospital, so how in the world did she get here?

Her hands on the floor, she pushed until she was up and on her feet. The dizziness returned and for a moment she swayed. Chills raced down her spine, and she was afraid she might crumple back down to the dirty floor. With effort, she managed to stay on her feet, her legs still trembling a little. She took a deep breath and coughed like an old smoker. Good grief. It smelled as bad as it looked. She put a hand over her mouth and nose, her eyes watering. Slowly she took her hand away and let the odor of the room wash over her.

She scanned the room, and as she breathed in and out, the scent of the empty room took shape. By all rights it should smell of dust and disuse, except what hit her with hurricane force was more than the dirt and mold of a long-unused space. Something very different assailed her senses. This, she decided, reminded her of unwashed bodies and stale sweat. Like an old locker room that hadn't been cleaned in weeks or months. The scent also held a freshness, as if those who had passed through to leave a trail of odor behind had exited mere hours ago. Deliberately she did a full circle, taking in the tall walls, old furniture, and the cobwebs hanging from the corners.

What exactly she was looking for, she didn't know, and frankly, nothing jumped out at her. It was an old, unused room, empty save for the black, dented frames of the numerous single beds that looked sad in their neglected, discarded state. Certainly those things accounted for at least some of the scent of decay and abandonment. It was what she didn't see that confused her. No tossed-aside clothing, no visible dampness or mold, nothing that would fill the air with the odor of a recently vacated locker room.

Her heart always in the game, she shifted from confused to work mode. Briefly, she considered how this room would play on film. Light and dark, shadows and sunshine, crowded and spare. That it would work on a number of levels sent a shock of excitement through her, and she wished she had her tablet in hand so she could take pictures and make notes. Then a shot of pain zipped through her head again, and all thoughts of work, cameras, and sets disappeared.

As she massaged her temples with her fingers it occurred to her that maybe it was all in her head. Judging by the way it hurt, she could have suffered a concussion, and if that was true, she might easily imagine things that weren't there. Yes, that must be it. She was suffering from a head injury, and that's why she couldn't remember how she came to be in this room. Or, for that matter, how she'd even hit her head.

The way she figured it, the best thing she could do was get outside and draw in a good long breath of fresh air. Get away from all the dust and God knows what else that was circulating in the air she was breathing in and out. Once her head cleared, she'd be able to figure out exactly what had happened. Come to think of it, her car was probably outside too, along with her cell phone and her tablet with mobile Internet access. Help was a quick call and email away.

At the opposite end of the room was a single closed door and, she realized, her only way out. It struck her a little odd as she made her way to the door that a room this large had only one avenue for ingress and egress. What kind of architect would design this type of room with only one door? Then again, it was an old building, and things in decades past didn't always make sense in today's world. With each step, her head pounded like someone was smacking her with a baseball bat. Whatever she'd done, she'd done it in a big way. This was going to take a bit more than fresh air. Probably more like an ice bag and a handful of ibuprofen. Or, though she hated to consider it, a trip to the ER.

At the door, she closed her hand around the brass knob and twisted. It was cold and hard in her hand, and it didn't budge, not even a centimeter. Well, now that didn't make a whole lot of sense, considering it had to have turned for her to get in here in the first place. She tried harder. Still nothing. She let her hand drop away and stepped back, biting her lip as she studied the stubborn door. Even though the pain inside her head was now pounding away at hurricane force, the truth pierced the fog: locked. Not just locked, either, but locked from the outside, as if whoever occupied the beds were prisoners more than occupants.

One more time she tried. "What's the definition of stupid," she muttered to the empty room. "Trying the same thing over and over and expecting a different result." Her self-incrimination fell on an empty and silent room.

Panic started to rise as the reality of her situation settled in, and her hands trembled as she patted her pockets. Maybe she hadn't left her cell in the car, but as she thumped her hands against her pockets, her heart sank; the cell phone wasn't on her. More than likely, she'd dropped it in the bag she used when scouting locations. She carried all sorts of things in that bag: a cell phone, her SLR camera, a sketch pad, some granola bars.

The bag went where she went, so it had to be here somewhere. Again, she surveyed the room. It wasn't anywhere in sight. No closed closet doors or cubby holes where she could have dropped it. In fact, the only thing in the room besides the skeleton bed frames was her. Her bag wasn't here.

Forcing herself to stay calm, Sadie looked around one more time. If she couldn't make a call, she had to find another way to get out of this place. The windows beckoned to her like the proverbial light at the end of the tunnel. That was it: she could crawl out a window. It made perfect sense. Once more ignoring the pounding in her head, she hurried over to the old, dirty windows. The sooner she got the hell out of this room, the sooner she could get home to her bottle of ibuprofen and her nice comfortable sofa, where she could relax and put her feet up. Most of all, she could give Anna a kiss and tell her how much she loved her.

At the bank of windows covering the south wall, she stopped and stared, and tears began to pool in her eyes. Even if she could find a way to open one of them, it was pretty clear she wouldn't be crawling out. If she managed to break away enough of the rusted bars to squeeze through—and she was coherent enough to realize that was a long shot—the four-story drop would more than likely kill her. Her back against the wall, Sadie slid to the floor and gave in to sobs.

❖

"No fucking way." Lorna Dutton stared at the phone and refused to touch it. While she understood it was an inanimate object, she had the feeling that if her fingers came in contact with the phone, it would burn them. She wanted nothing to do with it or the person on the other end of it, so she kept her hands clamped to her sides.

The very last person in the world she expected to hear from was Anna, yet that's exactly what Jolene Austin, her housekeeper extraordinaire who also happened to be her girlfriend's mother, was telling her as she held the phone toward her. Seconds before the phone rang, she'd been enjoying great coffee and great conversation in her bright kitchen, feeling optimistic about the start to the day. Talk about a buzz kill.

Jolene patiently waited, the phone held out toward Lorna, while her girlfriend, Renee, looked at her and raised an eyebrow. "Really?" she said with an edge of sarcasm. Renee was the best, and Lorna loved every minute she spent with her. Except maybe for this particular minute. She couldn't believe she was advocating that Lorna take the call.

Lorna pressed her lips together before blowing out a long breath, her hands still at her sides. This shouldn't require an explanation. "Yeah, really."

What the hell did she want to talk to Anna for? She'd dumped Lorna like she suffered from a contagious disease, and, Jesus, how she'd felt like shit for such a long time. In fact, she lived here on the coast of the Pacific Ocean instead of across the mountains in her hometown of Spokane because the future she'd thought she had with Anna had blown apart. Not in a pretty way either. No, it had blown like Mount St. Helens back in the eighties, covering everything with gray ash for hundreds of miles and making everything look like a barren, alien landscape. That's how she'd felt at the time, gray and lifeless. She'd come here to hide and wallow in her misery, though as it all worked out, she'd discovered a wonderful new life that the beautiful Renee completed.

Come to think of it, Renee should be supportive in this one. Of all people, she knew how badly Anna had treated her and how hurt she'd been. Renee was the one to help her come out of the darkness and back into the light. Step by step, day by day, Renee was there for her, and slowly she'd come to see that her life hadn't ended. In fact, it had just begun in so many ways.

Even given the happy ending to her tale of heartbreak, she didn't owe Anna a damn thing. She refused to let her cast a cloud over what was turning out to be a great morning, and she wasn't going to talk to her. Regardless of what Renee might think, she was going to hold a grudge, and that was that. She'd earned the right to dig in her heels on this one.

"No," she said firmly. "I'm not talking to her. Not today, not tomorrow, not ever." She turned her gaze away from the phone that Jolene still patiently held without bothering to cover the mouthpiece. Anna, she was quite sure, was hearing the conversation taking place in the kitchen. Perhaps the best thing she could do was have another cup of Jolene's excellent coffee, so that's exactly what she did. Her hands shook a little as she poured coffee from the carafe into the mug, and silently she cursed herself. She was not bothered by this; she was not. Holding the hot mug between her hands, she leaned against the counter and pretended nothing at all had happened to disturb their congenial conversation.

Renee shook her head before sticking her hand out. "Give it to me, Mom. If one of us is too childish to take a call, I'll have to be the adult here."

This time Jolene raised an eyebrow and a smile twitched at the corners of her mouth, but she still didn't say anything, just handed the phone to Renee. Lorna didn't move from where she continued to lean against the counter. She loved Renee, but her beautiful girlfriend wasn't going to make her do something she was dead set against doing. Right was right and wrong was wrong. She was right. Anna was wrong.

On the other side of the kitchen, Lorna's brother, Jeremy, was sitting at the kitchen table next to his pregnant fiancée, Merry. They looked at each other with expressions that seemed to say, "Oh, shit." It wasn't a stretch to figure out what they were thinking. The old Lorna might wig out, but they needn't worry. She hadn't been that person for a long time. Not that it changed anything about the current state of things. She didn't intend to talk to Anna; neither did she intend to let her call disturb her day.

"Anna," Renee said in a friendly tone as she put the phone to her ear. "This is Renee Austin. I'm…" She paused for a second as she looked at Lorna and then smiled broadly. Her eyes were dancing as she continued. "Lorna's fiancée."

Lorna felt her mouth fall open, and she came perilously close to dropping the freshly filled coffee mug she held between two hands. Renee just looked at her, smiled even bigger, and shrugged.

"Lorna isn't available right at the moment. Can I do something for you, or can I give her a message?"

Renee's smile disappeared as she listened, and her eyes narrowed in concentration. As Lorna watched her, she started to lose her righteous anger, only to have it replaced by curiosity.

Renee was nodding as she spoke. "I understand, and I'll talk with Lorna. I promise you, we'll give you a call back as soon as possible." Renee pushed the end button on the phone and stared at it as if it was the first time she'd ever seen one before she raised her eyes to Lorna's. She didn't move to replace the handset.

"I'm not calling her back," Lorna declared. If she was five, she'd have stomped her feet too, but since she was slightly older than that, she just stood her ground sans the foot-stomping.

Besides, it didn't matter what Anna had said to Renee. Lorna had no intention of returning that call. In fact, if she got her way, she never planned to speak to Anna again. True, she was incredibly happy right now, and it was way past time to let go of the hurt Anna had caused her. Knowing it and doing it, however, were two completely different animals. Each time she thought about Anna, fury rose in her chest and she couldn't seem to let it go. Her reaction was stupid, and intellectually she understood that fact. It was all pure emotion, and so far she'd failed to bridge the gap between pain and forgiveness. Someday maybe she'd be able to do it, but that day hadn't arrived yet. So whatever Anna wanted or needed, she was going to have to go somewhere else for help. She had plenty of friends on the other side of the mountains, and she could just tap one of them.

Renee studied her for a long moment, turning the handset

over and over in her hands, and then said quietly, "I think you have to."

"No, I don't." This was obviously going to be one of those rare times when they didn't agree.

Holding up her hand, Renee said, "Hear me out. I think you'll change your mind when you know why she called."

"I doubt that," Lorna muttered, knowing that she sounded like a pissed-off little kid. Still, she couldn't think of a single thing that would ever change her mind.

"Her wife is missing."

Of all the things she'd anticipated Renee saying, that was the last. No, not the last, because it wasn't even a consideration. Wife? What the fuck? Since when did Anna have a wife? She didn't let any grass grow under her feet, did she? Lorna brought her gaze up to meet Renee's. "And that concerns me why?"

"It concerns you because you're in a unique position to help."

"What exactly am I supposed to help with?"

Renee sighed, almost as if she were explaining something to a child. Okay, so maybe she was acting a little childish, but she figured she was entitled when it came to Anna.

"Look, I get why this is difficult for you. I really do. It doesn't change my feelings about this. Anna's wife went out to do some work and never came back. The police aren't helping yet because they don't think she's been gone long enough. You're in a unique position to help find her, to make a difference."

So far she wasn't convincing Lorna. "If she truly is missing, the police will step in."

Shaking her head, she said, "Not for at least another day, and you know how time can be critical. This has nothing to do with what happened between you and Anna and everything to do with helping to find an innocent woman before something terrible happens. I know you, Lorna. If something happens to Anna's wife and you could have a made a difference, you'll never forgive yourself."

"Crap," she muttered under her breath. Now she was starting to get to her. Too much of what Renee said rang of truth. It wasn't fair, and she shouldn't have to do something she didn't want to.

They'd just gotten home from spending time in Spokane helping Lorna's old friend, Theodora Lane, in a heartbreaking search for her twin sister, Alida. With the aid of a sheriff's department investigator, Katie Carlisle, they'd found her. Sadly, she was dead, as were a number of other women. The only upside to that trip was that their discovery had exposed a serial killer who was also a sheriff's deputy. They'd stopped him, and he'd never be able to hurt another woman again.

Not only did she not want to go back to Spokane right now, but she also didn't want to do a damn thing for Anna. She knew from firsthand experience that Spokane employed plenty of law enforcement for situations like this. In fact, the one thing she was willing to do was to call Katie and see how she could assist Anna. That was the extent of her inclination to help. She wasn't heading over the mountains again anytime soon. Period. Especially not for the woman who'd turned her back on her. Nope, not going to do it.

"Lorna." Renee reached over and took her hand. The look she gave her was full of compassion and understanding. "If there's a chance you can help her and save her wife's life, we have to go. It's the right thing to do and you know it."

"I don't owe her anything," Lorna bit out. She refused to bend to guilt or arguments that weighed on her sense of right and wrong. That wasn't playing fair, especially when it came to Anna. Where had right and wrong been when she was cheating behind Lorna's back? Where was it when she'd looked Lorna in the eye and said "I love you," knowing all the time it was a big fat lie? She was sorry Anna's bride was missing, despite the fact it grated on her that she'd gotten married about ten seconds after she'd dumped Lorna. In truth, it wasn't her problem, and she wasn't going to be guilted into making it her problem.

"No." Renee squeezed her hand. "You don't owe her one

single thing. Baby, this isn't about Anna, and it's not about you. This is about a woman whose life might be saved if you use your gift."

Reaching behind her, she set the coffee mug on the counter, spilling some of the hot coffee as she did. Emotion welled up, and she took three deep breaths, trying not to let tears fall. This wasn't fair. "I can't…" But she couldn't finish.

"Yes, you can," Renee said softly. "You can, my love."

Lorna looked over at Jeremy and Merry, hoping for a little help. Surely they would understand, as they'd both been there for the fallout. They'd seen firsthand how crushed she'd been and how difficult it had been in the days afterward.

Merry spoke up. "What did Anna tell you exactly? I mean, how does she know her wife is actually missing? Any number of things could have happened. From what I gather, they jumped into marriage pretty damn quick."

"You make a good point," Renee said. "Her wife Sadie went to work early yesterday morning and never came back. Now consider this. If Jeremy didn't show up tonight, was gone all day tomorrow, he didn't answer his phone, and he didn't check in, what would you think?"

Merry turned to stare at Jeremy, her eyes searching his face. "I wouldn't think anything. I would know something was very wrong. He would never do that to me." She reached over and took his hand.

Renee turned to look at Lorna. "Just as I would know if Lorna was lost or hurt or in danger, Anna knows something has happened to Sadie or she would never have risked a call to you."

Jeremy nodded ever so slightly, his eyes holding Merry's. "Gotta go with Renee on this one, sis. I'd know in a heartbeat if Merry was in danger."

"Wha…" She couldn't believe her own brother was turning on her.

He held up a hand. "Hear me out. You're right that you don't owe Anna anything, but this thing you can do is bigger than any of us. You're kind of the superhero here, and it wouldn't be very superheroish if you turned down a damsel in distress. If Anna believes something terrible has happened to her wife, I, for one, believe her."

He winked, and her heart lightened somewhat. He always had a way of bringing her light when the darkness tried to intrude. His wink made her smile…just a little. "You do have a way with words."

"To know me is to love me." His grin spread across his face while Merry shook her head and rolled her eyes.

"Blowhard that your brother is," Merry said with a smile, "he's right. I think it's important for a number of reasons to help Anna. We would all feel bad if she's harmed and we didn't at least try to help."

"Is this your legal opinion?" Merry was, after all, the one attorney in their family.

Merry's smile grew and she shook her head. "Nothing legal here. It's one hundred percent my personal opinion. It isn't about condoning what Anna did to you. That was wrong and always will be. That said, this is about providing assistance to another woman who could be in danger. You were given that gift for a reason, and I personally believe it was for situations such as this. So, for what it's worth to you, I say we go."

Lorna studied each face in turn and then nodded slowly. "All right. I'm not dense enough to not know when I'm beaten. I'll call her back, but you all talked me into this, and that means you all get to go with me."

Renee kissed her on the cheek as she pressed the phone into her hand. "Deal. You know we're all here for you. Always."

"Can I get that in writing?"

"We do have an attorney present," Jeremy said and patted Merry on the shoulder. "And she can come up with one mean contract." He winked at her.

"I'll work it up when I get back to my computer," Merry said with a laugh. "I'll start with 'all for one and one for all.'"

Lorna took the phone and studied it for a moment. She looked up and narrowed her eyes as she studied Renee. "So, before I hit redial, tell me about this fiancée I have."

❖

Anna Frye put down the receiver and stared at it as tears began to drip down her cheeks. The call had shaken her more than she'd imagined it would, and she'd imagined all sorts of outcomes. If Lorna had told her to go fuck herself, she wouldn't have blamed her. Lorna was entitled to feel that way. She'd treated her like shit, and what she'd done to her was unforgivable. If the shoe was on the other foot, she'd never have taken that call.

Still, she couldn't help but reach out for any and all lines of defense. She'd done the best she could at the time, because back then, she didn't know how to end it. Somewhere along the way she'd realized that they were far better friends than lovers. She saw it and felt it, but Lorna didn't. Anna remembered being a bit shell shocked by the truth of it before going into protection mode. Things hadn't been right between them, and every day it seemed to grow a little worse, a little heavier on her shoulders. When Sadie had come into her life, all the problems simmering between her and Lorna had become so glaring she'd never figured out how Lorna missed them. She didn't miss a thing and chose to take the coward's way out. No, more like grabbed it with both hands and ran. Her actions had hurt Lorna deeply, and no matter what had been happening at the time, it hadn't been fair to her.

Since then she'd wanted to go to her at least a hundred times and apologize. Lorna wouldn't talk to her and she didn't push it. Despite all her regrets, she knew she didn't have the right to insist, and to be brutally honest, she didn't push it because it was easier. She quit trying and told herself it was okay because if Lorna wouldn't talk to her, it wasn't her fault she couldn't apologize.

Lorna had always been the tougher of the two of them. Anna

knew she'd broken her heart and at the same time knew she'd recover. That was the way it was with Lorna. She could face any fire and come out stronger on the other side. She had the heart of a warrior. Anna did not.

Now, she was desperate enough to face a fire of her own and risk the burn that would surely come. Six months ago, when she'd married Sadie, her world for the first time ever had felt complete. Regardless of the poor decisions she might have made in the past, the act of saying "I do" to Sadie was one hundred percent right. Happily-ever-after was never something she figured would come her way, yet when she wasn't looking that's exactly what had happened.

Until twenty-four hours ago.

The morning had started like most of them, with coffee and small talk at the kitchen table. It was a routine that warmed her heart just by virtue of its simple normalcy. She loved their mornings together and the way they set the tone for the coming day. Anna had headed out to her office, and Sadie went to work as well. Then poof, it was as if Sadie had dropped off the face of the earth. Her iPhone was off, her car was nowhere to be found, and she didn't come home. Anna had waited for hours, watching out the front window for the telltale lights of her car, thinking that perhaps she hadn't called because her phone battery had died.

Finally, Anna gave merit to the rising tide of fear and called the police. They weren't a lot of help. Sadie was an adult. Sadie hadn't been gone even twenty-four hours. Sadie would probably call. On and on it went with not one, but three different officers. By the time she finished talking to the third officer, she'd wanted to scream.

The police might think she'd run off, but they were full of it. Anna knew better. They had their rules and regulations, and they had their theories based on, Anna had to admit, years of experience. But none of it changed what she felt in her bones: something bad had happened to Sadie.

She'd tried to explain her own theories to them, like the fact that the television series being filmed in Spokane afforded Sadie the opportunity to fully stretch her artistic wings. When she'd dropped out of sight she was scouting locations, and that, she'd told all three officers, was something that thrilled her. No way would she take off and give it up. This television series was the opportunity of a lifetime, and Sadie would never throw that away. She wouldn't want to leave town, because every time she went to work, she almost glowed with happy anticipation for what the new day would bring. When Sadie'd left the house that morning, she'd been really excited about the day.

After officer number three essentially blew her off, Anna felt she'd had no choice but to walk away from the police station. They couldn't, or wouldn't, help her at this point. But Anna wasn't about to let their lack of response deter her. Maybe law enforcement intended to wait, but she didn't. She had to think of some other way to find Sadie.

As she'd stood in the kitchen rolling it all over in her mind, Anna had looked down at the newspaper on the table and seen the article about Lorna and her newly discovered psychic ability. Frankly, she was surprised. In all their time together, Lorna had never admitted to so much as a twitch, let alone shown any sign of being a psychic. Still, the article was pretty flattering, as it described how she'd uncovered the truth about a hundred-year-old murder and helped capture a serial killer right here in river city.

She'd held the paper between her hands and stared at the words for a long time. If Lorna could do anything even close to what they'd written about her, it was worth a try. She'd do anything at this point to find her wife. Anything, and if that meant groveling to Lorna, so be it. Begging was absolutely on the table.

She started when Halle jumped up on the table and bumped against her shoulder. "You know better than to jump on the table." She scolded her cat but without any malice. The warmth of the little creature was a huge comfort to her.

The tortoiseshell cat rubbed up against her arm and purred.

She'd never been much of a cat person until she'd met Sadie. Before then, she'd always believed the furry little things to be aloof and without much in the way of personality. She'd considered herself a dog person. They were far friendlier and way smarter. Or so she'd believed. Boy, had she been wrong on all counts. Halle was a character, and that was putting it mildly. She was smart, friendly, and entertaining.

Sadie and Halle came as a package deal. Get one, get both, and she'd been so in love with Sadie, she was willing to give it a try despite her anti-cat mentality. It hadn't taken long for Halle to suck her in. After getting to know her, she couldn't imagine not sharing her home with a cat. It was a win-win. She got the woman and she got the cat.

"We have to find her," she said against Halle's neck. "I hope we have help."

Halle rubbed harder, her purr loud in the quiet kitchen. It was almost as if she were saying, "We'll find her."

CHAPTER TWO

R enee was a little worried despite her vocal show of bravado. She knew exactly how much Lorna had loved Anna and how deeply she'd been hurt at Anna's betrayal. It took a long time to bring her back from the despair that had turned her world gray, and the woman who'd emerged from that fog had captured her heart completely. In fact, she had realized not so long ago that she'd never loved anyone more.

Her road to this once-in-a-lifetime love had been long and bumpy and totally unexpected. She'd been the good girl, the one who did what was expected of her, like get married to a nice man everyone in her family loved. The last thing she'd ever wanted to do was disappoint the people who mattered to her. Her mother. Aunt Bea. They were so pleased the day she walked down the aisle.

Unfortunately, the marriage was a sham, and she'd realized it quite soon after she'd said "I do." Or if she was being really honest, before those two words had ever passed her lips. On her wedding day she'd stood in that dressing room staring at herself in the full-length mirror and didn't see a happy bride staring back at her. What she'd seen was a woman trapped and one too cowardly to set herself free. She'd stayed in the marriage because she'd believed it was the right thing to do. So what if she felt empty? So what if she felt like running away? She'd made a commitment and intended to see it through.

In the end, she had come to understand it was all an ugly lie that she couldn't continue to carry forward. She'd been incredibly unfair to her now ex-husband, Bryan, and unfair to herself. Both of them had deserved to be happy, and neither of them was. She'd left Bryan, and despite the hurt she'd caused him, she'd believed with all her heart it was the right thing to do.

Even now, she could recall how angry he'd been with her, and he'd been justified in his feelings. Particularly considering that, at the time, she still hadn't crossed over to embrace her own truth. That came later, when she was finally able to admit it to herself. Denial was so comforting, but truth had a way of making itself known despite all obstacles.

Peace, at least for her, came the day she'd stepped out of the proverbial closet and accepted what she'd dimly known all along. She didn't abandon her marriage because she didn't love Bryan. In her own way she loved him very much and always would. But she didn't want to be his lover; she wanted to be his best friend. Her ideal lover didn't sport the shadow of a beard or pee standing up. No, her heart had longed for another, who was soft and rounded, full breasted, and all woman.

As she'd evolved into the woman she'd always wanted to be, Bryan's bitterness toward her had grown. Once again she couldn't blame him. It was tough enough going through a divorce under normal circumstances, but finding out your wife had left you because she wanted to love another woman, well, that could be a hard pill to swallow. He was a good guy, but even good guys had their limits.

Today things were still a bit strained between her and Bryan, and though she hated it, she understood. Perhaps someday he would be able to forgive her enough to be friends once again, and she hoped that day would come. She still loved him and prayed he would find it in his heart to love her again too.

If Lorna felt that same reluctance to be around Anna that Bryan did toward Renee, she really didn't have the right to push it. Except this situation was different, and despite her own reservations, deep in her heart she felt they needed to help. It was unfortunate that the aid needed to come primarily from Lorna. Just the same, it was unavoidable. The universe in its infinite wisdom had seen fit to bestow the gift of sight upon Lorna, and all Renee, Jeremy, and Merry could do was be there to support her.

Gazing at Lorna now, her heart constricted. Being there for Anna was the right thing to do, yet she hated the thought of having Lorna in the same room with Anna. Renee had seen pictures of the woman, and she was beautiful. In fact, not only was she beautiful, but she was incredibly accomplished as well.

In comparison, what did Renee really have to offer? Her home and livelihood had gone up in flames. She was essentially jobless and homeless. Well, she did have a million-dollar offer for her property on the table, and that was something, except it was just money, and that wasn't likely to be the thing that would attract Lorna. She wasn't that shallow.

Asking her to be with Anna again was like throwing a match on gas-soaked logs. Who knew what kind of sparks still existed between the two women, ones that could potentially ignite? Their breakup had been ugly, but that didn't mean a reunion might not be tender or stir the sort of feelings that had brought them together in the first place. She could lose the life she was living now, the plans she'd made with Jeremy and Merry to rebuild her company after losing it all to a fire, and the dreams she had for a future with Lorna. By pushing this, she was putting everything important to her at risk.

She shifted her gaze to her mother, Jolene, who gave her a slight nod. Sometimes she had the feeling her mother could actually read her mind. It had been that way since she was a kid and hadn't changed in the years since. Mom knew the truth, just as she did, and she sensed the risks, just as she did. Turning away from this situation would be wrong. Her mom gave her another tiny nod, and Renee managed not to sigh. Sometimes a person just had to walk into the fire and hope to hell she walked out alive on the other side.

Her eyes went to the handset Lorna held. "Call her," she said. "And when you're done, we'll talk about the fiancée thing."

Silently she prayed she was making the right decision and wasn't about to lose everything she held precious.

❖

Jeremy would be lying if he said he was one hundred percent okay with this recent turn of events. Yeah, he totally believed Lorna needed to take the trip back across the mountains. Whatever this psychic thing was that his sister had developed, she rocked it, and it seemed like it had some greater-good element they couldn't, or more accurately, shouldn't ignore. Karma could be a nasty bitch if blown off.

So far, she'd solved a hundred-year-old mystery here at the house, and then she'd helped find a murdered friend back in Spokane and in the process stopped a serial killer who didn't appear to be in the mood to stop killing. Without Lorna's psychic gift, who knew if anyone would ever have recovered the body of Catherine Swan or stopped the killer in Spokane. Now, from what Renee told them, Anna's wife was missing and could be hurt or in danger. Anna's situation wasn't that very different from the other two.

Except it was different, at least in one very important way. Anna had hurt Lorna, and he'd been there during the aftermath. At one time he'd wondered if he'd ever get his sister back, and he blamed Anna for that. Yes, he got that every story had two sides, and honestly, he wasn't sorry they weren't together any longer. In his opinion, Anna wasn't the one for Lorna and never had been. That said, the way Anna had ended it was inexcusable, and a part of him would always hold that against her.

Despite everything, he didn't hold on to animosity. He could forgive even if he never quite forgot. He could be friendly with Anna even if he would never fully trust her. Did he wish her harm? No. Did he wish harm to the woman she married? Absolutely not. And, in reality, good people did not turn away from this kind of plea for help. He wanted to believe they were good people.

So he would urge Lorna to help and flex her super-power muscles and use them to get Sadie back home. He would urge Lorna to trek the high road, and he would be there beside her every step of the way. He didn't intend to take a bitch-slap from karma anytime in the near future.

Besides, in not too many months he was going to be a father, and that changed the rules of the game in a big way. He wanted to be the kind of parent a child looked up to. That meant doing the right thing, like helping out his sister's ex-girlfriend even when he wanted to tell her to fuck off. Oh, yeah, and he was going to have to clean up his mouth too.

"What are you thinking about, handsome?"

Merry came up beside him where he stood on the patio overlooking the expanse of ocean shoreline and put her arms around him. He loved the way she felt, her warm and swelling belly pressed against him. She was more beautiful than ever, and that was saying a lot considering she had been, in his opinion, stunning from day one. It was true what they said about expectant mothers. They glowed.

"I'm just thinking about this thing with Anna."

Merry kissed his cheek and then laid her head on his shoulder. "You were right, what you said in there. Lorna has to help. We all do. My new-mother intuition seems to be kicking in, and it's telling me it's important we all do this together."

"It's going to be painful for her."

"Probably."

"We have to be there for her."

"Without question."

"I have to marry you soon."

"Absolutely."

He wrapped her in his arms, and this time he laid his head against the top of hers. "I love you."

CHAPTER THREE

Clancy jumped up on the bed and grabbed a single sneaker out of her suitcase. Looking at her as if to say "ha ha," he jumped off the bed and carried it out of the room. Lorna laughed, knowing she'd find the sneaker, intact though slobbered up, near the windows in the living room. It was a game Clancy played with her daily. Usually he grabbed a shoe from the closet, but today he seemed to be making a statement by unpacking the shoe she'd tucked in the suitcase.

"I don't think Clancy believes I should make this trip," Lorna said to Renee, who was, like her, packing a small suitcase. "It would probably be a good idea to listen to him. Dogs have a good sense of right and wrong."

Renee cocked an eyebrow and shook her head. "Clancy's a smart dog, and he'd urge you to do the right thing. He's just showboating by taking a shoe out of your suitcase. Nice try, though."

Lorna smiled because even though she didn't like it, Renee was right. Clancy was playing, and Lorna enjoyed the game as much as he did. Turning, she stared out the master-bedroom windows. Outside, twilight was settling in and darkness was following close behind. It had taken her hours to make peace with this trip. She should have left shortly after taking Anna's call, but she couldn't get herself moving, and everyone had wisely let her work through her slow start in her own time.

"Why don't I feel anything?" she asked Renee. Honestly she wasn't sure if she meant she didn't feel anything toward Anna or that she didn't feel any psychic pull at all.

Renee walked up to stand beside her at the window. "I don't know," she said after a moment. "Maybe there's more to this than what you experienced with Catherine Swan and Alida Canwell. Who knows, considering there's no user's guide for what you can do. Or maybe we just need to be closer to Spokane for you to start picking up vibes."

Those two names Renee said so casually sent chills through her whole body. Catherine Swan was the murdered Makah woman Lorna had been led to by the ghost of her love, Tiana McCafferty. Alida Canwell was her childhood friend who fell victim to a vindictive serial killer. She had found them both and brought them home. As heart-wrenching as it had been to find the bodies of the murdered women, it had also been satisfying to know they were no longer lost and alone. Since she was stuck with this thing, whatever it was, it was comforting to know she could bring the lost home.

Which led right straight back to the original question: could she really turn her back on Anna's plea for help in finding Sadie just because her heart had been bruised? If she could, what did that say about her? Nothing good, that was for certain. No matter what direction she came at the question, she had to go, and she knew it. The knowledge didn't make this trip any easier. Having Renee at her side was the only thing that did.

Slowly she turned and looked at Renee. "So, tell me again about my fiancée."

A look somewhere between sheepish and delighted crossed Renee's face. "Well, it seemed like the right thing to say at the time."

"Really? That's what popped into your mind when you were talking to my ex?" The thought sent warmth flowing through her. Though they'd never talked about marriage, the idea was not unpleasant or unwelcome.

Renee's smile lit up her eyes. "Well, how was I going to get Anna's attention if I didn't give her something to think about? After all, she ran right into the arms of another woman, and I didn't want her thinking you were just sitting around moping, now did I?"

Lorna couldn't help but return her smile. "I kinda *was* sitting around moping, if you remember, and it wasn't pretty."

Renee put her hand against Lorna's cheek. "You know that and I know that, but she doesn't need to. This is what's called having your back."

"God, I love you."

"Right back atcha."

Lorna put her hand over Renee's where it still rested against her cheek. "So let's talk about this fiancée thing…"

Renee's smile grew, but before she could say a thing, Jeremy came winging into the room. "Come on, you two. Quit with the lovey-dovey stuff and get your butts moving. We've got pavement to burn. I hate driving the pass in the dark, and it's going to be dark really soon."

Renee grabbed her suitcase, gave Lorna a peck on the cheek, and zipped out of the room. Apparently, they'd be talking about it later. Lorna grabbed her own suitcase and headed toward the front door. Later was fine, but they would talk about it.

Anna tried Sadie's cell phone again and, just like every other time she'd called, had no luck. Over the last few hours she'd called everyone she worked with. Nobody had seen her since bright and early yesterday morning, but according to her coworkers, that wasn't unusual during this phase of the project. When Sadie was scouting, it could be several days before she checked in. She'd been known to cover hundreds of miles gathering pictures and making sketches of places she thought would work for a given movie or, as in this case, a weekly television series. No one in her office had given it a second thought that she hadn't called in yet.

Apparently the only one who knew something was wrong was Anna. The police didn't believe her. Sadie's coworkers didn't find it odd. She felt it deep in her stomach, and the sensation made her ill. Was this her penance for taking the coward's way out when it came to ending her relationship with Lorna? Maybe she had it coming, but to take it out on Sadie wasn't right.

From her point of view, they couldn't waste any time before trying everything possible to locate Sadie. Obviously from her fruitless efforts so far, she couldn't do it alone. Until the call she'd made to Lorna, nobody wanted to extend help of any kind, except Lorna. Anna wasn't entirely convinced she had bought into the idea that Sadie was in trouble either, but unlike the others, she was willing to help. It said a lot about the woman she'd turned her back on.

It also said a lot about her that she would walk away from someone like Lorna. Not in a good way, either.

Getting caught up in her own character flaws was a waste of precious time. It was water under the bridge. She couldn't change any of it now, and even if she could, Anna didn't believe she would. The realization that she and Lorna weren't the forever kind of couple hadn't dawned on her in a flash of understanding but rather in a gradually growing understanding that she had to be free.

At the time, she'd realized they were on different sheets of music. Clearly she could have found better ways to handle breaking away, but she chose a path that was selfish and self-serving. It was easier, but then again the coward's way usually was.

She frankly didn't deserve the help that was on its way. Lorna could, and probably should, have told her to go to hell. That she didn't made Anna want to start crying all over again. Once Sadie was safely back home, she would find a way to make amends.

Now, staring out the window into the darkness punctuated by the stream of golden glow of the streetlight, she waited for headlights to pull into the driveway. Each and every approaching vehicle made her jump. Each time another car passed by, her heart sank.

Again and again her thoughts turned to Sadie. She could see her as she was the morning she left, cheerful and full of life. She was always that way, and it was one of the things that had drawn her to Sadie. She needed that spark of positive energy in her life, and it made every day a little better because of it. The fact that Sadie was also beautiful and sexy and smart as hell didn't hurt either. For Anna, she was the total package, that once-in-a-lifetime chance that she'd grabbed with both hands. She wasn't going to let go now either.

After hours of watching the comings and goings of traffic out her front window, hoping each and every car held Lorna, her vigil paid off. The lights of a vehicle glowed in the distance, growing ever larger and brighter as they came slowly down the street. They were extinguished when the SUV turned and then came to a stop in her driveway. Her breath caught in her throat, and her heart felt as though a band had tightened around it. Help was finally here.

She forced herself to move from the window and out the front door. The doors of the SUV opened and four people emerged. Three of them she recognized: Lorna, Jeremy, and Merry. The fourth woman she'd never seen before. The fiancée? She had to believe it was the woman she'd spoken with on the phone, and a flutter of something she didn't want to name hit her heart. She ignored it and charged out the door.

Without giving herself a chance to change her mind, she hurried to the driveway and threw her arms around Lorna. Tears streaked her face, and in the back of her mind she thought she looked tired, drawn, and well, just plain awful, and maybe that wasn't so bad. At least Lorna wouldn't have any questions as to how worried she was. "Thank you," she cried as she hugged the woman she'd once lied to when she'd told her she would love her forever. "Thank you."

❖

The streak that came flying across the sidewalk to envelop Lorna in a hug was tall and beautiful. Slender in blue jeans and a white shirt, she was barefoot and devoid of makeup. Though she looked exhausted and stressed, she was lovely in a way Renee would never be. She hated her instantly and had to stifle the urge to scream, "Get away from my woman!"

As it turned out, Lorna gave her a brief, tight hug, then stepped out of the embrace. Her movements were calm and cool, and something about that quality put Renee at ease. Lorna casually slung an arm around the woman's shoulders and turned her to face the three of them. "Renee, this is Anna."

Her face was tear-stained and distraught, her poise and grace were alluring, and Renee wanted to load everyone back into the SUV and race straight back to the coast. All along, she'd convinced herself she was giving wise counsel to Lorna. Now that they were here, she realized how wrong she'd been. Anna was everything Renee was not. Tall, willowy, lovely, and from the looks of the house, wealthy. Of course, Renee had to remind herself she wasn't exactly destitute after the sale of her downtown Seattle building, so at least on that score she could stand neck and neck with the amazing Anna.

On every other score, she was sorely lacking, which made her heart hurt, and she desperately wanted to run and hide. Lorna hadn't wanted to come here and she'd been the one to push her. Now her own stupid ideals were going to be the very thing to take away the first real happiness she'd known. She was going to lose Lorna, and it was her own stupid fault.

It was more than just the way Anna looked. Her aura flowed around her like a rainbow cape of colors. In it, Renee glimpsed the soul of the woman Lorna had loved with all her heart. In it she detected not evil or hatred, but the mind, body, and spirit of a basically good woman. True, she'd done Lorna wrong. At her core, however, she wasn't a bad person, and that made Renee hate her all the more. She'd wanted to find her ugly and mean.

"Anna," she managed to say in a deceptively calm voice. It was amazing what she could dredge up when she had to. She solemnly shook the other woman's hand. "It's nice to meet you," she lied. "I'm so sorry it has to be under these circumstances."

"Thank you for coming. You have no idea how much this means to me. All of you." Her gaze took in all four of them. Though Anna sounded sincere, Renee wouldn't quickly forget how she'd just fallen into Lorna's arms like lovers reunited after a long absence. No, definitely not going to forget that.

Jeremy came from around the SUV and gave Anna a quick hug. "I'm so sorry," he said. "Let's figure out how we can help you bring Sadie home. You remember Merry?"

Anna nodded and held out a hand. "Merry, you look wonderful."

Merry took both of Anna's hands in hers. "I wish we were here for just a plain old visit, Anna. I'd tell you all about the baby. Once we find her and bring her home, that's what we'll do. I promise."

"A baby," Anna whispered softly as her gaze swept over Merry.

Merry nodded. "Yes, Jeremy and I will be parents in a few months, but we'll have time enough to talk about that once we get your wife home."

"Thank you." Anna's eyes brimmed. "I'd like that."

Renee wished she could feel the friendliness that came so easy to Merry. It helped under these difficult circumstances, but it was hard not to be tense around the woman who had hurt Lorna so deeply. It was hard not to feel inadequate when face-to-face with such beauty. Sometimes life could be such a bitch.

"Come inside, please," Anna said to all of them.

Though Lorna kept her arm around Anna's shoulders as

they headed toward the house, she turned her head and looked at Renee. That little bit of eye contact told her a lot and made her feel better. A little better, anyway. She still wanted to run back home, dragging Lorna with her.

❖

The Watcher was confused. Standing at the edge of the ocean, the waves hitting his feet, he was disturbed and, for the first time ever, frightened. Something was in the air, but he did not know what it was. It was different and so far away he could not clearly make it out. It was like an ominous shadow that continually shifted in the wind.

She was gone from the big house, called across the mountains once more, and his heart knew she would again put something right. It was not evil that stalked her. Not like before. Nor did he sense the darkness and the pain that had come to her on the other occasions seeking to be brought into the light.

No, this was something far different, and he did not know how to help because he did not know where to start. Something beckoned from the world beyond, and it stayed just outside his touch and sight. Frustration made his hands shake. How could he guide her if he did not know the path?

In his ears, the sound of sobs echoed. Despair pulled at his heart at the mournful echo, and resignation weighed down his spirit. Somewhere beyond his vision, beyond his help, souls beckoned. Where? Why?

Lightning slashed across the sky and thunder roared. He tilted his head to the night sky and watched as the light show danced and crackled. Above the stars the answers awaited, if only he could reach through the veil and touch them. He raised his arm and stretched his fingers toward the night sky. He touched nothing.

Would she be lost forever if he failed to help her now? He worried it would be so. He wanted to guide her hand and, by guiding her, walk his own path toward redemption. They were part and parcel of each other; of that truth he was most certain. Through this last year he had come to understand they must take this journey together, and by doing so they would come to discover a truth that would open up heaven to both of them. Yet he could see nothing, hear nothing, and the way was blind to him. She was in this alone.

For tonight, all he could do was pray.

CHAPTER FOUR

Sadie stayed sitting on the floor with her back against the wall for a long time after her tears stopped. As she sat there thinking about the strange events, it occurred to her that, in a way, this was some sort of twisted fate. She'd come here to scout locations for a television series that had the supernatural at its core. Everything about what was happening to her felt supernatural. If it was coincidental, she'd be very surprised.

It made sense in a weird way, if she bought in, that is. Except she didn't believe in the paranormal, the mystical, or the magical, despite the project she was currently working on. Quite the opposite, actually. Sadie believed in what she could see, hear, and touch. She was very much grounded in the here and now. Hers was a world filled with a reality she could touch and feel. But that didn't mean she couldn't appreciate the concept of the mystical, even if she didn't take it to heart.

The series she was location-scouting for was great, and she loved being a part of it in spite of its reliance on a supernatural premise. It was intriguing, the actors were all a joy—and she knew from experience that was not always the case—and for a change, she could stay home and work. Too often she was off on location somewhere, staying in hotel rooms and eating at bad restaurants. When she was single, being on the road for weeks and months on end was no big deal. Now that she was married, being home was important. Leaving for extended periods didn't hold the appeal it used to. This gig was the greatest ever because it gave her the best of both worlds, and she appreciated every minute of it.

Until right now, that is. Trapped in this room—and she couldn't find any way to describe it other than by unseen paranormal forces—was not cool. She couldn't explain any of it. Not how she got here and not how she ended up locked inside a room four floors up. It was straight out of one of the show's amazing scripts. She was smack-dab in the middle of a case of life imitating art. Just her freaking luck.

As she sat there, resting her head against the wall and listening to the wind whistling by the barred windows, she watched shadows dance across the ceiling. Outside, the sun had dropped below the mountains to the west, and the daylight had gone with it. The room had plunged into darkness.

Would Anna wonder where she was? A better question would be, would she care? Lately things had been strained between them, and she really didn't know why. Or perhaps she did. Though she never said much about it, Sadie knew Anna harbored a great deal of guilt over her breakup with Lorna. In a lot of ways, so did Sadie.

Right from the beginning, Anna had been up front about her involvement with Lorna. Despite an immediate attraction to Anna, she'd stepped away. Sadie hadn't been interested in stealing a woman from her current love, and that was the last thing on her mind with Anna. She'd liked her a great deal yet knew it could never evolve into anything serious. As far as she was concerned, they would be friends. End of story.

Of course, everything went sideways the moment she touched Anna's hand. Despite all her good intentions, she'd been drawn to Anna like a magnet. She'd never felt that kind of desire before, and it was intoxicating. Before long, she'd come to realize it wasn't a case of simple attraction, and all her well-intentioned rules went out the window. She was flat-out in love with her.

If what she'd been feeling had been a one-sided thing, she

could have found the fortitude to let it go and get over Anna, though it would have taken her an eternity to heal. It wasn't long before she learned it was far from one-sided, and she wasn't embarrassed to say she rejoiced. Anna was right there with her, passionate and loving. Together they dived into a relationship that was hot, intense, and the best thing that had ever happened to Sadie. For her and Anna it was a bit of heaven.

Never did she imagine she would turn out to be the "other woman," yet that's exactly what she was. She should have felt terrible, and on one level she did, at least when she was alone and her thoughts turned to the woman Anna had still lived with. She hated the sneaking around and the lying. When she was with Anna and staring into her gorgeous eyes, she knew they were meant to be together and nothing else mattered. It was fate, and who could argue with fate? What being with Anna did to her heart was life-altering. What it had done to Lorna was ugly and unforgiveable. By the time it all shook out, she got Anna and Lorna got a broken heart.

Though she'd always pushed it to the back of her mind, she did feel more than a little guilty. No matter how she looked at it or how she tried to justify what they'd done, it hadn't been fair to Lorna. But none of it changed how she felt about Anna. Love happens, usually when least expected, and she couldn't have walked away from Anna even if she wanted to.

Now she wondered if the recent distance between her and Anna had something to do with the guilt Anna harbored for the way she'd treated Lorna during their breakup. It was possible she was reading something into what was an incredibly busy time for them both. Her schedule was nuts, and Anna was, likewise, really busy. She wanted to believe that Anna still loved her as much as she did on the day they exchanged their vows. In her case, she knew she loved her even more than on that very special day. She hoped and prayed Anna felt the same way and that the unease of late was nothing more than growing pains of a normal relationship.

"Please come for me," she whispered to the ever-darkening shadows. "Please find me, my love."

For a moment she closed her eyes and concentrated on breathing in and out. If she could stay calm, her mind would focus. She used the technique time and time again when dealing with difficult producers, directors, and other industry professionals. It worked so well in those high-tension situations that surely it would help her now. She focused her mind and pictured Anna's face, her smile, her sparkling eyes, and soon her shoulders relaxed and her breathing became even. Slowly she opened her eyes and then screamed.

❖

As they reached the front door, Anna stepped away from Lorna, who'd stood unmoving when she'd enveloped her in a hug. It might have been better not to throw herself at Lorna like that, yet it had happened as if she had no will of her own. She pushed the door open and then stood back, unable to stop wringing her hands. For someone who prided herself on control and decorum, she was out of control. Everything in her life at the moment was messed up in a big way, and she had no one to thank but herself.

Lately she'd been a huge bitch, and she knew it. So did Sadie. She'd been able to see it in her eyes and did nothing to make it better, even as she saw the effort Sadie was making to ease the tension. Selfishness was the name of her game lately, and now she was suffering the consequences. As her mother liked to say, "You reap what you sow." *Got that one right, Mom.*

In the back of her mind a tiny little voice was whispering that maybe this was her fault. If she'd been a little less moody and a lot more communicative, perhaps none of this would be happening. Maybe the police were right and she had, in fact, driven Sadie away.

She stopped wringing her hands. That little voice could just go to hell because no one would ever be able to convince her that their love wasn't strong enough to weather a few ups and downs. It was, and her faith in Sadie was as strong as ever. Only something terrible could keep them apart like this. She had not driven her away.

The only ray of hope in the whole mess was Lorna. The second she stepped out the car, it was all Anna could do not to burst into tears. It was more than the fact that Lorna was able to set aside the justified bitterness of the way things had ended between them. Until she saw her, Anna hadn't realized what it would mean to see her one more time. She had grown apart from her and had most definitely fallen deeply in love with another woman, yet in that moment she realized she would always have a special place in her heart for Lorna.

It also warmed her to see that the time apart had done wonderful things for Lorna. She'd always been a striking woman. Not beautiful, at least not in the conventional sense. No, Lorna was athletic, strong, and attractive. Now, all of it was intensified. Part of it, she knew, was the result of her training for the upcoming Ironman triathlon. The hours and hours of work showed, and she'd never looked stronger, healthier, or more attractive.

The athletic training accounted for a lot of the change in Lorna but not all of it. Her walk was different. The way she talked was different. Her very essence was different. This was not the woman Anna had turned her back on.

And that broke her heart just a little. She hadn't lived with this woman, and she wondered how things might have turned out if she had. Then she almost smiled because she realized it wouldn't have altered a single thing. The end result would have been the same. Regardless of how either one of them might have changed in the intervening time, they were still two very different people, and their destinies were separate as well. Hers was with the woman who had stolen her heart, and Lorna? Well, Anna had to believe that perhaps her heart belonged to another as well.

The epiphany of the moment didn't make this meeting any

smoother. She stood shifting from foot to foot, trying to think of what to say in order to break up the uncomfortable silence. The truth, her mind kept repeating. The truth was the only thing that could make this right. She opened her mouth to give voice to what was inside, yet before she could utter a single word, Lorna's quiet voice stopped her. "It's water under the bridge. Let it go."

The tears she'd managed to hold back earlier now dripped down her cheeks, and she swiped at them with the back of her hands. "I owe you an apology," she insisted. She'd promised herself to do the right thing if Lorna was able to set aside her bitterness in order to come help. In a perfect world, she should have done it a long time ago and not waited until now, when it would look like she was apologizing only because she needed her help. She had never been really good at the perfect-world thing.

Lorna shook her head. "That's not what I came here for. I don't expect or need an apology."

"I know that's not why you came, and you don't realize what it means to me that you're willing to do this, considering what I did. Even so, after everything I put you through, I still owe you an apology. I should have done it a long time ago."

Lorna shrugged but didn't meet her eyes. "Duly noted. Now what we really need to worry about isn't ancient history but current events."

Anna deserved the cold shoulder, and she owned it. Lorna had come when she called, and for that she'd always be grateful. Her hope that they could mend the rift between them at the same time was perhaps a very unrealistic dream.

"Agreed," she said softly. She would have to learn to live with the fact that some sins could never be atoned for. It was one of those big-girl-panty moments, and as much as she hated it, she was pulling hers up. "The here and now."

Lorna finally met her eyes. It surprised her to see no hardness in them. It hurt her to see no trace of warmth. Once upon a time those lovely eyes were filled with joy and caring, and every time she'd gazed into them, she'd smiled. The day she'd started avoiding that gaze was the day it all changed. Expecting to see that warmth of emotion in them now was stupid, as she was the one responsible for wiping it all away. It was as if the universe was aligning all of her sins and bringing her to atonement in one come-to-Jesus moment. What a world it would be if one didn't have to live with regrets.

If she focused on the positives it would probably go smoother. She'd extended the olive branch, and that's all she could do. She was grateful for the kindness Lorna was showing her. Friendship was probably off the table for good, and that was something it was far too late to change. Lorna was here, and that was a godsend. She could be bitter and angry, but from all appearances she wasn't. That too was a godsend. All in all, it was more than she deserved.

She gave her a slow nod. "Yeah, the here and now."

Anna took a deep breath. "What can I do to help? What do you need from me to help find Sadie?" Her mind whirled with a thousand thoughts, none of which seemed very helpful. If they were, she'd have already brought Sadie home.

Sticking her hands into her pockets, Lorna rolled back on her heels and seemed to consider her answer, her head tilted back, her eyes focused somewhere beyond those in the room. When her gaze returned to meet Anna's again, she had a different look in her eyes, one she'd never seen before, and she couldn't put a name to it. Yes, this Lorna was so very different from the woman she'd turned her back on, and she didn't consider it a bad thing.

Lorna bit her bottom lip as she appeared to think. "Tell me everything that happened the day she didn't come home."

Running her hands through her hair, Anna tried to pull her thoughts together. If this was going to work, she was going to have to be in it one hundred percent. No more dwelling on the past and no more focusing on regrets. This was about Sadie and the reality of today. This was about taking all the small details and putting them together to form a picture that would help Lorna see Sadie, wherever she was. It was starting right here, right now.

She shook all over and her chin trembled. "All right. Where do I start?"

Lorna put a hand on her shoulder, her touch gentle and warm. "Just start at the beginning. Tell me everything from the first moment you realized something was wrong so we can figure out how to find your woman."

Anna calmed as she stared into Lorna's eyes. Something in the depth of her gaze filled her with strength. Her words flowed.

❖

The Watcher jolted upright. Power unlike anything he had experienced before struck him with the force of a hurricane. At first he didn't understand, and then it came to him. This was it. He had waited millennia for this, and it was almost too much to take in.

Tears came into his eyes, and he fell to his knees on the damp, sandy beach. Wind whipped his long hair around his head, the wet strands stinging his cheeks. His heart pounded against his ribs, and he curled his fingers into the wet sand as if holding on so as not to be swept out into the angry sea.

The restless spirits came to him, their screams and moans filling his ears. Their needs so long denied, their ignored cries, beat at him like the ocean waves that pounded on the beach he kneeled on now. No one heard them and no one cared, not then and not now.

In his mind's eye he saw them as they had been. Forgotten and unloved, and hidden away as if they were something to be ashamed of. The tragedy of it filled him with pain and despair that tore at his heart. Tears brimmed in his dark eyes. For far too long they had wandered through eternity lost and hopeless, searching for the one that never came. It was to be no longer, for they had found their champion at last, and they would not release their grip until justice was theirs.

He raised his head, and the cool, damp air kissed his skin.

His faith in her was rewarded once more, for she had heard the call and taken the higher path. When she could have turned her back on the one who needed her, she did not. She embraced the gift God had given her and now walked the path of righteousness. The faith he had assigned to her the moment he first saw her was not misplaced. She was special. She would once again bring the lost home, and this time she would also bring light into darkness.

Pushing his tall frame up from the sandy beach, he stood, his cloak billowing in the gusting wind that ripped across the ocean. In the distance, the sun had slipped below the horizon, and total darkness had fallen.

He put his hands together and bowed his head. "Go with God," he whispered. "Go with God."

Chapter Five

Lorna wanted to take the high road, she really did. But that was easier said than done. A wide range of emotions rose to the surface the second she saw Anna. Only a few hours ago it would have taken a whole lot of coercion and most likely a fair amount of alcohol to get her to even talk to the betrayer, and now here she was face-to-face with the woman who had broken her heart. Not much in the way of coercion and no alcohol at all. The weirdest part of all was that she wasn't filled with blinding anger or even a tinge of resentment. Not exactly what she was expecting.

All the way over here, her body had buzzed, and she'd been so jumpy she'd had to force herself to stay seated in the car. She'd been anticipating the fury that seeing Anna again would ignite. Yet the moment she stepped out of the car and took one look at Anna's face, all she could think of was helping her. It hit her in that moment that none of this was about her or Anna. This was all about Sadie. She was here to help someone in trouble, just as she'd done back at the house for Catherine and Tiana. Just as she'd done for her old friend Alida. A failed relationship, lies, and betrayal were all ancient history, and they simply didn't matter.

The secret to her newfound freedom wasn't much of a secret at all. She gave Renee one hundred percent of the credit for it. How she'd changed Lorna's life over the months since she'd first glimpsed her having coffee in her kitchen was huge. If someone had told her on that morning that Renee would rock her world like this, she'd have called them nuts. Funny how things had a way of turning out. Her life since leaving this place had changed so much, and all of it was good.

Quite a relief to realize she could concentrate on trying to find Sadie and not have to worry about managing lingering emotions directed at her ex. That wasn't the only eye-opener either. As much as her feelings toward Anna, or lack thereof, surprised her, she was equally amazed at how much she wanted her psychic abilities to kick in. When had she shifted from wanting them to go away to wanting them to appear on demand? Her trepidation on the way over here aside, now that they were here, she wanted to get rolling. She wanted to be able to part that veil and see what the universe could show her. Wow, what a mind-blowing revelation.

Her desire to get rolling was as much personal as it was to be the savior riding in on her white horse. Whatever was going on with Anna's wife, Lorna wanted to find her quickly, as much to restore Anna's life to normal as her own. She found that she truly wanted to help, and then she wanted to go home. Why? Her mind was whirling and one thing kept coming back around: she wanted to marry Renee.

"All right, let's figure this out," she said once they'd all taken seats in the living room. Just as Anna had shed her relationship with Lorna, she'd done the same with the house they'd shared. This was a new place, in a new neighborhood, and miles apart in location and in style from the one Lorna had run away from.

Inside, the surprises kept coming. When she'd pulled up in front of the big house she figured she'd be very uncomfortable in this place where Anna had built a life with a new woman, but she wasn't. In fact, she was shocked to realize that nothing about it bothered her. Not being here with Anna, not the unfamiliar rooms that nonetheless held some familiar objects, or the changes that so clearly demonstrated how Anna had moved on without her. It was like visiting the home of an old friend. *Friend*...now wasn't that a fine twist? It wasn't a term she'd ever expected to use in conjunction with Anna. The last few hours were turning out to be brimming with the most surprising self-realizations.

She turned her attention away from her internal thoughts and back to Anna, who perched on the arm of the sofa and chewed on a fingernail. She recognized the familiar habit for what it was: nerves. Hindsight being twenty-twenty, it struck suddenly that Anna had been doing the same thing for weeks before their relationship blew apart. Funny how she hadn't seen it at the time. Then again, thinking back, she had been pretty much in denial about everything that had happened back then. She'd told herself for months that Anna had blindsided her, and now she realized that wasn't exactly true. The signs had been there, but she'd chosen not to see them.

Now it was a different relationship in that Anna's lover was in peril, and Lorna's heart unexpectedly, surprisingly, ached for her. She couldn't wrap her head around how she would feel if it was Renee who was missing. Not something she even wanted to imagine.

Renee sat next to her with her hand on Lorna's thigh. The gesture was both comforting and possessive, and it gave her a sense of security she'd never experienced with Anna. In the back of her mind she'd always worried she wasn't good enough for Anna. It had been a recurring thought that beat against her confidence day in and day out. Looking around this room in the home Anna had made with Sadie, she realized this wasn't a place she'd have been comfortable with or that she'd have wanted to live in. Yet it seemed to envelop Anna in a way that obviously fit. That fearful whisper of inadequacy and insecurity had never so much as flickered when it came to Renee.

"I don't even know where to start." Anna's eyes filled with tears.

Looking at Anna's pale face, Lorna thought again of how devastated she'd be if Renee suddenly went missing. It would crush the life out of her. She placed her hand over Renee's and squeezed gently. "Just start at the beginning," Lorna said with kindness. "Tell us everything one more time and we'll sort it all out."

Taking a deep breath, Anna related the events of the last few days for the second time. When she finished, silence fell over the room, and Lorna had the sense that, just as she was, everyone was thinking through the odd situation. It wasn't like what had happened with the ghosts of the two women inhabiting their house back on the shores of the Pacific Ocean or anything even close to what had happened when her dear friend Alida was abducted and murdered. With Sadie, it was as if she had vanished into clear air. No abandoned car, no obvious signs of abduction, no nothing. Lorna didn't even know where to begin with this one.

Lorna decided to go for what was becoming her preferred starting point because she couldn't come up with a better place to begin. "Do you have something personal I can hold?"

Anna looked at her quizzically. "Something personal? Like what?" Her hands fluttered as if she was trying to grab something imaginary.

Honestly, she still didn't have a good handle on what would trigger her visions. It had been dumb luck so far. Still, it made sense that if Sadie had touched an item or worn a piece of clothing, she should be able to pick up something. A vision would surely come to her if she could hold an item of Sadie's, and it could potentially give them clues as to where she was.

"Like a brush or a jacket she might have worn recently. Even better would be something she'd been wearing or holding the day she went missing." Yeah, that sounded good, and hopefully it would work. Not hopefully. It would work because it had to.

Anna paused to think for a moment and then got up and disappeared down the hallway. Her footsteps were a muted thump, thump, thump against the hardwood floor. A few minutes later, she reappeared holding a necklace. It was a delicate gold heart with a hefty sparkling diamond in the center. Impressive piece and nothing Lorna would ever wear. She wasn't the sparkly diamond kind of woman. She was more the type who got excited over a shiny new wetsuit or a carbon-fiber road bike. Another reminder of how far apart they were in their separate lives.

"She was wearing this the morning she disappeared, and then before she left, she changed her mind and took it off. I hope it helps." Anna's eyes filled with tears again as she hesitated before dropping the necklace into the palm of Lorna's hand.

Lorna jumped as the metal touched her palm. Yeah, her plan was going to bear fruit. The bolt of energy that roared through her was immediate, and darkness charged across her vision.

The woman standing in the open door was backlit by soft glowing light coming from the hallway. A black apron covered the ankle-length white skirt, and a sharp-white nurse's cap covered her dark hair. Her expression was one of deep disapproval, her eyes narrowed and her thin lips pressed together in a hard line. The whole effect was to give her a menacing bigger-than-life appearance that sent chills down Sadie's spine.

Involuntarily, Sadie shrank back against the wall as her pulse surged. In that flash of a moment when she'd closed her eyes and willed herself to relax, everything had changed. She'd opened her eyes to a sight that couldn't be, and yet it was. The empty room was no longer empty. The bed frames were no longer rusted shells.

Against the long wall, the beds were evenly spaced, crisply made with snow-white linens, and on every one a single pillow rested against each headboard. At the foot of the beds stood a black locker, held secure with a brass latch. All except one. A woman with disheveled long red hair and her blue-striped blouse untucked from her full navy skirt sat on the floor frantically throwing items from the opened chest. One shoe lay in the middle of the floor, one on the foot not tucked under her body. Her stockings were smudged and had fallen in waves at her ankles.

"Who took it?" she cried. "Who took it?" Despair colored her words, and tears traced down her shadowed cheeks. Her face was as colorless as the linens on her bed.

"Stop, Rose," whispered another woman, small and pale as she put a restraining hand on her arm. She too wore a blue-striped blouse tucked into an identical long navy skirt. Unlike Rose's, her stockings were tidy and intact. "You do not want to go into the brass."

The woman called Rose immediately stopped her frantic searching and peered up at the other woman with tear-filled eyes. "It's gone," she said in a voice filled with such anguish it tore at Sadie's heart. "Gone. Where could it go?"

"Enough," bellowed the nurse, who still stood, imposing, in the open doorway. "Rose, clean up that mess, right this moment. I will not tolerate this type of disorder in my ward."

Every woman in the room except Rose scuttled to her bed, each of them sitting with her clasped hands in her lap, eyes downcast. Rose stared with sadness at the clothing, books, and scarves littering the floor. She picked up one of the scarves, stared at it, and then let it flutter back to the floor.

"Now, Rose. You are trying my patience. I have told you before that this type of behavior is not acceptable."

Shoulders shaking once more, Rose began to retrieve her belongings from the floor, slowly placing them back in the chest with great care. When she finished, she closed the lid and engaged the brass latch. She pushed up from the floor and, like the other women, sat on the one empty bed in the room. She leaned down and put her missing shoe back on. She didn't pull up her stockings. With her hands clasped in her lap, she lowered her eyes.

"Good," the nurse said in a harsh, clipped voice, her hands in the pockets of her apron. "There will be no further outbursts of this nature. Need I remind you of what will happen if there is another?"

Every head in the room, except for Rose's, shook from side to side. "Rose? Must I remind you of what will happen?"

Slowly Rose brought her head up, and her eyes met those of the nurse. She shook her head. "No, ma'am." Defeat dropped her shoulders and clouded her eyes.

"Very good then, you all understand. You must obey the rules. You must behave. It is not for me that it must be so. It is for your own safety," she said with a smile. "Now, you must all be ready for the evening meal in twenty minutes. Rose, do tidy your hair and fix your clothing. I will not have you in the dining room looking like riffraff. This is a fine institution, your families pay a great deal to provide you with the very best of care, and I will not allow you to show disrespect by looking as though you live in a gutter. One never knows when a family member might stop by for a visit. You must always be prepared."

"Yes, Nurse Thompson," Rose said without looking up, her voice flat and lifeless.

"Twenty minutes, not one minute longer." Nurse Thompson turned from the door and took a step away, but not before Sadie saw the smirk that crossed the woman's face and the glint of a gold and diamond locket she pulled from her pocket.

Sadie got chills again. Something about this was so very wrong. The way the nurse talked to the women, the look on her face as she chastised Rose, and the obvious perverse pleasure she gleaned from possessing the locket. Though she wasn't certain, she believed the locket was the thing the red-haired woman was so frantically searching for. She wanted to run through that door and snatch the jewelry out of her hand.

It took a second for the importance of that thought to sink in, and when it did, Sadie jumped up and started to run toward the still-open door. She focused her gaze on one single element: the open door. As her feet pounded against the hardwood and the door drew closer, hope surged that her nightmare was over. As quickly as it rose, it crumbled because, in the space of an eye blink, everything that had given the room life dissolved. Her steps slowed and finally stopped. She reached up and put one hand on the door, closed and locked.

Her hand fell away. "What in the hell is going on here?" Sadie turned a full circle as tears began to slide down her cheeks. Once more she was staring at empty bed frames and mold-stained walls, and with her back against the locked door, she slid to the floor.

❖

She was screaming and trying as hard as she could to tear herself free from the grip of the tall, frowning man who held so tightly to her arm that bruises were already beginning to appear on her pale flesh. "I will not go," she cried. "You cannot force me to step inside. I am not sick. Let me go!"

He sighed loudly, and his grip grew stronger and more painful. "Stop! You are making a spectacle of yourself. Have some dignity, woman. Do what you know you must. Stop shaming us. Do you want our children to hear of this? They will be mortified."

Her hair was coming loose from its pins, and her clean white blouse was pulling free from her skirt. Desperation poured from her like water from a fountain. The look in her eyes mirrored that desperation.

"It is you who lack dignity," she snapped as she tried to wrench her arm free. "You who create a spectacle. How can you do this to me? You only want me gone so you can send our children away to boarding school while you live with that child." She almost spat the last word.

He shook his head and continued to drag her toward the front door even as she stumbled and nearly fell. His step didn't falter. "This does not concern me. I do this not for myself but for you. It is for your own safety. We have talked of this many, many times. You know you must have help. You must be protected."

"I am perfectly safe. I am sane. It is you who needs help. Not I. Let me go."

"You are a danger to yourself. To our children. Do not fight this."

"I am fine. You just want me out of the way."

He stopped at the bottom of the entryway steps. She stumbled again, crashing into him and dropping to one knee. He yanked her back up to her feet. "Please," he said with icy calm. "Do not fight this." She continued to try to wrench herself free from his iron grip, tearing the shoulder of her blouse as she did.

Two large men in white pants and crisp white shirts came scurrying down the steps of the big brick building. At the sight of them, she screamed again, "NO!"

Lorna dropped the necklace to the floor, and relief flooded over her in a whoosh. While she appreciated the fact that her psychic powers had kicked in powerfully as she held the piece, she didn't want to hold the thing one more second. The despair and agony transmitted through the diamond were in absolute contrast to its sparkling magnificence. How could something that beautiful hold such sorrow? The strength of emotion in that small piece was so powerful she felt as though it actually burned her palm.

She blew out a long breath as she rolled through her mind the meaning of what she'd seen. With her thumb, she massaged the palm of her hand, trying to rub away the lingering sensations. "Wow. That was weird."

Anna didn't even glance at the precious necklace lying discarded on the floor. Her eyes stayed on Lorna's face. "What? Did you see her?" An edge of hysteria threaded through her voice, and all color had drained away, not that there had been much color in her face to begin with.

Lorna wished she had a better answer, one that would wash away the brittle emotion in Anna before it broke her. Nothing she could say would ease Anna's worry. Her strategy of holding something of Sadie's had worked, just not in the way she'd hoped. She'd expected to see Sadie and to glean some clue as to where she might be, but that hadn't happened at all. Whatever she saw had nothing to do with Anna's missing wife. This new twist on her *gift* was frustrating. She was just getting used to how things worked, and now it was taking an unexpected turn. This wasn't the best time for things to change.

Shaking her head slowly, Lorna said, "No, and that's what was so odd."

"You didn't see anything?" Anna's voice trembled.

"The necklace gave me a vision, only it wasn't about Sadie."

Tears pooled in Anna's eyes. "I was so hoping…"

"Yeah, me too." A thought occurred to her, and she studied the piece as it lay on the floor. Without looking back up, she asked Anna, "Is the necklace old?" It didn't appear to be antique, either in style or design. In fact, it seemed to be just the opposite. It looked contemporary.

Anna shook her head. "No, it's brand-new." She paused and her gaze met Lorna's. Slowly she said, "It was a gift to Sadie for our wedding."

On the floor the diamond sparkled, its quality undeniable. The gold setting was intricate and beautiful. A twinge of pain sliced through Lorna's heart. Not once in all their time together had Anna gone to such extremes to impress her. Again that little shock hit her. So much about the relationship between Anna and Sadie was deeper and more intimate than the one she and Anna had shared. For a second she wanted to be pissed off, but then the feeling faded away. This wasn't something for her to be upset over. It was another revelation showcasing how mismatched they'd been. At every turn she seemed to be hit with reminders of what was never meant to be.

She shifted her gaze away from the jewelry to Renee's face, and any remaining twinge of regret evaporated. Not so long ago, discovering what Anna had done for another woman would have immediately sent her spiraling into deep despair. Not so any longer. What she'd had with Anna was a mere shadow compared to what she'd found with Renee. It was incredible how things could change when least expected. She was grateful beyond words.

Shaking off thoughts of past slights, Lorna turned her mind back to what she'd seen and tried to make sense of the vision. "I don't get it. Since this psychic thing hit, if I touched something, I saw the person it belonged to. What I saw when I held Sadie's necklace was nothing about the present, and Sadie was nowhere in the vision. It was odd and strange and seemed to be of another time and place."

During those few seconds of sight, the words and images had had nothing to do with today or, for that matter, the recent past. It was far more like what she'd experienced with Catherine and Tiana. Everything in the vision was old, as in decades or perhaps even a century or more in the past. Everyone in the vision wore clothing seen only in museums. Why had that possession of Sadie's taken her back in time? Argh, it was so frustrating. It would be so much easier if this psychic thing kept to a pattern she could recognize.

Anna leaned down and picked up the necklace. She stared at it, rubbing her thumb across the beautiful diamond. "What do you mean, Lorna? What kind of different place and time?"

"Judging by the clothing of the people, I would guess what I saw to have occurred at the turn of the twentieth century, give or take a few years." She could still see the woman's starched blouse and long, heavy, dark skirt. It had been at least a century since anyone had worn clothing like that. A bit of déjà vu hit her, and all she could think of was "here we go again." She'd come to help find someone lost in this time and place, yet the vision seemed to beckon toward a past sin. Maybe her purpose was to bring light to scales long out of balance. Regardless, she still had to try to help bring Sadie home.

Anna was shaking her head and then abruptly stopped. A

quizzical look crossed her face. "The diamond," she said slowly. "It's the diamond, it has to be. It's the only thing that makes any sense."

The diamond what? Lorna waited for Anna to say more, but she didn't. Her eyes were focused somewhere beyond her. "The diamond? What about the diamond?" Lorna asked her.

Anna's eyes came back into focus. "The setting of the necklace is new." She held it up for Lorna to see. "The diamond is old. Sadie's mother gave it to me before we got married. She told me it had been in the family for years, so I had it reset as a gift for Sadie. I thought it would be special to have something of her family as part of our wedding. You know, something old, something new—"

"How old?" Lorna was aware of how rude she sounded, but she didn't care. This was important. Like a-trail-of-bread-crumbs important and possibly making sense out of the vision.

Anna shrugged. "I'm not sure. It belonged to a grandmother or a great-grandmother or something like that. From what I gathered from Sadie's mom, it's been handed down a few times. It was just such a spectacular diamond I had to make a special piece for Sadie out of it."

Her earlier frustration at the confusing vision began to fade as she embraced hope that her powers were still keeping true to form. One of those grandmothers was most certainly a sad, red-haired woman who'd been dragged into a red-brick building. The odd vision was starting to make a little bit of sense in a figure-out-the-puzzle kind of way. She might get the hang of this psychic thing yet. "Can you find out exactly who it belonged to and when?"

"You think it's important?"

Oh yeah, she really did. "I believe it's critical." No sense mincing words. They didn't have time for subtlety. The necklace held something important that might very well be the key to finding Sadie, she was sure of it. Maybe her *gift* wasn't going wonky on her after all.

"All right, I'll find out." Anna pulled her phone out of a pocket and then stopped as a shadow passed over her face and tears filled her eyes. She held the phone in her hand without moving to place the call. Her hand began to tremble. "I forgot. Sadie's mother is in Europe, but I have no idea where or when she'll be back."

Crap. That wasn't what Lorna wanted to hear. She needed more information and she wanted it now. It was probable that what she had seen when she held the necklace was residual emotion from a long-ago owner and had nothing to do with what was going on with Sadie. It would make sense in her weird psychic kind of world. Then again, given how everything had happened so far, she didn't believe in her heart that it was actually that simple. The diamond was attempting to tell her something important, and she was trying really hard to listen. So far, everything that came to her had played a part in solving the mysteries. She had no reason to think now was going to be any different.

Her gaze was steady when it met Anna's. "If not her mother, then someone else. You need to track down a family member who knows the history of the diamond. Now."

CHAPTER SIX

Renee paid attention to everything Lorna was telling Anna and was paying even more attention to her aura. Since the moment they arrived, the colors that surrounded Lorna had been shifting in waves of changing hues. The threads of black, gray, and brown testified to the conflicts raging inside her heart. The residual feelings were unsettling to witness. Though she'd never say it out loud, she wished she'd never encouraged Lorna to come here. She wanted those threads of black, gray, and brown to disappear and Lorna's aura to return to the pleasing colors she witnessed when they were at home.

Needing reassurance, she reached over and took Lorna's hand. The reaction was automatic and comforting. Lorna didn't look at her and neither did she hesitate. Her fingers linked with Renee's, and that simple gesture made the uneasy feeling inside her fade just a little.

"Do you have any idea where Sadie was going when she disappeared?" Renee might not have Lorna's psychic ability, but she could help by hitting the ground and doing the more physical work of searching. It was very simple. She would lend assistance in any way she could. The sooner they found Sadie, the sooner they could go home.

She wanted to get back to where life felt normal and she didn't have the urge to comb her hair or put on makeup every time she looked at Anna. Usually she was comfortable in her skin. She didn't need to be the pretty girl, didn't typically care that she was a little curvier than most. But that was before she laid eyes on Anna. Lorna's ex-lover was tall, slender, and classically beautiful. Her dark eyes were framed by enviable long, thick lashes, and her lips were full and enticing. No wonder Lorna had fallen for her. Shoot, if she'd seen her across a room, she'd have been attracted to her too. That made it even worse.

What did she have to compare to that? Not a hell of a lot, if she was honest. She twirled a length of hair with the fingers of her free hand, and for the first time she noticed that one strand threading through the thick dark hair was long and white. Great, she was getting old and gray as she sat here. Good gods, she needed something to do. Anything to get out of this house and away from the lovely ex.

Anna turned and nodded at Renee. "The production company she works for sent me a list of possible locations she was to have scouted that day. I have it in my bag."

"Well, what are we waiting for? Grab the list, Anna, and we'll start hitting the places she was supposed to scout." This came from Jeremy, and Renee had never wanted to kiss him more than at that moment. This sitting around was getting nothing done and increasing her anxiety by the minute. She'd feel better once they were out and moving.

Renee nodded at him. "Jeremy's right. We can divide the list so we can cover the spots quicker."

Anna didn't move, and as she spoke, her voice broke. "I've already gone to them all. I drove by every place on that list and found a big fat nothing. Not her car. Not the bag she always carries. Nothing."

All right. Now she felt like a big shit for the way she'd been thinking. The break in Anna's voice told her a whole lot about the relationship dynamics at work here. Anna's heart was with Sadie and not, repeat not, with Lorna. Renee didn't have to worry about her still carrying a flame because it simply wasn't there. She was obsessing about herself when she should really be thinking about how to help. Mom would not be real proud of her at the moment. Basically it boiled down to one truth: whatever had happened between Anna and Lorna was history. Sure, Lorna was still pissed, but it suddenly occurred to Renee that it wasn't because she was still pining for Anna. Oh, no. It was because her pride was hurt.

She could work with hurt pride. She could heal wounded pride. Oh yes, she could.

She let go of Lorna's hand and moved to put an arm around Anna's shaking shoulders. Now that was a move to make Mom proud, and it made her heart feel a little better too. "This is what we're going to do. We're going to take your list and go to all these places again."

"What good will it do?" Her watery eyes regarded Renee with such sadness she felt guilty for being so bitchy. A little bit anyway.

"Fresh eyes. We've never been to these places, so we'll see them a little differently. It might be all we need to find a clue." She wasn't saying it just to make Anna feel better. In her heart she really did believe it could help. Besides, with her only-too-human skills to help, it was all she had.

"Renee's right," Lorna said, and Renee wanted to kiss her for the show of support. "We could very well see something you missed."

"I looked." Anna's chin came up a little and her eyes cleared.

Lorna took one of Anna's hands and stared into her eyes. For the first time, Renee noticed softness come into Lorna's. Made her wonder if forgiveness was starting to touch Lorna's heart. "Yes, you did. But you're upset, and rightfully so. Any of us would be if we were in your shoes. We're less emotional, and that gives us a little bit of an advantage."

Anna took a deep breath and looked for a moment as though she might argue. "You might be right. I've been so frantic it's hard to think straight. My stomach is rolling and I've barely slept."

Renee gave her shoulders a light squeeze. "If Lorna was

missing, I'd be a basket case. All things considered, I think you've kept it together pretty well. Now it's time to let us do what you called us here for. We'll find her."

"We will find her," Merry said, rising from the sofa and heading back toward the front door. "We might not look like detectives, but finding the lost has turned out to be the thing we do. So far, Anna, we've done a pretty good job together. We'll help you now if you let us."

Jeremy was already standing at the door and shaking the car keys. "Ladies, we're wasting daylight. Let's go find Sadie."

"Uh, Jeremy," Merry said from the open front door. "It's not daylight yet."

Merry was right. They'd driven through the night to get here and it was still dark outside. It wasn't like they could do much searching now.

Jeremy slung his arm around Merry's shoulders and said to the rest of them. "Details, my love. It's," he looked at his watch, "four. By the time we reach the first place, daylight will be upon us. Let's rock and roll."

❖

Jeremy was certain of one thing; they needed to get the hell out of Anna's house and start traveling down the road. The tension building among them was palpable. Or as was often written in books, it was so thick it could be cut with a knife. That phrase had always seemed stupid to him, yet as he'd stood there watching and listening to the interactions among Lorna, Renee, and Anna, it had taken on new life. From the expression on Merry's face, he was pretty sure she was on the same page as him.

Despite the growing tension, Lorna wasn't as bitter as he'd expected her to be, particularly considering how down she'd been after the breakup. Oh, she was still showing her reluctance to be here, but she just didn't seem as angry as he thought she might be. Good for her. He liked seeing the metamorphosis that was taking place. Anna had never been the one for her, and it appeared that Lorna was finally beginning to embrace that truth as well. He'd known it, her friends had known it, and it seemed everyone except Lorna had known it. Better late than never.

Renee, on the other hand, was a complete surprise to him. In the time he'd had to get to know her, he'd come to like her more and more. No, that wasn't right. He'd come to love her. She was a glowing spirit who brought something special into all their lives. Her positive take on life was infectious.

When he'd first arrived at Lorna's house on the ocean, he'd been lost. Merry had been too, he suspected. They were both jobless, rudderless, and in the spirit of really bad timing, pregnant. He'd been excited and scared all at the same time. He loved Merry with all his heart, wanted to marry her, and was thrilled to be starting a family with her.

He'd also been without a single prospect for a new career to support his growing family. Lorna, always his number-one champion, had kept telling him it would all work out, and indeed it had. As it turned out, for all of them. Renee had stepped into their lives and changed everything. She'd fallen in love with his sister and given her the hope she so desperately needed. She'd come up with a start-up business plan that not only put Renee, Merry, and Jeremy to work but also gifted them with a project that put the fire back into his heart. She was a gem who consistently visualized the good in every situation.

Until now. Though he'd give her props for working to hide it, he could see shadows in her eyes when she gazed between Anna and Lorna. The only thing Jeremy could make of the look was fear, and that scared him. For months now, Renee had been their rock. She'd lost her home and her business, and still she was the steady, calm influence that drew them all together. Throw in her awesome dog, Clancy, and it was a family made in heaven. So to see her floundering bothered him, and he felt like he had to do something fast.

In his years doing business, he knew that many times the

best course of action involved time and space. In his opinion, this was one of those times. He was going to do whatever he could to wipe that fear right out of Renee's eyes. She'd been the one to give him back hope and purpose, and he intended to do the same for her. Putting some space between her and Anna was job number one. The best way to do that was to start doing something constructive. Besides, the quicker Lorna worked her voodoo and found Anna's trophy bride, the quicker they could jet back home.

Funny how he thought of it as home. He'd spent his entire life here in Spokane, with the exception of his college years—born right up there in Sacred Heart Hospital, and then he'd gone to kindergarten through high school in good old District 81. He was a Spokane boy through and through.

Or he had been anyway. With startling clarity he realized this place was his past. Lorna's past too. A piece of his heart would always belong to Spokane, but his future lay across the mountains where the rain came often and the sound of the ocean waves crashing against the shore was a lullaby. How quickly things changed, or maybe not so quickly. It just seemed that way. Didn't matter one way or the other because it was all good, and he was more than okay with that. He smiled as he turned away and headed outside. Everyone followed.

When they got out to the car, he took the list Anna had pulled out of her bag and scanned it, then looked up at four expectant faces. "I thought there'd be more, but this list isn't huge. I recommend we hit them all as a team, get everybody's impression at the same time." It made sense to him, and given the short list, it wouldn't take them long.

"It would be quicker if we split up," Lorna said. "We covered a lot more ground that way when we were looking for Alida. Time is an issue here."

Lorna was right in one respect. When they'd not long ago come searching for her childhood friend, they'd opted to divide and conquer. It should have worked great, but it didn't. Ultimately, their strategy hadn't yielded much that helped them in their quest to find her friend. It was only when they came back together as a group that the final piece of that puzzle had popped into place. He believed staying together was the way to go now. They were more powerful as a team.

Jeremy shook his head. "Time is absolutely important. So is getting eyes-on at each spot. We're better together, especially since there aren't nearly as many locations as what we had last time."

"Jeremy's right," Renee said as she put a hand on Lorna's shoulder. "Think about it, Lorna. You need us all with you. You're turning into an incredible psychic, yet if we've learned anything over the last few months, it's that we *are* better together."

Merry grabbed his hand and squeezed. "I second that. The stronger we are, the quicker we'll find Sadie."

It was no wonder he'd been so quick to jump on Renee's proposal to create a new business including Renee, Merry, and him. They often seemed to be in sync when it came to thoughts and ideas, just as the three of them were in sync right now. His sister might be convinced she could do this Lone Ranger style. Like him, Renee and Merry were not. They understood the power that linked them together, and it made them a pack of sorts. Wolves did better when they ran together, and they were going to run this together.

Lorna opened her mouth to argue with them and then snapped it shut, her lips pressed together. He could almost see the wheels turning in her head. She could be stubborn when she felt like it. And she could be a very reasonable and rational woman as well. Her nod was all the affirmation Jeremy needed that she was taking his advice. Reasonable and rational was winning the day. He leaned over and kissed Merry on the cheek, then opened the back passenger door for her. "Everybody pile into the Yukon. Let's pool our powers and get this done. Let's get Sadie home."

❖

Sadie closed her eyes and counted to twenty. This couldn't be happening. The only explanation that made any sense at all was that she had to be sick or hurt. What else could explain the hallucinations that seemed oh so very real?

"Twenty," she murmured and opened her eyes. A sob escaped her throat, the sound reminding her of a hurt animal. Dim light filtered in through the dirty windows, highlighting a swirl of dancing dust mites. With her back against the closed door, she reached up and tried the doorknob. *Please let it turn.* As it had the previous hundred or so times she'd tried already, the knob refused to move even a millimeter.

Think, Sadie, think! There is a way out of here. With shaking arms, she pushed herself up from the dirty floor. Slowly she walked around the room, forcing herself to stay calm and focused as she studied every inch of dusty floor and faded walls. Despite the fact that she worked on a show predicated on a belief in the paranormal realm, she didn't buy in. In her mind it was all fantasy and nothing more.

But whether she liked it or not, whether she wanted to buy in or not, she had been thrown into a paradigm shift. And if she was going to make it out of this hell, she was going to have to unleash a heretofore untapped part of her imagination. She was going to have to consider the idea that things happened outside of the explainable world.

Okay, if that's what she needed to do to get out of this hellhole, then that's what she'd do. Her hands still trembling, Sadie rubbed her palms over her face. It occurred to her that she'd probably just wiped dirt all over herself. Then again, what did it matter? There wasn't anyone around to see or care. Nothing mattered except figuring out what was happening to her and why.

Oh, and getting out of here. Alive.

What would Anna do? Sadie was the creative one of the pair, and she liked to see the possibilities in the world around her. Anna was the logical one who made sense of everything. Their personalities blended in a way that was perfect, and she loved the symbiotic nature of their relationship. It was dependable and heart-warming, and she wished with all her heart that Anna was here now. She'd know what to do; she always did.

Except Anna wasn't here. Sadie was locked inside this crazy dream and had to find a way out. She had to find her way back to Anna.

As she walked the length of the room studying the cracked and peeling walls that she suspected had been a bright white once and running her fingertips over the ancient bed frames, her mind turned back to what she'd seen in her *vision*. For reasons she couldn't explain, the face of the sobbing woman stuck in her mind. Something about her hit a distinct chord with Sadie. It was like finding that perfect set location. She couldn't always pinpoint what made it special; she just knew it when she saw it. Something about the woman was like that.

At the far end of the room, she reached for the bed frame where the crying woman had been seated. As her fingertips met the cold, rusting metal, a shock went up her arm, and once again the room turned black.

CHAPTER SEVEN

Anna's sense of panic rose higher with each stop they made, and each one they left without coming any closer to finding Sadie. She couldn't speak to the wisdom of Jeremy's plan for searching each location together. They could certainly have covered more ground if they'd split up, and maybe that would have been good. Except it wouldn't have changed the results. Of the seven locations on Sadie's scouting list for the day she went missing, they'd covered five and were just now arriving at number six. One through five had yielded nothing more than when she'd searched them on that first day, which was a big fat nothing. She'd been crushed the day she went alone. Now she wanted to scream. She'd believed Lorna when she suggested that fresh eyes might see something she'd missed. It had drawn her in and filled her with hope that was rapidly fading with each stop.

Instead of screaming, she tamped down the urge, jumped out of the passenger's seat before anyone else even had their seat belt unbuckled, and started toward the massive buildings of the abandoned factory. It struck her as odd on the first day and did so again today that Sadie would pick this for a potential filming location. It was old and dirty, and many of the buildings were clearly falling apart. Anna thought about how excited she'd been when she told her about the place. Sadie had been confident it would be perfect for the show. To Anna it looked like an accident—and a lawsuit—waiting to happen.

Jeremy followed her and stood staring up at what had once been a thriving factory employing hundreds of local people. "How the mighty fall," he muttered.

He wasn't wrong. A couple of decades ago it had been a major coup to grab one of the coveted jobs with the company that once had made the building hum with work and pride. The massive parking lot had been perpetually filled with late-model cars and shiny pickup trucks. The steady flow of activity surrounding it in its heyday had gone on twenty-four seven. Now it was a ghost town. Discarded drink cups, empty booze bottles, faded newspapers, and other assorted trash floated across the asphalt, where weeds and spindly trees were shoving up through the cracks. Its post-apocalyptic atmosphere was depressing.

Without saying anything, they all began to walk in different directions. It was even more of a wasteland once she skirted the perimeter. If anyone had been here lately, she'd be surprised. If anyone had wanted to be here lately, she be even more surprised. It was dangerous and sad, though perhaps that's what had drawn Sadie to the place. Often in her work she searched for locations that evoked emotion. This place certainly did that.

Within fifteen minutes they were all once more gathered around the Yukon. Their faces were all grim and her heart sank.

"She's not here," Anna said and couldn't suppress the despair that filled her words and her heart. She felt as desolate and defeated as the old factory looked.

Lorna stepped up next to her and put an arm around her shoulders. The gesture was as welcome as it was shocking. She would always be grateful Lorna had come when she called, yet she realized that forgiveness was doubtful. To have her be the one to offer comfort in this moment made her want to believe in miracles. If Lorna could forgive, then surely God would see fit to bring Sadie back to her. Her sins could be absolved.

"Don't give up, Anna. We'll find her."

"Promise?" She wanted to believe Lorna. How she wanted to believe that any moment Sadie would come strolling around the corner of one of the crumbling buildings, her bag slung over her shoulder, her cell phone pressed to her ear. It was a sight she longed for more than anything in the world.

Lorna squeezed lightly before letting her go. "I promise. Now, when you came here before, did you search the place?"

The confidence in her voice was encouraging. "Yes and no. I was alone, so not every nook and cranny, but I pretty well walked the whole grounds just like we all did now. I didn't see Sadie's car here, and because of that I figured I wouldn't find her here. I still looked around just in case and found nothing."

With her hands stuffed in her pockets, Lorna stood staring up at the dilapidated buildings. Merry, Renee, and Jeremy flanked her and also were studying the buildings. Whatever the three of them were seeing passed her by. All she saw were decrepit buildings threatening to fall to the ground in giant heaps of rubble, and if an earthquake hit the area, these would surely be the first structures to crumble. All she heard were the birds that now claimed the highest peaks as their own personal domains. It was as empty and desolate as the first day she was here.

No one said a word for few minutes until, unable to stand the silence any longer, she asked no one in particular, "What? Are you seeing something?"

Lorna shook her head, the first to look away. "I'm getting nothing. I don't see anything, I don't feel anything." Her gaze swept across the others. "You guys?"

Anna thought Lorna was the psychic, yet she spoke to the rest as though they held the same powers. Did they? She hoped so. Four psychics had to be better than one, and she'd take power in numbers. Surely one of them would be able to find Sadie.

Jeremy spoke up first and, like Lorna, shook his head. "I don't believe she's here. It feels empty. Like real empty, if you know what I mean. What do you think, Renee? You getting any aura vibes?"

Renee reached out and took Lorna's hand. For a moment, she closed her eyes and stood very still. Then she opened her eyes and shook her head. "No, she's not here. How about you, Merry? Do you have any thoughts?"

Merry shrugged. "You all know I have nothing in the way of superpowers beyond the expectant-mother thing combined with a good eye for detail. I've walked all over the place here, and I've got nothing at all to contribute that might be helpful. I don't believe she's here. I didn't see anything indicating that Sadie, or anyone for that matter, is or was here."

Anna held back tears, just barely. She didn't want to hear any of this. Number six of seven locations and still nothing. Sadie had to be somewhere. Why couldn't she be here? Why couldn't this nightmare end? It was like she was a lost hunter who'd fallen off a cliff in a wilderness area. Or a fisherman who fell from a boat and was caught underwater.

She had to tell herself she was thinking about it all wrong. Sadie had been out doing her job in a series of urban locations, and people didn't vanish from places under circumstances like that. They were going to find her. That's all there was to it.

Silently she followed everyone back into the Yukon. No one said a word as they buckled in and Jeremy drove them out of the parking lot. Anna focused on the scenery outside of the windshield, watching as he left the downtown corridor and pulled onto the freeway. She saw shadows at every corner, her eyes searching for the one face she longed to see.

The last place on the list was the farthest away. Miracle Lake was twenty some odd miles west of Spokane proper. Of all the locations it was the least urban, though it wasn't exactly wilderness either. A small community had grown up around the lake, and a few hundred people called the area home. It was a quiet, family-friendly place very different from the crumbling factory.

They made the entire trip in silence. It didn't surprise her. What was there to talk about? Sadie was gone, and they weren't any closer to finding her than they were when they started. Anna was as silent as the rest. She didn't know what to say, even if she'd felt like talking. She massaged her temples with her fingertips and wished they were already there. Sadie had to be at Miracle Lake, and it seemed like it was taking forever to drive the twenty miles to get there.

Behind the wheel, Jeremy's eyes were focused on the freeway traffic. Lorna sat in the passenger's seat, her head tilted back and her eyes closed. Beside Anna, Renee peered out the side window, and Merry sat quietly in the third-row seat behind her. From all appearances, they were relaxed and unconcerned. Maybe they were quiet and calm because they didn't believe her. Perhaps they'd concluded she was crying wolf over nothing. Sadie could have bailed on their relationship and, as the police had not so kindly suggested, just taken off. People did that sort of thing all the time, and whether she liked it or not, it was actually true. Adults walked away, it was that simple. But in her heart, she'd never believe that's what had happened with Sadie.

In a way she was screwed. If that's what they were thinking, how was she going to make them believe it wasn't the case when she'd been the one to pretty much do exactly the same thing to Lorna? While she hadn't physically taken off, she most definitely had checked out mentally and emotionally. She had walked away from Lorna in every way that counted.

This was different. Sadie was different. As much as she'd loved Lorna at one time—and whether Lorna believed her or not, she had loved her—when Sadie had come into her life she'd discovered the difference between love and destiny. Sadie was her destiny, and she'd be damned if she was going to lose her now.

It didn't matter what any of them thought. Not really. She knew the truth and she'd make them see it one way or the other. Something terrible had happened to Sadie, and it was up to her to save her. No way was she going to not find her woman. It would be easier with their help, but she would go it alone if she failed to convince them that Sadie was in trouble. Giving up wasn't an option.

After what seemed like a couple of hours, Jeremy took the exit toward Miracle Lake. Usually she would enjoy the winding road that bridged the distance between the I90 and the popular lakeside town. It was bordered by small farms, rolling hills with occasional outcroppings of basalt rock, and beautiful swaying wild grasses. The trees were an interesting mixture of pines, evergreens, maples, and aspens. Today she saw the scene as more of an obstacle between her and Sadie.

A few more miles on the country highway and the little lakeside town finally popped up. The main street was lined with small shops and a couple of mom-and-pop cafes. A high school with an expansive football field and fenced-off tennis courts was close in. A nicely maintained county park with a nicely groomed public beach appeared at the edge of town. They drove past it all as they followed the directions they'd pulled up off the Internet for the old hospital complex that was the final location on Sadie's list.

They made a few wrong turns before they found the tall brick pillars that stood sentry on either side of the long driveway into the abandoned mental-health facility. A tall, curving sign that read HEALING WATERS SANITARIUM hung suspended over the driveway. It was old and rusted, and little about it felt healing.

This, she realized now, was the one location she hadn't found when she first went out in search of Sadie. Actually, she'd thought she'd found it, but she'd been in the wrong place and about a mile off course. She wasn't sure what the other building was; she only knew it wasn't the location Sadie had been interested in.

Now as she studied the beautiful red-brick structure that was the main piece in a compound of at least half a dozen buildings, she realized why it would appeal to Sadie. It had the design and structure popular a century past, and it was solid and interesting. Massive lawns bordered by shrubs and trees that once were probably well-tended were now yellowed and grown over. When green and trimmed, the yard must have been an impressive sight. Today it looked sad and neglected. With the exception of the large carved sign over the front entrance, its pretty façade didn't hint at the tragedies of the lives spent inside the four walls.

"No car," she murmured after Jeremy brought the Yukon to a stop and she'd swept her gaze over the large, empty parking area. Emphasis on empty. This was no different from any of the other locations they visited. Her stomach turned and she wanted to sit and cry.

This time it was Jeremy who shifted around in his seat, reached back, and gave her a reassuring squeeze on the shoulder. "Anna, if you'd seen the things the four of us have over the last few months, you'd realize that doesn't mean squat."

"But…" Tears started to well up in her eyes. She couldn't help it. The vast emptiness of the place had just crushed her last hope.

"He's right," Lorna said. "Don't focus on the car. It's not the most important piece of the puzzle. Come on, let's look around."

From the back, Merry added, "You'd be surprised what this group sees when us regular folks see nothing. Trust me, Anna. Go with them."

They all seemed so unconcerned by the lack of concrete suggestion that Sadie was here. Even Merry, who of the group seemed the most like her. She didn't get it. The first thing she'd expected to see was Sadie's car. It made no sense to her at all that she could be here without her car being somewhere close by. It wasn't exactly a leisurely walk from town. "If the car doesn't matter, what does?" she asked once she was out of the Yukon and standing on the cracked sidewalk leading to the front entrance. The place looked as though no one had stepped foot here in decades, let alone a couple days ago.

Lorna's face was pale as she studied Anna, and it made her nervous. She wanted her to be animated and full of life, not looking as though she'd seen a ghost.

"This." Lorna patted her hand against her chest. "It's less about what we can see with our eyes and more about what we feel."

Anna ran a hand over her hair. It would be nice to feel comforted by Lorna's apparent confidence. She didn't feel much beyond pure growing panic. "I thought you had psychic powers and could see things that would lead us to Sadie. None of this makes any sense, Lorna. Can't you just try to see something so we can get Sadie home? I don't understand why you can't just do what you did for the others and find her."

"It'll all make sense sooner or later. You just need to trust me, Anna. Trust all of us. We've been through this a couple times already."

God knows she wanted to put all her trust in Lorna, but at this point, she was too frantic to blindly believe. Nothing was going like she'd envisioned when she put in that call. She'd thought Lorna would show up, do her psychic mojo thing, and lead her right to Sadie. The article in the paper that led her to make that call made it sound like Lorna could conjure up visions that walked her right to the missing. It wasn't happening like that at all, and she wanted to scream.

"Trust me," Lorna said again. "We will find her."

Anna bit her lip and met Lorna's eyes. The way she saw it, she didn't have a whole lot of options here, and despite what she'd done to Lorna, she did trust her. It was all she had left, and she had to hold on or she'd lose her mind. She nodded.

Jeremy trotted over from his side of the car to put a hand on Lorna's shoulder. "Son of a bitch," he muttered. He might have thought he said it loud enough for only Lorna to hear, but he was wrong. In the quiet, it was as if he'd used a loudspeaker.

"What?" Anna's head snapped up and her eyes swept over the building. She didn't see a thing.

"You feel it?" Lorna was gazing up at the building.

"Damn straight. Merry, come here." Jeremy stretched out his hand to take hers. "Tell me you feel it too? It's so strong it's like electricity buzzing through the air."

They were soundly ignoring Anna as they talked to each

other, and she didn't appreciate it. She wanted to know what they were discussing.

Merry shook her head and frowned. "Sorry. I'm not getting a thing. My new-mama mojo isn't tuned in apparently."

Lorna held out her hand to Renee. "You?"

Renee's eyes were on Lorna as she took her hand. Something dark swept across her face. "Oh…"

"What?" Anna screamed, unable to stand it any longer.

Lorna's gaze came back around to meet hers. "She's here."

❖

Renee almost snatched her hand away when the shock hit her like a baseball bat to the back of the knees. She truly did have a talent for seeing auras, and it was a darned handy talent in her line of business because it often hinted at those people who would turn out to be trouble. More than once it had saved her from taking a wrong turn. That, however, was the extent of her preternatural or paranormal abilities, and it was enough for her.

In the time she'd been with Lorna she'd experienced the psychic phenomenon secondhand. Some people might find the ability to see beyond the world of the here and now as a blessing. Lorna fought against it like a tiger. Actually it was probably more accurate to say she had been fighting it. Lately, she'd noticed a grudging acceptance come into Lorna's spoken and unspoken bond regarding her psychic ability. It wasn't that she no longer harbored reluctance toward her gift. It was more that she seemed to be growing to accept it as a permanent part of her life, and with that acceptance came a dawning sense of responsibility.

It struck Renee suddenly that's why they were here. It wasn't because she still had a torch going for Anna and wanted to see if they could start over. On the contrary, it was because she felt responsible for giving the benefit of her gift to the world at large. She was paying it forward even when it came to the woman who had broken her heart. The realization filled Renee with an overwhelming sense of pride.

As she held her hand now, the unwelcome fear and bitterness she'd been consumed with since they arrived in Spokane faded completely. It suddenly all made perfect sense, and as the negativity flowed away, something magical replaced it. A feeling of being in perfect harmony with Lorna filled her. Maybe that's why the second her flesh touched Lorna's, energy roared through her body and she understood, despite not possessing an ounce of psychic ability. Maybe she personally didn't have a psychic bone in her body, but she was very certain of one thing: Sadie was here.

"Wow," she said, her eyes on Lorna and her body vibrating with the energy that infused the air around them. It wasn't like anything she'd experienced back at the house or at the cemetery where they'd found Lorna's friend so recently. No, the air almost seemed alive. "I've never felt anything like this."

"Yeah." Lorna agreed with her. "Freaky, isn't it?"

The way her body buzzed was incredible. "Is this the kind of thing you feel when *it* happens?" While she had been fascinated since she'd met Lorna by what she could do, it had never occurred to her that she would be able to experience it too.

Lorna nodded, her lips pressed together. "Kind of. This is more subtle. It's like the universe is letting me know she's here, but it's up to me to push the envelope and find out where. At least we now have a place to start."

Renee squeezed her hand and looked around at everyone. Heavens, if this was more subtle than what Lorna usually experienced, she was blown away. It was pretty incredible. "Well, what are we waiting for? Let's push the envelope."

Even with her sudden epiphany about why Lorna was here helping Anna, Renee didn't particularly enjoy lingering here with Anna and Lorna side by side. In fact, she had a very simple plan in mind: find Sadie and directly afterward load up her woman, drive like a bat out of hell back to the west side, and once across those mountains, locate the nearest county office so she could marry her.

❖

The second Sadie's fingers met the cold metal of the bed frame that belonged to the woman the nurse had called Rose, the room shifted and swayed as if the building were on a fault line in the throes of an earthquake. When everything finally steadied again, the light inside the room was gone, filled instead by darkness broken only by the light of a full moon spilling through the barred windows. In the long rows of beds, still forms lay beneath pale blankets. The rise and fall of the blankets told her the occupants slept, some silently while some snored softly.

At first Sadie thought she was the only one not lulled into slumber, and then her gaze fell on the bed closest to the window. Rose sat on the edge of her still-made bed, her back military straight, dressed in a starched white nightgown, her feet bare, her long hair tumbling down her back, and her hands clasped in her lap. Her head was down as if she was intently studying her hands.

Slowly Sadie walked around the bed, and it was then she realized that Rose didn't have her hands clasped together. Instead, she held a copper receptacle about the size of a can of coffee. As Sadie drew closer, she realized Rose was whispering something. Until she stopped near the windows and directly in front of Rose, she couldn't make out the words. When she was close enough to make sense of the whispers, what she heard sent chills down her spine.

"Yea, though I walk through the Valley of Evil, I shall not fear, for thou art with me..."

What the hell? The twenty-third Psalm? The only time Sadie could remember hearing that one was at funerals. This did not bode well in any dimension.

"...thy rod and thy staff they comfort me..." Rose continued to pray.

Under her breath Sadie said the remembered words. "Surely goodness and mercy…"

A far-off sound made her stop and turn her face toward the door on the other side of the room. As the sound grew closer and louder, she spun as she realized it was the click of heels. The staccato rhythm was already becoming familiar. It was Nurse Ratched again. Did this vision take its timbre from *One Flew Over the Cuckoo's Nest*? The lady certainly could have been in that movie, and she wouldn't even have needed to act.

Sadie watched as the devil in white and black opened the door, crossed the room, and then stopped in front of Rose. "Give me that," she snapped and held out her hand. "Right now."

Rose looked up then as she clutched it to her chest, her arms protectively crossed over the container. "The copper steals the soul."

"Do not be ridiculous. Hand it over right this instant. I will not tolerate theft of any sort. I do not care how rich and influential your family is."

"The copper imprisons the spirit. The spirit deserves to be free." Rose's words were soft, yet Sadie felt that they came straight from her heart.

Nurse Ratched reached over and roughly jerked the can from Rose's arms. "Now get in that bed, and I do not want to hear a single peep out of you. If I do…"

Terror came into Rose's eyes at the whispered threat. Sadie had no idea what lay behind it, but Rose obviously did and it wasn't good. What had she done to Rose and others to spur that kind of terror so quickly? Spinning on her heel, the nurse, copper can in hand, left the room.

Slowly, Rose pulled back the thin covers and stretched out on the bed, her dark hair like spilled oil against the snowy bedding. For a second her eyes closed, and then they opened once more. She turned her head and her eyes seemed to meet Sadie's. She knew it was just an illusion because she'd already figured out she was a mere observer in some bizarre reel from the past. She could see Rose and the others, but they couldn't see or hear her.

Or could they?

As Rose's eyes held Sadie's gaze, Rose quite clearly said, "Help me. Help them."

Chapter Eight

Lorna felt a thrum of electricity in every fiber of her body. Yeah, it sounded corny, but damned if that wasn't what it felt like. Nothing like this had assailed her at any other location they'd stopped at today. Hearing Renee and Jeremy hit the same note had confirmed what she already knew. Sadie was definitely here. The fact that her car was nowhere to be seen didn't lessen Lorna's conviction. With all the weirdness they'd encountered so far, the lack of a vehicle was just a blip.

"Let's check this place out and find her." Lorna was ready to roll. "She's here. I can feel it."

Anna was still shaking her head. "How can she be here? I don't see her car anywhere. I'm telling you, she wouldn't have walked all the way out to this place."

While she didn't blame Anna for stubbornly refusing to let go of the car thing, she had to get past it. Lorna turned and put her hands on either side of Anna's face. She stared into the eyes that had once made her heart melt. It certainly wasn't happening now. The anger that had lingered all the way over here was fading, and not slowly either. It was flowing away like the outgoing tide she watched so often these days from the deck of her house. Anna's eyes were as beautiful and soulful as ever; they just no longer spoke to Lorna's soul.

"You have to trust me, Anna. Sometimes you have to let go of what you see and trust in what you feel."

Tears pooled in Anna's eyes. "I don't feel anything and her car isn't here," she said again. "How would she have gotten here without her car?"

Despite every fiber of her mind and body screaming that Sadie was here, Anna actually did have a point, at least in the logical world, and until she acknowledged it for Anna, they weren't going to move forward. Theirs was the only car in the parking lot. Granted it was an old, cracked, and weedy lot, and looking at it made her wonder if anyone had driven across it in years. She needed to listen to all her senses and not get caught up in simple visuals. Just as she'd said to Anna, she had to search beyond what the physical evidence seemed to be telling them. Her heart screamed that Sadie was here somewhere, and that's all there was to it. If she'd learned anything over the last year, it was to trust her instincts.

This time she pulled Anna close and gave her a hug. Over her shoulder, she caught Renee's eyes and nodded ever so slightly. Renee was looking quite serious, and that wasn't something she was accustomed to seeing. Renee was by far the brightest light in Lorna's life, and to see her so somber touched her heart. Whatever was on her mind, she wanted to help bring back the sunshine that never failed to soothe Lorna. The sooner they could find Sadie, the sooner she could do precisely that.

"Let's just not worry about the car for the moment. Let's track down your wife. We're going to find Sadie and we're going to find her here. I know it. This is what I'm good at, Anna. What you called me to do."

Anna stepped out of Lorna's embrace and let out a shaky breath. With the back of her hand, she wiped away tears. It struck Lorna at that moment that she'd never seen Anna cry. "God, how I hope you're right."

Even without a clear vision, she was confident in what she was feeling. "I am. I'm sure of it."

They all jumped when Anna's cell phone rang, its cheerful chiming-bell tone jarring in the quiet of the day at the long-abandoned building. Anna hastily dug it out of her pocket and answered it.

As she watched, Anna leaned against the car with the small phone pressed against her ear so hard, her fingers looked almost ready to break. Beyond the initial hello, she said very little, and Lorna had no sense at all of who was on the other end of the call. After a few minutes, she muttered a thank you and returned the phone to her pocket. Her head came up and her eyes met Lorna's. Once more they were filled with tears. "That was Sadie's mom."

There was more to the story; beyond the spilling tears she could see it in her eyes. "Did she have anything helpful?"

Anna bit her lip and then said, "Maybe, but I don't think it's much."

"Spill. It might not come across as important to you, but it could help us a lot." Lorna had a deep feeling that whatever Sadie's mother had shared with Anna, even if it seemed minute, it was important.

Again she wiped away the tears with the back of her hand and appeared to gather herself. "The diamond in Sadie's necklace belonged to her great-great-grandmother, Rose."

Ah, now that explained a great deal about what she'd seen when she held the cold, hard stone in the palm of her hand. It seemed to her that this weird gift of hers had a certain pattern to the way it worked, and discovering that the stone belonged to a long-dead family member fit right into that pattern. It didn't, however, explain everything she saw in Anna's face. Pain, or perhaps sorrow, still cast shadows. "What else did she tell you?"

Anna's gaze moved up the red-brick building with the wide steps, and she was shaking her head as she said, "She was involuntarily committed to this place and never left. Sadie's great-great-grandmother died here under circumstances never fully explained to the family."

❖

The Watcher's head snapped up, and a jolt of white-hot energy raced through his body. For a moment he stood motionless as he listened to the whispers on the late-afternoon wind. The universe was speaking to him, and it had much to tell him. Then he smiled.

At last she'd found her way. He could sense the change in her, and it was the very thing he'd been praying for since the moment she'd arrived at this beautiful place by the sea. She'd come here lost and brimming with sorrow. The ice was finally melting from her heart, and her spirit was once again free. He'd known she had it in her, and his faith had not been misplaced.

Despite the change that was about to free her soul, she was on a dangerous journey that would take her to a very dark place. As he touched her spirit he felt the darkness pushing back. It wanted her with a ferociousness that was frightening, and somehow he had to find a way to keep her safe. He would not allow harm to befall her as long as he continued to draw breath.

This journey was not like the others she'd navigated thus far; he could sense the difference as if it were something he could hold in his hand. Air whispered across the hair on the back of his neck, feeling like icy fingers. Whispers floated through the breeze that beseeched him to beware. He closed his eyes and turned his head toward the sky.

"What are you trying to show me?" he asked of the heavens. "What must I do to protect her?"

A few moments later he opened his eyes, his heart heavy and his prayers unanswered. He turned in search of the shadows that always gave him solace and then stopped, not moving his tall frame. With sudden clarity he understood at last. This was his final test, and he would be on his own during it. No help would be offered, not from above, and not from this world. He alone would succeed or fail. If he succeeded, after all the years of walking his path alone, he would finally be able to leave this world and go home.

If he failed, she would die.

❖

"You." Jeremy pointed a finger at Merry. "Wait in the car." She'd been a real trouper all day and had walked right along with him at the six other locations. It didn't escape him now that she looked very pale, and dark circles had formed under her beautiful eyes. He wasn't going to let this search wear her down and put either her or the baby at risk.

"I'm fine," she said, and gave him a small smile. "You need my help."

"Jeremy's right," Lorna said as she took Merry's arm and turned her toward the Yukon. "Take a few minutes to recharge. I don't want you running on fumes. By the time this is done, we may need you, and right now, you look like you can use a bit of rest."

"You guys are treating me like I'm too delicate to help. I'm not. I'm okay." Her hand went to her midsection. "We're okay."

Jeremy opened the car door and just stood silently staring at her. She was going to sit one way or the other. Ha, big talk from the guy who would cave the second she smiled at him. He waved his hand toward the seat inside the Yukon.

"Get in, Merry. You're going to sit this one out, at least for a while. Please. If we really need you, we'll yell."

She opened her mouth for another protest and then blew out a long breath. "You're going to pull out your baby-daddy-knows-best lecture if I don't get in the car, aren't you?"

"You know it, my beautiful bride-to-be. I don't honestly know best. I just know what would make me more comfortable and able to concentrate better. I can't give Lorna my best if I'm worried about you and the baby."

She put her hand on his and squeezed. "I don't want it going to your head, but sometimes you do know best. As much as I hate to admit it, I really am feeling a little tired. Closing my eyes for a little while doesn't sound all that bad."

He leaned over and kissed her. Resting his forehead against hers, he said softly, "Thank you. I love you, baby mama."

She touched her lips to his. "Back atcha, baby daddy."

When Merry was settled in the Yukon and leaning back with her eyes closed, he shut the door and turned again to Lorna, Renee, and Anna. It was a lot easier to concentrate when he didn't have to worry about Merry. Something tickled his subconscious, as if to let him know they weren't here alone and now he could give it his full focus. "I'm pretty sure we're all on the same page with Lorna on this one. Sadie's around here somewhere, so let's check this place out and get her home."

The building was old but in pretty good shape, considering the years of weather that had ranged from flaming hot to glacial cold. It had been built to last, and indeed it had done just that. The ravages of Mother Nature had not been enough to take it down. Even given its refusal to bend to harsh weather conditions, the four-story red-brick building had the sad look that structures earned when they were out of use for long periods of time. Shingles curled on the roof, moss clung to bricks in the shady areas, and the windows were caked with years of dust and rain. Despite its tired, neglected appearance, he could sense something alive and disturbing beneath the façade. It was time to let Lorna work her magic, and the best way to do that was to give her some space. That meant doing so without the distraction of Anna.

He turned and spoke to Anna. "You come with me." He shifted his gaze to his sister. "Lorna, we'll start on the west side of the main building if you and Renee want to start on the east side." He would have Anna out of sight in a minute, and that would leave Lorna space enough to do her magic.

Lorna's eyes were narrowed and her body suddenly very rigid. If he hadn't been feeling the juju in the air already he'd have known by one look at his sister that they were on to something. All she had to do was tune into those invisible vibes, and that would give her a clearer vision. Then they'd be in business. She was already one step closer, and if he got Anna away, she could take it all the way.

He laid a hand on Anna's arm, the tension in her body making her feel as hard as stone. She'd never been his favorite, yet he didn't wish this one on her. No one should have to deal with something like this, even selfish, self-centered heartbreakers. "Come on, Anna. Let's get to looking."

From all appearances, Anna wasn't particularly enthusiastic about leaving Lorna to go search with him. At first he found her attitude irritating. They'd come hundreds of miles to help, and after what she did to his sister, that was saying a lot. Then again, as he thought about it, he realized she was exhausted both mentally and physically. It was more than possible her reluctant attitude was far from personal, and so he needed to not take it personally.

It wasn't just Anna who was emotionally weary. All of them were still feeling the pain of their last trip across the mountains. The journey back to Spokane to help find Lorna's childhood friend Alida had left them reeling when they did, in fact, locate her. They'd hoped to find her alive, but she'd fallen victim to a serial killer who'd been infatuated with her and had embraced the if-I-can't-have-you-nobody-can philosophy. He prayed they wouldn't find themselves faced with a repeat situation here.

He might not have the psychic skills of his sister, but he was beginning to understand that he possessed his own bit of magic. The upside to that was he didn't believe Sadie was dead. The vibes he was picking up here seemed to embody life, not death. It was almost as if he could feel her heart beating, which was encouraging. She was alive, for now.

Anna finally overcame her reluctance and followed him around the back of the building. The grass was brown and sparse, crunching beneath their feet as they walked. They peered into grimy windows as they worked their way down the long building. The interior was dim and their vision hindered by the decades of wind, rain, and dirt that covered the wavy glass. The few doors they encountered were not just locked but chained and padlocked. The county was going to make darned sure nobody used the place for squatting, parties, or any other unauthorized use. Great for security, not so great for trying to locate a missing person.

By the time the four of them covered the entire exterior of the main building, he was as confused as ever. Anna had been right that there wasn't a trace of Sadie's car, and she was also right when she'd said it would need to be here. When they'd first arrived, it hadn't concerned him much, though now, he began to question its absence. This place was too far out of the city for Sadie to have gotten here any way except in her car. So where was it?

It didn't really matter because the feeling wasn't diminishing. Car or no car, Sadie was here.

CHAPTER NINE

This was frustrating. Sadie was here; Lorna could feel it all the way to her toes. They'd covered the entire exterior of the main building and then moved to the three nearby smaller buildings. There was no trace of Sadie or her car—no open doors, no broken windows, no signs of recent visitation by anyone human or otherwise. It was an old blank slate that seemed to be mocking her strong belief that they weren't here alone.

Now they all stood at the front door of the main building, including Merry, who'd made it clear she was done sitting around in the car. She'd almost laughed when Merry had come bounding out of the Yukon. If their child had even half the spunk Merry did, Lord help them both. It was going to be fun watching them run after that child.

They stared at the locked door. The dust on the entrance was undisturbed except for the tracks the four of them had just made. How could that be if Sadie was inside? Surely they'd see some evidence of her presence. It was like everything else they'd run into, locked up and seemingly untouched for years.

Everything intangible screamed "she's here" to Lorna, and at the same time everything concrete screamed "liar." It didn't make sense if she looked at it rationally. That thought almost made her laugh out loud, given that lately rational hadn't been in her toolbox. Since she'd reached the conclusion that her reality was forever changed, she was beginning to get the hang of looking at things through eyes open to mystery. The lack of physical evidence wasn't going to deter her. This place, and she was becoming even more confident about this building, was the key to finding Sadie. All they needed to do was get inside.

Unfortunately, the building had other ideas, and the old heavy lock set refused to budge. It had been designed to last, and indeed it had. She stood back and stared at it, trying to decide what to do next. She wanted to kick the shit out of it and get inside, but good sense kept her from taking that course of action because she had no desire to see the inside of a jail cell. Whether this was state-owned or private property, they didn't have permission to go inside. Without it, they would be guilty of breaking and entering. There was a way to do this right, even if it cost them a little bit of time. She was pretty sure that wasn't going to sit well with Anna, who would more than likely be all in favor of the kick-the-shit-out-of-it tactic.

"What next?" Jeremy asked as he trotted around the side of the building and came back up the front steps, taking them two at a time. He'd decided on a second run around the exterior just to give it another once-over, though Lorna suspected he'd wanted to do it without the company of Anna this time. "All the exterior doors I could find are not only locked tight, but they're also secured with chains and padlocks. Somebody was making sure nobody gets inside."

Lorna grabbed the door handle and tried to gain entrance again, even though she knew it was a wasted effort. It was kind of like hitting the elevator button over and over, hoping it would come a little faster. Didn't work on elevators and it wasn't working with the door. "We can't break our way in."

"Why not?" Anna said as she pushed Lorna aside, grasped the brass door handle, and violently shook it. Or tried to anyway. It didn't budge, wiggle, or open. "If you say she's here, then we've got to get to her. We can break a window, something." She kicked the door as she continued to try to shake the handle.

Lorna reached down and gently took Anna's hand away from the door handle and moved her a step away. "We can't break and enter. We're not going to be able to help Sadie if we're sitting in jail. We have to do this right. And if you kick this very solid door again, you're likely going to break your foot. We don't need to call emergency services for you on top of everything else."

As she spoke she realized how true her words were. They had to do this legally, and that meant they had no legitimate way to enter the property. Not right now, anyway, but she had an idea. Not to mention, she didn't want to take the time to fix a broken foot if Anna kept kicking it the way she was.

Renee must have been thinking along the same lines because her face brightened. "We could call Katie, couldn't we? She could get us access to the inside pretty quickly."

Katie Carlisle was a deputy sheriff here and the girlfriend of Lorna's friend Thea. Thea's twin sister, Alida, had been murdered by a serial killer, and Lorna had used her gift to stop him. Katie would certainly help them now. She came from a long line of cops and knew everybody who was anybody.

Nodding, Lorna said, "Yeah, I was thinking the same thing. Katie's our ticket inside this place." She glanced up at Anna. "Legally."

Anna frowned. "I still say we force our way in."

"Legally," Lorna told her again.

"Fine." Anna stepped back and stared at the door with tired, sad eyes.

Lorna pulled her cell phone out of her pocket and punched in Thea's number. She didn't have Katie's number programmed into her phone, not that she was worried about getting ahold of her. Her faith was rewarded when Thea answered, and she wasn't a bit surprised to find the two of them together. Her conversation was quick once Thea put Katie on the phone. When she slipped the phone back into her pocket the news she shared wasn't what any of them wanted to hear. Hell, it wasn't what she'd wanted to hear either.

"Katie will be able to secure permission for us to enter the grounds, but it's not going to happen tonight."

"What?" Panic vibrated through Anna's single word, and her face went even paler than it already was. Lorna felt bad for her, and if she could do more to help ease her worry, she would.

"She'll get us inside as quickly as she can tomorrow. The State of Washington owns this whole complex, and she'll have to jump through a fair amount of hoops before she can get us inside."

Anna was shaking her head. "She can make calls. She can rattle some cages. Give her another call and nudge her some more."

Lorna shook her head and put a hand on Anna's shoulder. "It won't change a thing. She's doing what she can for us as fast as she can. Katie understands how important this is and will make it all happen as quickly as possible."

"Maybe I should try," Merry offered. "You know, lawyer to cop? Sometimes the professional-courtesy thing comes in handy."

It wasn't a bad idea, and maybe under different circumstances she'd say "Go for it." But this wasn't one of those times.

Lorna shook her head again. "It would be a great idea if Katie was reluctant to help. That's not the case here. She's working to get us in as soon as possible, so I say let's let her do what she needs to make sure once we're in, we won't have any problems. This is not an official search so we have to tread carefully. I know it's not ideal. It's just the best we can do. Okay?"

Merry nodded and took Jeremy's hand. "You're right, of course."

"Yeah." Jeremy agreed. "It sucks to wait, but I don't see that we have a better option."

They all silently accepted the situation, even if Lorna could tell no one was happy, particularly not Anna. She certainly wasn't thrilled that they would have to wait until morning. Given the way she was feeling, she really wished she could get into this place tonight. But it simply wasn't going to happen.

"Come on," she said gently to Anna as she turned her in the direction of the Yukon. "Let's get some rest, and as soon as Katie calls to tell us she has the keys, we'll find Sadie. Trust me. She'll be calling before you know it." They were big words that sounded hollow. Even if it took only an hour for Katie to work her way through all the red tape, it would seem like an eternity in a situation like this.

She expected more of an argument from Anna and was quite surprised when it didn't happen. In fact, Anna's body language radiated defeat as she trudged back and silently climbed into the passenger seat of the Yukon. Part of her resented the attitude; they were doing the best they could. Another part of her understood. She'd feel the same way if Renee was missing. No one else spoke as they drove back to Anna's house. Not surprising, as there was little to say.

When Jeremy pulled into the wide driveway, Lorna felt like they'd come full circle. In so many ways they were right back where they started. For a moment after the car stopped, no one moved and they sat in silence, each apparently wrapped up in their own thoughts. She suspected she wasn't the only one feeling this way.

Anna finally opened her door and got out. She stopped before closing the door and leaned back in, addressing all of them at once. "You're welcome to stay here."

Oh, hell no, she thought. "Thanks" was what came out of her mouth. Lorna spoke up before anyone else. Partly because it just burst out of her mouth and partly because she wanted to make sure no one said yes. "It's really kind of you, but we've already booked hotel rooms." The last part was a white lie. There were no reservations.

While it was nice of Anna to offer her home, Lorna wouldn't consider staying at her house under any circumstances. Her reconciliation with the past they shared did not extend to the sort of hospitality that included sleeping in Anna's guest room. A hotel room would be just dandy, preferably on the opposite side of town.

As they drove away, she discovered, much to her relief, that they were all of a like mind. Her posse didn't want to stay at Anna's house any more than she did. That made her feel better and less like it was all about her.

They decided to splurge on rooms at the historic Davenport Hotel. Designed by famed architect Kirkland Cutter and built by Louis Davenport in 1914, the hotel had been fully restored in 2002. Just as it had been back in the early days of the twentieth century, when the likes of Mary Pickford, Clark Gable, and Babe Ruth had stayed in the comfortable rooms, it was once again one of the sparkling gems of downtown Spokane. In the midst of chaos and tragedy, a bit of elegance was soothing.

Lorna wasn't wrong either. The lobby's Spanish Renaissance design was beautiful, as were the hand-painted frescoes, the marble, and the gorgeous woodwork. She loved the gold leaf that surrounded the lobby hearth. Yes, this was definitely a better idea than staying at Anna's house.

After they said good night to Jeremy and Merry, Lorna took Renee's hand and they headed to their own room. Until the moment she shut the door to their room, she'd thought she was too tired to do much beyond falling into a heap on the bed. She was wrong. After she took one look at Renee, her heart thumped and her breath came fast. Suddenly she wasn't tired at all. The term "second wind" took on a whole new meaning.

❖

Sadie had watched Anna and the four people who'd come with her get back into the big white SUV and drive away. For a long time she stood staring at her hands as she turned them from side to side. Her nonstop pounding on the windows had caused bruises that were beginning to color her flesh purple. As hard and as long as she'd beat against the glass, it should have shattered into dust, yet she didn't see so much as a single crack. All she'd accomplished was to make her hands hurt.

Not a single one of them had noticed her pounding or heard her. If she tried to talk now, her voice would be hoarse from all the screaming. She didn't bother to talk; there was no one to talk to. From her vantage point on the fourth floor, she'd been able to watch as they tried doors and checked each building on the grounds. She'd hit the windows over and over as she yelled in an attempt to get their attention. When they'd disappeared around the corner of the building, she'd quieted, and as she strained to hear the sound of their footsteps on the stairs she felt certain they would come at any moment. Instead of what she hoped for, she was met with only silence, for not one of them had come to her rescue.

The key that the woman at the state office responsible for the buildings had given her was still in her pocket. She wrapped her fingers around the cold metal so hard it bit into the flesh of her palm. The cuts it would leave would match the bruises, and at least the pain reminded her she was still alive. It shouldn't have made any difference that the key remained in her possession, because even though she didn't remember coming in, surely she'd left it unlocked. Why would she lock it up behind her? She was certainly the only one around, and it wasn't exactly the kind of place people came to hang out.

It had been unused for decades, and people throughout the local area knew of the stigma of its history as an insane asylum. Even Sadie had heard the stories, and she was a California transplant. Ghosts, random lights, noises, and screams. Those stories hadn't deterred her and, truthfully, had intrigued her. A haunted hospital was perfect for her show, and she'd been excited to come and give it a look-over.

It never occurred to her that any of those tales could hold even a grain of truth. They were simply stories evolving over the years until they were bona fide folk legends. That's what she'd believed until she found herself an inmate inside the brick walls and witnessing replays of the past—until she'd watched her saviors drive away.

What shocked her even more than the fact that they never came inside to check for her was that one of the four people with Anna was Lorna Dutton. They'd never met face-to-face, and she certainly didn't blame Lorna for not wanting to meet her. Still, she'd seen her from a distance and even in some pictures that Anna possessed. To see them together now was surprising and a little scary. She wanted to believe she and Anna were rock solid, yet if the first person Anna turned to in a crisis was Lorna, rock solid would appear to be the last thing they were. For the life of her, she couldn't figure out why Lorna would be here with Anna.

That quirky question aside, when she finally could see that they'd approached the entrance door, she'd breathed a sigh of relief and waited for them, believing at any moment they would walk through the unlocked front door and free her from this prison. She'd gone to the door of the room where she was trapped and begun to pound and pound and pound. Again nothing happened, just like when she'd beat against the glass windows as they all stood below her. Her ear pressed against the heavy wood door, tears pooled in her eyes as she realized no footsteps approached from the hallway outside and no voices floated on the air to announce their arrival.

Once more she tried to make noise, sure that if they heard her, they'd come. Her frantic pounding had slowed and finally stopped. It was a waste of energy and hope. No one was coming inside for her. She'd given up her vigil at the solid door and returned to the window just in time to see them loading into the SUV and driving away. Even then she'd tried a few halfhearted knocks on the window, knowing in her heart that it wouldn't do a bit of good. They were gone, and nothing she could do would bring them back. Tears slid down her cheeks and panic washed over her. This situation was absolutely crazy yet terrifyingly real. She was a prisoner inside this place, and she didn't know how to get out. She didn't even know how she got locked in here in the first place. Nothing made any sense.

After a moment, she swiped away the tears with the palms of her hands and then wiped her hands dry on the legs of her jeans. Crying wasn't helping a damn thing. *Buck up, Sadie.*

Slowly she turned and surveyed the room. If something was keeping her trapped inside, there had to be a reason, right? All she had to do was figure out what it was because it had seemed pretty clear as Anna drove away that she was on her own. She was good at problem-solving, which was why she was never at a lack for work, even as far away as she was from the Los Angeles and New York City hubs. Production companies loved her get-it-done work ethic and didn't hesitate to contract her, despite her decision to relocate to the Pacific Northwest. That's what she needed to do now, get it done.

So, she thought as she stood looking around, if she was a character in her own TV show, what would she think and do? She just needed to approach it like one of the writers would. Haunted hospital. Visions. Imprisonment. A classic horror movie, and, she considered, classic movies were always about the young girl. She might not be the young girl, but all of a sudden she wondered if something about this whole thing was linked to her. It didn't seem possible, yet given how nothing about this seemed probable, it also didn't feel impossible. *Open your mind, Sadie.*

She swept her gaze over the room and stopped when she reached the last bed frame: the one closest to the barred windows and the bed she now knew had belonged to the sad-eyed woman they called Rose. Her steps were slow as she moved from the window to the bed. At the footboard she stopped, and her hands shook as she reached toward the metal with its rust and chipped paint. With a grimace, she took hold of it with both hands, feeling its roughness beneath her palms.

"Oh, hell..." she breathed out as the room faded into black.

❖

Anna paced the living room, holding her cell phone in a death grip. So much for appealing to the goodwill of Lorna. That tactic had produced precisely nothing. Well, almost nothing. Lorna, Renee, and Jeremy were convinced Sadie was at the old mental hospital, which was all fine and dandy, except if that was true, then they'd left her there.

How could they do that?

A better question was why had she let them? She hated herself for walking away. Now that she was here and alone at the house, the more she thought about it, the more she was convinced she'd done the wrong thing. She got that Lorna had friends who would be able to gain them access to the building legally. In a normal situation that was absolutely the right course of action. This wasn't a normal situation, and thus normal rules didn't apply. If she were a good wife she would have stayed and found a way into the place, legal or not. It didn't matter when it came to getting Sadie home safely. That she had so willingly driven away with them made her sick to her stomach. She was a coward and Sadie deserved better.

She wandered into the kitchen, finally released her hold on the silent cell phone, and popped a coffee pod into her machine. It wasn't that she was thirsty; she just needed something to do. As she stood and watched the dark liquid pour into her mug, her mind raced through every option she could come up with. Every avenue she explored circled around to the same point, and she made a decision. Perhaps Lorna could wait until morning to find a way into the old mental hospital, but she couldn't. If Sadie was in that big brick building, as Lorna said she was, then Anna was going to get her out of there…now. She refused to wait around for something to happen.

From the cupboard she grabbed a go mug and poured her freshly brewed coffee into it. Snapping on the lid, she was about to leave when she decided to make a second cup. Sadie loved a good cup of coffee, and when Anna rescued her from that building, she'd have one waiting for her.

Once she was in the car and on her way back out to Miracle Lake, she called Lorna. When she didn't pick up, the call went to voice mail.

Lorna, I'm sorry. I know you believe you're doing the right thing, and I can appreciate that. But I can't leave Sadie out there by herself so I'm going back to Healing Waters. I will get into the building one way or the other.

Chapter Ten

Renee put her hands on both sides of Lorna's face and stared into her eyes. "I love you," she said, and her voice trembled.

"I love you too," Lorna said, but in her eyes there was a question. "You know that, right?" She put voice to what she saw.

Since they'd arrived in Spokane she thought she was hiding her uneasiness, but apparently not quite as well as she believed. "I…"

"Is it Anna?"

She wanted to deny it now and to tell her she was confident in their love. But it would be a bit of a white lie. All day she'd been feeling a little off center. She even questioned what she was seeing in Lorna's aura. It was hard to tell if what she was seeing was real or an interpretation colored by her own insecurity. Her world was swaying, and more than anything she wanted to put it all back on firm ground.

"Yes," she finally admitted. "I can see the connection you two have."

"Had." Her voice was firm.

Renee gave her a wry smile and appreciated that single word more than she would ever admit. "Okay, had."

This time it was Lorna who reached up and took Renee's face between her hands. "I love you. Period, end of story. I thought, a long time ago, that Anna was who I wanted to spend the rest of my life with. She betrayed me and I was hurt. Poor little me, but I got over it. I got over her. The thing is, my darling Renee, when I met you, I discovered a truth."

Her heart started to beat more rapidly at the look in Lorna's eyes. The intensity was breathtaking. "A truth?"

Lorna smiled and her eyes grew soft. "I discovered that I really didn't even know what love is. You showed me what it meant, what it is, and my life will never be the same."

"Really?" Hearing those words took away the pain that had been with her since she stepped out of the car at Anna's house. Everything felt a little lighter. "She's so beautiful and accomplished. I don't have anything like that to offer you." She still couldn't escape her own truth. In comparison to Anna she was pale and lifeless.

"Are you kidding me?" Lorna seemed genuinely surprised. "You are incredible. Don't get me wrong, Anna is pretty on the outside. I think everybody would agree on that score. It's what sucks you in to begin with, and trust me, I'm not the only one who got pulled into that orbit. It's not until you're in deep that you realize how shallow she can be. That's not what I need or want in my life. I learned that lesson the hard way. You, on the other hand, are beautiful through and through. Nothing about you is just skin deep, and that blows my mind every day. The fact that you tell me that you love me makes me feel like the luckiest woman in the world."

Tears welled up in her eyes and she wrapped her arms around Lorna. "Thank you." Relief, joy, and passion rolled through her with each word. It was a little embarrassing to think she was so needy she had to cling to reassurances, yet right at this moment, it was exactly what she needed.

"Oh no, baby, thank you."

Lorna kissed her deep, pushing her tongue between her teeth. A fire warmed her as passion took control. She didn't want to be anywhere else in the world except right here in the arms of this woman.

Lorna pulled back and gave her sly smile. Her hand slid down Renee's cheek, her neck, and came to rest on a breast. The heat made her nipples grow hard. "You know," she said, and raised a single eyebrow. "There's a really nice bed in this room, and it's awfully tidy right now. What say we mess it all up?"

Renee grabbed her hand and dragged her toward that nice, tidy bed.

❖

Jeremy didn't like how pale Merry was looking at all. So far everything in her pregnancy had gone really well, and it made him happy knowing she was feeling great. The glow she had about her made his heart swell. Today was different. Her eyes were drooping and her skin was devoid of color. As the day wore on, it made him more and more nervous. The rest he'd insisted she take while they were out at the abandoned mental hospital seemed to have helped a little. But not enough. Her normally beautiful face was still pale and drawn.

Even now, as she rested on the comfortable king bed in their hotel room, she didn't look a hundred percent. It sent knots of worry right to the pit of his stomach. She, of course, refused to complain and was more concerned with the welfare of Anna's wife than her own well-being. That was his Merry and just one of the reasons he loved her so much. It was also why he took the role of protector all the more seriously.

He was standing at the small coffee machine making her a cup of chamomile tea when she suddenly jolted up and grabbed her midsection. "Oh good Lord," she squeaked. The alarm he saw in her eyes tore at his heart.

The tea bag he'd been holding went flying as he raced to her side. If he'd thought she couldn't get much paler, he was wrong. Her face was now ghostly white, and he thought his heart would stop beating right then and there. "What's wrong?" It was impossible to keep the panic from his voice. He'd never seen her look like this, and holding her, he could feel the tremors racing through her entire body. This was terrible; his Merry was confident and fearless.

Tears formed in her eyes. "I don't know. Something's wrong," she told him as her eyes met his. Fear, deep and dark, filled them. "Oh, dear God, I think something's wrong with the baby."

Terror flooded his whole body. No fucking way. Not their baby. He wouldn't let anything happen to either one of them. He scrambled for his cell phone and hit Lorna's number. His hands were shaking so fiercely, it took two tries before the call went through. Her voice sounded almost sleepy when she picked up, and he wondered briefly if he'd awakened her. Only for a second though, and then he snapped, "Bring the car around front. Now. I'm taking Merry up to Sacred Heart."

He knew he wouldn't have to say more, so he shoved the phone into his pocket and scooped up Merry. The hospital that was at the core of a major medical center was only a couple of miles south of the hotel. They could be there in a matter of minutes. Holding her close to his chest, he carried her from the room to the side entrance of the hotel, where cars could pull in to load and unload. If she weighed an ounce he couldn't tell. He was so scared he could have easily carried her those few miles to the hospital. Instead he held her close and waited for his sister. It seemed like he'd waited for an hour before Lorna pulled in front of the sliding-glass doors.

"What's going on?" she asked once they were all inside and headed up the south hill toward the tall white buildings perched above the city like guardians. Lorna's eyes were steady on the traffic, and as if the gods were pulling for them, she was making all green lights. Three minutes and they'd be there.

"Something's happening," he said, with Merry's head resting against his chest. Her body continued to shake and he stroked her hair, hoping his touch would help in some small way. It helped him just to touch her. "We've got to get her to the ER quickly."

He hugged her even tighter as Lorna negotiated the downtown traffic as easily as if she still called this place home. The ease with which she drove through the busy streets was comforting. Nothing was going to happen to his girls. He'd always thought it would be the coolest thing in the world to have a little boy, yet the moment they'd learned their child was a girl, he'd felt like the luckiest guy around. First, because Merry had accepted his proposal and very soon would be his wife. Second, because he was going to have a beautiful baby girl he just knew was going to be as beautiful as her mother. He was a lucky, lucky guy, and he didn't take that for granted.

Now, something was trying to mar the joy surrounding his little family, and he wasn't going to have it. Spokane had some of the best medical care in the country, and by God, his girls were going to take advantage of the skill and expertise available. It was too soon for their baby to make her appearance, and he was pretty damned sure there was a doctor up on the hill who could make sure she met her family only when it was the right time.

Though he dreaded going to the emergency room for any reason and expected an intolerable amount of run-around and waiting, he was surprised. While he took care of the admittance info, they immediately wheeled Merry back through the double doors with the two square windows. He didn't have to wait around wringing his hands and doing nothing while frustration built and fear wrenched his heart. He was incredibly grateful for what felt like a true gift, even though he hated being parted from Merry for even ten minutes. Letting go of her was almost impossible. Still, he wanted her taken care of right this second, and that's precisely what they were doing, so he managed to stay calm as he let go of her hand and stayed out front in order to give the intake people what they needed.

By the time he finished with what seemed like a million questions and they finally took him back to the small curtain-draped cubicle, Merry was dressed in the ubiquitous blue hospital gown and was reclining against white pillows on a rolling bed.

Her face held a mere touch more color than the pillowcases, and just that little evidence of bloom in her face made his shoulders relax a bit.

"How are you doing, babe?" He bent and kissed her forehead. Her skin was cool, which was probably good. No fever. He hoped.

She held his hand very tightly. "I'm scared out of my mind. Other than that, I'm great. I'm better now that you're here."

"Yeah, I'm scared shitless too. But it's gonna be all right. There are some really good docs here, and they'll take care of you and our little princess." He wiggled his fingers so that she'd loosen her death grip and he'd get some blood circulation back.

"I can't lose her," she said, and tears began to flow. The color in her cheeks just a moment ago disappeared as what appeared to be despair leached it away. "I'm so scared."

He put both hands against her cheeks and stared into her eyes. If he knew anything right now, it was that his job was to be strong, for both of them if need be. He was scared too, but she was the one who carried their child inside. The fear he was experiencing had to be magnified a hundred times for her. "We are not going to lose her."

Her eyes held his, and what he saw in them made him want to weep. "You promise?"

He kissed her, saying against her lips, "I promise." God forgive him, he hoped it wasn't a lie.

❖

Lorna sat holding Renee's hand in the waiting room while she tapped her foot as if she were hearing some up-tempo music. She couldn't remember the last time she'd felt this afraid. After Jeremy's call, she and Renee had thrown on their clothes and raced to get the Yukon. Merry had looked so small and pale in Jeremy's arms when they'd pulled up at the sliding-glass doors of the hotel. She didn't look any better when they arrived at the emergency room and they sat her in one of the ever-present wheelchairs. Jeremy worked hard to stay calm for Merry, but Lorna saw through his brave front. He was truly alarmed, and that scared her even more. Jeremy was always the bright light in any room, and to see darkness flowing over him hurt her heart.

She didn't much believe in prayers. Had never been able to understand the point in them if she was being honest. But if there was ever a time to start believing, she figured this was it. Given her psychic powers that popped up, for which there was no rational explanation, it wasn't impossible that prayers might be answered too. Silently she sent a plea into the universe, asking for help. If a higher power did exist, she hoped like hell it heard her. She was so looking forward to welcoming her little niece into the world and into their growing family, and the thought of losing her was too much to even consider.

"It will be all right." Renee kissed the side of her head. Funny how she always seemed to know the right thing to say at the right time. In all her time with Anna they'd never been in sync like this.

She tilted her head into Renee, appreciating her soothing touch. She loved the way she smelled and the feel of her thick hair against her cheek. "God, I hope so."

"It will, I feel it here." Renee leaned away to tap her chest. "This is a bump in the road, and that's all it is. Merry and the baby will be fine."

Hearing those words from Renee actually made her feel better. She might not be psychic, but Lorna had been around her long enough to know she had her own special powers. In their own right, they were as important as what Lorna could do. "Did you see an aura around her?"

Renee's ability to see auras was incredible and, as far as she'd seen, pretty damned accurate. She could detect the powers of good, bad, sickness, and health as they surrounded people. It was pretty cool, in Lorna's humble opinion.

Renee squeezed her hand. "I did. What I can tell you is that all day she's been fine and nothing suggested tragedy around her. She was tired earlier and that's all. Remember, it's normal for a pregnant woman to be fatigued. It doesn't mean there's a problem. If something was wrong, I'm absolutely certain it would have shown up around her. It didn't, and so I'm telling you, she'll be fine, and so will our little girl."

The band around Lorna's heart loosened a couple of notches. How she wished Jeremy were here to hear Renee. He could use the encouragement as well. "Good," Lorna breathed out. "You don't know how much better that makes me feel."

Renee squeezed her hand, smiled, and stood. "You want some coffee? You must be a little tired." She winked and her smile grew.

Lorna flashed back to their earlier hot and passionate lovemaking. She could feel the flush that rose in her face as she thought about it. "You know, for someone who looks all sweet and innocent, you're actually a pretty wicked woman."

Renee winked again. "Only with you, baby. Only with you."

That comment warmed her all over and made her want to run back to the hotel. "Good to know. Let's keep it that way."

"No worries, I'm all yours." She leaned in and gave her a peck on the cheek. "Now, coffee? Yes? No?"

She had to think about that for only a second. "Well, thanks for the offer, but I'm going with no. This scare has me plenty wide awake without any artificial stimulants." All she needed to do was wind herself up with a caffeine rush. Besides, she'd never been in a hospital yet that had decent coffee.

Renee sat back down next to her. "All right, we'll forego the coffee for the time being. I have a hunch this is going to be a long night, and it might come in handy a few hours from now."

Lorna shifted in her seat and pulled the cell phone out of her pocket. She didn't wear a watch, but then who needed to these days when everyone had a cell phone to keep time. She looked at the display and frowned. "That's odd. I have a voice mail, and I didn't even hear the phone ring. Did you?"

Renee shook her head. "No, I didn't hear a thing. Do you have it on mute by any chance? That's my favorite trick, and then I miss a bunch of calls before I realize what I've done."

She looked at her phone more closely and was dismayed to see that somewhere along the line, she had, indeed, flipped the little switch that turned the phone from ring to mute. "Damn it," she muttered as she put it back on ring.

Now to see who'd left her a message. As she listened to the voice mail, her heart sank. Oh, hell no, she thought. This was the last thing she needed right now. Here they were in the middle of a family crisis, and damned if Anna wasn't making it worse. God had probably been looking out for her when Anna dumped her because she'd forgotten how big a pain in the ass the woman could be and how her timing on everything was the worst. She slipped the phone back into her pocket and turned to Renee.

She tried to keep the irritation out of her voice but figured it was an epic failure. "Anna has gone back out to Healing Waters armed with a pry bar and who knows what else. She's going to break into the place."

Renee turned in her seat, a shocked expression on her face. It confirmed her feelings about Anna's poor timing. "Oh dear, that's not good. What in the world is she thinking?"

Nothing good was an understatement. They'd be bailing Anna out of jail before the night was done and maybe, or maybe not, finding Sadie in the midst of the chaos. Anna didn't realize the danger she could be in or what it could mean to Sadie if something otherworldly was going on out there. She got the emotion that was driving Anna, she really did. At the same time, she wanted to shake her and make her understand the danger.

Lorna had come up against some weird shit since she'd evolved into a psychic or whatever in the world she was. It made her cautious and willing to think outside the box. Oh hell, she didn't think she ever even thought inside the box these days. So much of what she'd seen couldn't be explained in the rational world. Just like the troubling sensations she'd encountered out at Healing Waters. She didn't know what they'd find once they got inside the building. It might be perfectly normal. Or it could very well be something more along the lines of the paranormal. Bottom line, it was no place for Anna to be alone.

"No, it's not good," she muttered. "Not at all."

Renee took her hand. It was warm and soft, though the pressure of her grip was all business. "You know we have to follow her back out there."

Lorna nodded. Yeah, she knew exactly what they had to do, and it pissed her off. The most important thing right now was to stay right here for her brother and her sister-in-law-to-be. It wasn't fair that Anna once more was causing havoc in her life. So much for taking the high road. Wasn't she supposed to be building some good karma by coming to Anna's aid? Sure didn't seem it, or she wouldn't have to leave Jeremy in his hour of need.

She blew out a long breath. "As much as I hate to say it, yeah, we do. We can't leave her out there alone, but I have to tell you, I'd really like to. If she wants to be a dumbass, why is it up to me to save her? I could easily leave her out there all night and not feel the least bit guilty."

"You'd hate yourself if you did."

Damn it if Renee wasn't right. The old Lorna with the broken heart and bruised pride would love to tell Anna to knock herself out if she couldn't wait a few hours and do it right. The new Lorna, the Lorna loved by the wonderful Renee, would do the right thing. She would go and save Anna from herself.

"First, I've got to tell Jeremy we're heading out. Do you have any idea how much I hate leaving him alone? It's so wrong to bail out on family because of Anna. She's messed up my life in so many ways."

Renee kissed her on the cheek. "I have a pretty good idea how much this bothers you. I also know Merry and Jeremy are in good hands. They'll be well taken care of until we can get back here. If anyone will understand what you're doing and why, it's those two. You know as well as I do they'd be angry if you turned your back on her."

As if he'd heard them talking about him, Jeremy pushed through the double doors leading from the brightly lit waiting area to the emergency exam rooms. To see that some color had returned to his face made the tension in her shoulders relax a little. But it didn't make her irritation with Anna go away one iota. She would still love nothing better than to sit her butt back down in the chair and let the chips fall where they would for Anna. She stayed on her feet.

"Is she okay?" Lorna blurted before he got more than a couple steps outside the doors. "Tell me Merry and the baby are okay." Geez, she sounded like she was about to burst into tears. Maybe because she almost had.

He smiled and nodded, and the tension in the back of her loosened. The tears that were so close to the surface faded as quickly as they'd surged forward. "She's going to be fine." She saw the glimmer of tears in his eyes, and they were tears filled with light.

"And the baby?" she asked in a whisper, afraid for the words to pass her lips. She almost felt as though if she said the words too loudly, it would make them more powerful. As she studied her brother's face, she hoped her prayers would be answered.

His smile grew, and the light in his eyes pushed away the threat of tears. "The baby is wonderful. Healthy and happy right where she is. The doc told us it was a little premature labor and that's all. They believe they've got it stopped. Mama and baby are both going to be fine. The good news is that after a day or two in the hospital just to make sure it doesn't happen again, we can trek back across the mountains to that nice comfortable home you've made for all of us."

"Oh, thank God," Lorna breathed out at the same time Renee stepped forward and gave Jeremy a big hug, along with a kiss on the cheek. She followed suit and wrapped her arms around both of them. "I'm so glad."

When she stepped back, she frowned and told him, "I'm so sorry. I want to stay here with you, but we've got to go."

He nodded and seemed very calm about the idea of being left at the hospital. That surprised her until he started explaining. "Might as well go back to the hotel. You can't do anything more here. I'm going to stay with Merry though. I don't want her to be alone. You two get some sleep. I have a hunch you'll be back at it bright and early in the morning. I'll bet Katie has her hands on those keys before seven."

Her fault he didn't understand because she didn't explain at all. Lorna shook her head, "Unfortunately, we're not going back to the hotel, and tomorrow morning is out too. We have to race back out to Healing Waters tonight. Like right now."

"What the hell?" His forehead scrunched. "Why on earth would you go out there at this time of night? Katie said she couldn't get the key until morning. What's she doing, dragging some poor state employee out of bed in the middle of the night? That's gonna go over big. We don't need people pissed off at us."

She closed her eyes for a moment and then opened them. The evening had started out so wonderfully in the lovely and very comfortable hotel room. She'd felt alive and loved and hadn't wanted to move one inch. How quickly it had turned from being sweet to being painful. Not that she considered what was happening here in the hospital a pain. Merry and her niece were as far from that as possible. Anna, on the other hand, had pain in the ass written all over her. "Anna is on her way out to Healing Waters with a pry bar."

Jeremy blinked and blew out a long breath before saying slowly, "Son of a bitch. You two better haul butt out there."

❖

As Lorna drove, Renee punched in Katie's number on Lorna's cell. Not too surprisingly, the ever-vigilant cop picked up on the second ring. If Renee had to guess, that phone was right next to the bed. After apologizing for the late-night call, she explained the details of the message Lorna had received from Anna. The consummate professional, Katie didn't even seem flustered despite the ungodly time. She told Renee she'd meet them at Healing Waters with a key one way or the other. Renee was incredibly relieved to hear it, but felt sorry for whoever was going to get dragged out of bed.

Lorna's face was tense as she stared out the windshield. If she heard any of the conversation between Renee and Katie, she didn't give any indication. She was intent and focused on the road. The lights of city faded behind them as Lorna pushed her speed well past the posted limit. "You're worried, aren't you?" Renee asked as she put the cell phone on the seat. "I mean, really worried." At first she thought Lorna's intensity was because she was so focused on driving. Then she realized there was more to it than that.

Lorna nodded and kept her eyes on the road. Her jaw was tense, and Renee could imagine her teeth grinding together. "The whole time we were out there earlier I kept picking up a bad vibe coming off the main building. It's a bit like the feeling I got when John McCafferty's spirit made its presence known to me. You remember when he crawled inside Jeremy and tried to kill me. Or kill Catherine, actually, but you know what I mean."

"I do." And she did. She would never forget how close she came to losing Lorna so soon after they'd met. John McCafferty was the wicked, bitter man who'd built the gorgeous house on the ocean shore that they all lived in now. Even after he'd died, he would do anything and everything he could to make sure his daughter bent to his will. His iron rule transcended death just as Catherine's devotion for Tiana did. His evil had ended the lives of two good women simply because, in defiance of his mandate, they loved each other and refused to relinquish that love. He, or rather his spirit, had tried to do the same to them when Lorna's psychic powers uncovered the truth. As they brought to light the proof of his misdeeds, and when they were close to reuniting the spirits of Catherine and Tiana, his black spirit had returned from beyond the grave in an attempt to once again assert his will. He'd almost succeeded, *almost* being the key word. Love and kindness had won the battle that night. The spirits of the tragic lovers were reunited, and John McCafferty was silenced for eternity.

To now hear Lorna say she was sensing that same level of evil made Renee feel a little sick to her stomach. She never wanted to even come close to someone like that again. The man was bad through and through, his spirit even worse. Healing Waters was supposed to have been a place for help, and she had the distinct feeling it was, or had been, quite the opposite. She worried about what they might find once they stepped inside that old, abandoned building. It could hold the spirit of something far worse than John McCafferty, and that gave her chills.

In the bit of time they'd spent in the waiting room at the hospital, she'd been able to do a little research into Healing Waters and into the woman who, as it turned out, was Sadie's great-great-grandmother. All she could say was thank goodness for smartphone technology. She'd been one of those people who'd resisted the trend to have the kind of phone that could do it all and then finally broke down and bought in. She was a businesswoman, after all, and it wasn't very good business to let technology pass her by. Finally, she had her very own smartphone, and she'd never looked back. It made everything easier, including doing research while sitting in a hospital waiting room. At last she understood what the big deal was, and though she'd be loath to admit it, she loved her phone.

What she'd found in her Internet search at the hospital was quite interesting, especially what she learned about the grandmother. More accurately, what she didn't find about the grandmother. Sadie's family was quite prominent in the city, and her great-great-grandfather's name was on buildings, schools, and parks. So, it was very curious to discover that so little was written of her great-great-grandmother while volumes were available on her great-great-grandfather. Especially since he was the same one who had committed his beautiful, wealthy wife to an institution designed to treat the insane.

It didn't escape her that back in the day, women had little to no power, even if they were far wealthier than their husbands. It galled her to think that perhaps Sadie's relative had been put in such a place simply to get her out of her high-profile husband's way. It would have left him free to do as he wished and given him unguarded access to her money. She couldn't say that was what had happened, just as she couldn't say that wasn't what had happened. How she wished she could see the man and read his aura. Then she'd know if he'd been a concerned husband or a bastard.

On the way out to Healing Waters, she filled Lorna in on what she'd found in her search. Given everything they'd learned since Lorna's evolution into a psychic, they both decided that something otherworldly was indeed waiting for them at the big red-brick building. Whether or not Sadie was caught in its net, they didn't know. Whether or not it involved Sadie's long-dead relative, they also didn't know. All they were certain of was that a force with unseen powers was making itself known.

As it stood, they were going into the situation blind. Lorna had only fleeting images that didn't let her get a clear idea of what they would find inside, and Renee's particular skill wasn't useful at all in this setting. There was no telling what they would encounter once they walked through those doors. When she thought back to what they'd discovered the last time they were in the area, namely a serial killer's burial grounds, it chilled her to think about what they might come face-to-face with now.

She was absolutely confident that whatever it was, Lorna's powers would uncover it. As the days, weeks, and months passed, Lorna was coming more and more into her powers. Her confidence level was grounded in a growing understanding of what her powers could do, and she also appeared to be finding a comfort level in them that hadn't been there when they first stumbled upon the spirits of Catherine and Tiana.

It warmed Renee's heart to witness the ever-evolving change in the person she loved with all her heart. When she'd first come to the house on the sea, the woman she'd met had carried such a burden of sadness with her it was heartbreaking. It was ingrained in every fiber of her being, and her aura had shown it just as clearly. Renee had felt so bad for her and at the same time understood Lorna would have to be the one to embrace her own peace. The woman who sat next to her in the car now was infinitely more comfortable in her own skin. Lorna was discovering her way in the world that was now hers, and that made Renee love her all the more. That she was able to overcome her bitterness toward Anna and had come to help made her proud. That she was doing everything she could to find the woman Anna had left her for made her even more proud. It took a generous soul to set aside the depth of feeling that situation had created.

At the same time, Lorna's growing acceptance of her psychic powers scared Renee. Lorna was more open to her powers than ever before, and while that let her see beyond the veil separating the worlds more easily, it also gave evil a wider door to enter and attack. Lorna's heart was a good one, and evil detested people like her. Renee didn't want her hurt, and she worried that what was inside the doors of that building might go straight for her beautiful heart.

During the centuries past, people had often been brutal in their treatment of mental illness, and she feared that brutality still thrived inside those walls, that it had soaked into the floors, the ceilings, the windows. She would do anything to make sure it didn't touch her love. Unfortunately, she had few resources with which to battle that kind of evil. In fact, she had nothing.

A flashing light came up behind them. "Shit," Lorna muttered. "This is all we need right now."

Renee couldn't argue the point. The more time Anna spent

out there alone, the more likely she was to get herself into trouble. Delays were not helpful, yet this one appeared unavoidable. "Better pull over. Maybe if we're nice and polite, this will be a quick stop."

"God, I hope so." Lorna steered the car over to the side of the road.

The dark sedan continued around them and stopped right in front of the Yukon. Renee studied the taillights, thinking it was the first time she'd ever been stopped and had that happen. The cruisers always stopped behind the car. The unusual maneuver made sense a moment later when Katie's head appeared out of the open driver's side window. She waved and yelled, "Follow me." A second later, Lorna pulled her car off the shoulder and back onto the highway. They were driving in the direction of Healing Waters once more.

Thank the heavens for small favors. Katie's appearance lifted a huge load off Renee's shoulders. Katie making her timely arrival as backup was comforting on a number of levels. She was a good friend who understood the special gift Lorna brought to the table, and she was local law enforcement, always a handy thing to have on hand when on state property in the middle of the night. This whole thing could go south in a hurry, but with Katie joining them, that was less likely to happen.

As instructed, Lorna followed Katie, who continued on with the lights of her car flashing bright red and blue. The fields and scattered farmhouses rushed by in the darkness, the lights of Katie's car giving them the look of carnival grounds. A single car passed them as they raced toward Healing Waters well in excess of the fifty-mile-an-hour speed limit on this particular stretch of roadway. Katie was apparently of the same mindset as Lorna. Faster was better, even if it meant a possible ticket. Well, a ticket for Lorna anyway. Katie's lights gave her a free pass.

The relief of Katie's appearance faded as they drew closer to Healing Waters. Tension flowed back into Renee's body with each mile they covered. She couldn't help it; she feared what they might find once they arrived. The air carried a charge that seemed to grow stronger and stronger. It seemed like the longer she was around Lorna, the better able she was to pick up on her ability to tune in to their surroundings. It was a handy thing to be able to do.

As if she sensed the same thing, Lorna took one hand off the steering wheel and reached over to squeeze her hand. "We got this," she said. "We got this."

Renee squeezed back. "I hope so."

Chapter Eleven

The room was dark, the beds empty, the air cold and it reeked of a bitter disinfectant. The smell was so intense it made her eyes water. A flicker of light made Sadie's head snap around, and she sucked in her breath. Could she be going crazy? She'd never been one to see things before so the most logical answer was yes.

In the corner shrouded in shifting shadows, Rose sat at a writing table with a small journal open in front of her. A small lamp with a flickering bulb threw a little light across her face. She held a pen midair in one hand and with the other held down the corner of the journal. Her hair was pulled up and pinned in a sloppy knot on top of her head, tendrils of dark hair curling damply around her face. Under other circumstances, she might have looked pretty. In the off-and-on glow of the lamp she looked sad. Her skin was pale as a ghost, which nearly made Sadie laugh because she knew the only thing Rose could be was a ghost.

"Rose," Sadie whispered and was surprised how loud her voice sounded. It was as if she was in an alternate dimension where no echo or reverberation existed. As weird as everything was around her, she wasn't expecting to hear herself speak.

Rose turned her head and her eyes met Sadie's. She jumped as shock thundered through her body. No way, it couldn't be. Yet she was certain it absolutely was true. Rose knew she was here. She could hear Sadie's voice just as she could hear it herself.

Somewhere in this bizarre nightmare, she had become a ghost whisperer. With an insane little laugh, she wondered if she could put that on her resume…provided she ever emerged from this rabbit hole. This experience could spawn her very own reality series.

"Yes," Rose said quietly as she turned her entire body in the small chair so she was looking directly at Sadie. "I am so glad you have finally arrived. I have been waiting a very long time for you, my dear."

"You see me?" Her question was barely above a whisper. Sadie still couldn't quite wrap her head around the idea that she was having a conversation with a ghost. The notion that perhaps she really had hit her head and now her hallucinations were taking on sound was seizing on a pretty strong foothold.

Rose nodded slowly, and a smile fleetingly crossed her face. "I see you very clearly indeed, my child."

My child? Why, the ghost in front of her couldn't be much more than a year or two older than Sadie. Child wasn't exactly an accurate characterization. "You hear me?"

She smiled again and this time it didn't fade away, her teeth straight and very white. But the beautiful smile didn't erase the deep lines of sadness in her face. "I hear you as well. You have a very lovely voice. I am so glad."

"Why?" Sadie was so stunned it was all she could do to get the one word past her lips.

"Why do I think your voice is lovely?" She looked confused. "Because it sounds like Christmas bells to me. It has been quite some time since I have heard something so sweet."

Sadie shook her head. "No, not my voice. I mean, why can you see and hear me? You're a ghost." She wondered if Rose even knew she wasn't real. Telling her she was a ghost might make things worse.

Rose's face cleared, and she gave her another beautiful smile. This time, it did seem to chase away a few of the shadows. "Oh, my dear girl, I am real, or—" She paused and looked off into the darkness. "I was once. In some way I do not truly understand, I still am. It could be because, as I said, I have been waiting for you quite a long time. I knew you would come if I was patient, and I have to be real to see you and to speak to you."

Chills raised the hair on her arms as something indefinable whispered to her. "Who are you?"

A sad expression crossed her lovely, thin face and chased away the fragile sweetness that had been there a second before. She held out her hand to Sadie. Her fingers were long and slender, like those of an accomplished pianist. "Come, my child."

Again with the child thing. Either she was blind or delusional, and given where they were, both were a possibility. Sadie looked down at her own hands, and the sight stopped her. A shiver ran down her spine as she curled her fingers into a ball and then stretched them back out. She repeated the motion several times, staring in amazement. It couldn't be and yet the sight that greeted her eyes was undeniable. Their hands were the same, with identical narrow, long fingers and delicate smooth nails. Hands that could, indeed, play the piano well.

Okay, her fears were confirmed. She was obviously losing it after being trapped in this place for God knows how many hours. It had started with seeing ghosts, followed by hearing them, and now they were asking to hold her hand. Worst of all, she was seeing her hands on the apparition. Not just similar either. No, their hands were identical, as if they were twins. There was no denying what was happening to her; she was losing her mind.

"Do not be afraid of me. I would never hurt you, my child."

Stop it, she wanted to scream. Stop calling me child. This was all so surreal. Her mind was going, and yet strangely she wanted to talk with this spirit. She wanted to touch the hand still held out to her and that looked just like her own. "You're a ghost." Her protest was pretty darned weak.

She was surprised when Rose nodded slowly. "I am most assuredly a ghost. My life faded away years before my body could no longer stay grounded in this place of hell." She continued to hold her hand out toward Sadie. She motioned Sadie closer with her fingers. "Come with me. I have something I must show you. It is why I have waited all this time for you to come."

Part of her wanted to step forward and accept the outstretched hand. Another part of her was screaming, *Run, Sadie, run.* Neither part won the battle. Instead of doing either, she continued to stand rooted in place. Her feet refused to move and her hands stayed at her side. The part of her brain that worked toward self-preservation was still fine. She might very well be losing her mind, but that didn't mean she had to go willingly.

"Just tell me, please." Yes, the frightened whine she was hearing did come out of her mouth.

Slowly, Rose shook her head and her hand dropped to her lap. "I cannot tell you, for you must see to believe. You do not think this is happening to you right now, do you? You imagine you are hurt or are dreaming. Am I correct?"

Undoubtedly she was quite correct. Sadie was under the impression she had some kind of head injury and was seeing things brought on by severe trauma to the brain. She'd heard stories of things like this happening to people who'd suffered brain damage. The fact that her head didn't hurt anywhere was a minor inconsistency to what she thought of as a solid theory. Then again, if she was suffering from an injury, her being able to come up with any kind of theory was shaky at best. "No, I'm hallucinating. You're a figment of my imagination. Nothing about this is real."

Rose's laughter was brittle and far from warm. "Trust me, child. You are not having visions. I would know. Come with me now. Let me show you what you need to see. You will understand why all of this is happening to you."

Her reluctance was fading away because the draw to Rose was almost magnetic. Something about the ghost was irresistibly compelling, and fear was nowhere in the equation. Her previously uncooperative feet started to move, and the next thing Sadie knew, she was standing next to the apparition called Rose. Almost as surprising was when she put her hand into Rose's and then almost as quickly snatched it away. It couldn't be. Her touch felt as real and as alive as her own. Damn, but this was going so far beyond hallucination.

"What do you want from me?" Her trembling question was so soft she barely heard the words herself. The faint scent of lavender enveloped her as she stood next to Rose. It was sweet and soothing and totally frightening, as it hadn't been there a minute before. Sights, sounds, and now smells. She was going deeper and deeper down the rabbit hole.

For a brief moment, Rose closed her eyes and breathed deeply. Then she opened her eyes and stared directly into Sadie's. "It is very simple, my dear. You will set me free."

"I will set you free? What does that even mean? It doesn't make any sense." Like any of this made sense. "How in the world can I accomplish that, considering you're not real?"

She glanced down at Sadie's hand. "Once, so long ago, I was flesh and blood just as you are now. I lived and I loved and I laughed. I had a life with a family, with children, and then it was all ripped away from me." The last words came out on a sob. She breathed in deeply and then blew out the breath, long and slow. When she spoke again, her voice was once more steady. "Everything was taken from me and I nearly lost all hope, but God told me that one day you would come and give me back my life and my name." Her head came up, and she once more met Sadie's eyes. "God sent you to me."

"How?" Sadie asked again. "I don't even know who you are."

Rose ran a hand over Sadie's hair. "You will know how to help me, and you will know why when you see it."

Yeah, well, that narrowed it right down. She was already seeing ghosts. What more could there possibly be? "How?" Lord, she was beginning to sound like an owl. Who, who. How, how.

Rose took Sadie's chin in her hand and turned her head toward the mirror. When their heads were side by side, her hand dropped away.

"Oh, dear God," Sadie whispered right before her vision went black.

❖

Anna jammed the car into park, turned off the motor, and got out. From the backseat she grabbed the pry bar she'd dug out of the garage. She hadn't even known they owned a pry bar but was damned glad to see it tucked back on a shelf behind a can of motor oil. Before she left the house, she'd also grabbed the big flashlight they kept on hand for emergencies like power outages. This was, in her opinion, one giant emergency, and she doubted there would be electricity once she got inside the building. She was going in prepared.

Ahead of her the main building in the complex loomed dark and ominous in the night. The smaller buildings stood out in the darkness like guards to the larger, more imposing one. There were no lights in the parking lot, or at least none that worked any longer, and likewise for the building. It was as black and somber as everything else in this seemingly forgotten land. It was as if everyone wanted this place to fade away in silence. Out of sight, out of mind.

How she wished it had disappeared because maybe then she wouldn't be here in the middle of the night preparing to break and enter for the first time in her life. Committing a felony wasn't exactly her thing, and she didn't feel good about it now.

Regardless of how she felt about the action, she was barging full speed ahead. Sadie was in this building somewhere, they'd all said so earlier, and she was determined to find her one way, legally or otherwise. As long as she found Sadie safe, she didn't care if she was arrested and thrown in jail. It would be worth the charge. Besides, she knew a couple of good lawyers who'd have her bailed out in no time. Having friends who were licensed professionals came in handy.

Pry bar in one hand and flashlight in the other, she mounted the steps of the building. She balanced the big flashlight on the brick balustrade so that it illuminated the door. For a moment she studied the oval glass in the center of the thick wooden door. It was undeniably beautiful, and she believed it had stood in place for a century or more. It was unfortunate that she was here to destroy it, and a part of her regretted what she was being forced to do. Another part of her couldn't have cared less. It was simply glass, and glass could be replaced even if it was a hundred years old. Sadie could not. She walked up close to the door and, holding the pry bar high in a batter's swing, prepared to shatter the workmanship that had barred entrance to this building for so long. Time to get this party started. As she started into her swing, Anna paused and then slowly lowered the pry bar to her side. A thought had occurred to her mid-strike, and she decided why not give it a try. She reached out, grasped the door handle, and pushed.

It opened.

Anna gasped, and her hand flew off the handle as if she'd suffered third-degree burns. She rubbed her hands together, the lingering effects of an unexpected shock disconcerting. How in the world did that happen? Earlier three of them had tried this same door, and it had been locked up as tight as a prison. The door wouldn't budge no matter what they tried. She didn't imagine it earlier when it was locked up tight, and she wasn't imagining it now as it swung open on silent hinges.

She stepped back without crossing over the threshold and considered the ramifications of what had just happened. It was a simple thing that filled her with trepidation. After all the decades of misuse, after all the years of wind, rain, snow, and heat, the door should squeak like a scared rat when opened. It didn't make even a whisper, as if it had been installed yesterday. Silent was the very last thing this door should be.

As much as she wanted to charge through and find Sadie, rancid fear began to creep up her spine. Something about this was very, very wrong. Suddenly, despite all her earlier bravado, an urge to turn around and drive back home as fast as she could assailed her. She longed to pretend that when she arrived back at the lovely home with the white shutters and wide deck, Sadie would be waiting for her, wineglass in hand and a smile on her face. If only it could be that easy.

That wasn't going to be a reality, and she had only one choice. She closed her eyes and took several long, deep breaths. This wasn't the time to be timid or frightened, and she couldn't pretend it wasn't happening because it most definitely was. Denial wasn't an option she was willing to embrace. Her wife, wherever she was being held, was depending on her to be strong, and that's exactly what she was going to be. It didn't matter if things between them lately had been a little strained. One thing she knew with certainty, Sadie would do everything in her power to find Anna if she was the one in trouble, so that's what she was going to do now. Love was about being there for the other person no matter what. No matter what, she repeated. Anna dropped the pry bar and reached back to grab her flashlight.

"It's now or never," she muttered, then stepped over the threshold. When the door slammed behind her with a loud bang, she jumped and just managed to choke off a scream that rose in her throat. Whirling, she grabbed the door handle and pulled. It wouldn't move. The quirks of an old, abandoned building, right? It had to be, because anything else…well, she wasn't going there. She didn't have the time or the energy to waste on going there.

Anna gave up on the door and turned back around. She swept her light over the entryway. Once it had probably been quite spectacular with its oak-paneled walls, terrazzo tile, and a tall ceiling with an ornate dropped light hanging in the center. Imposing in the middle of the room was a massive reception desk, and it was clear that it was the defining element of the space. Visitors must have waited on the side she stood on now.

Patients—or were they inmates—kept on the other side. The barrier it created was as effective as if it were a solid wall. Behind the desk was a long stairway leading to the upper floors, and the once-polished steps appeared to stretch up into a yawning black hole.

As she moved the flashlight, shadows swayed in the beam of her light, and dust motes kicked up by her feet danced as if music were playing somewhere. Once again, despite the eerie and unsettling silence, she had the feeling that something was very much alive here. It further strengthened her conviction that coming tonight was the right course of action. At every turn her decision to be here was confirmed. It wasn't a wise idea to leave Sadie in this place.

"Okay, Sadie," she whispered while she turned full circle and studied the tall windows, the bare walls, and the stone floor in the beam of her flashlight. "Where are you?" Though her words were soft, they seemed to echo in the large room. More shivers assailed her body. In day-to-day business she always considered herself a pretty tough competitor. Right at this moment she was beginning to think she was far from tough. This place gave her the creeps.

Studying her surroundings, Anna decided the best and only way to do the search was to go one floor at a time. Clear the main floor and then go up to the second, the third, and finally the fourth. If there was an attic, she would hit it last. She really hoped it wouldn't be necessary. She hoped she'd find Sadie quickly and they could get out of here. *Please let her be on the first floor.*

Anna's work style had always been of the OCD methodical variety, and so she would use that philosophy here too. At times, being a bit obsessive-compulsive could come in handy. It had driven Lorna crazy, yet with Sadie, it always brought a smile. Another thing she loved about Sadie: unconditional acceptance.

Once more she did a full three-sixty, sweeping her gaze over everything the beam of her flashlight highlighted. She was hoping for something that would give her a clue as to where to start. If only she could find a switch that would light the place up. No such luck, not that she really believed she'd find a light switch. Even if she did, odds were that the electricity had been turned off for years.

There was nothing obvious in the lobby for anyone to hide behind, with the possible exception of the reception desk. It was as good a place as any to start. As soon as she stepped behind it, she was essentially done with the lobby, because it was empty. Not so much as a paperclip on the dusty surface. When they cleaned out this place, they obviously did a complete job. It didn't appear that anyone planned on coming back.

She shined her flashlight down the hallway behind the reception desk. Closed doors lined the darkened expanse that stretched beyond the beam of her light, along with silence and shadows that gave her the shivers. She tapped her foot as she stared. She could stand here and think about what to do next, or she could get in gear. She opted for kicking it up a notch. It was time to check out the inner sanctum of the Healing Waters Hospital.

As Anna started to move away from the reception desk her light caught something on the floor. Apparently she was wrong when she'd decided the area was clean of everything except years of dust. She kneeled down to see what was beneath the counter and reflecting back the beam of her light. When her hand closed around a familiar object, her heart nearly stopped. Slowly she pulled her hand from beneath the counter, clutching the small item in her hand. Opening her clenched fist, she immediately recognized the black fob with the gold star on one side and the single key dangling from the silver loop. It was Sadie's.

"Oh my God," she gasped. "Where are you?" Tears pooled in her eyes and her heart took a leap. She had been right to come here.

"Visitors are not allowed unescorted beyond the desk."

Anna screamed at the same time she jerked upright. When she did, she smacked her head soundly on the underside of the reception counter. For a moment, she saw stars and wasn't sure she wasn't going to black out. When the stars receded, she slowly rose to her feet. Rubbing the back of her head with one hand, she turned in the direction of the disapproving female voice that had come out of nowhere. She hadn't heard a single footstep.

Halfway down the stairwell, with one hand on the banister, stood a dour-looking middle-aged woman in an ankle-length white skirt, black apron, and white nurse's cap. Shiny black hair was tucked beneath the cap in a style she'd seen only in books. The woman's expression telegraphed loud and clear that she wasn't happy to see Anna. News flash. Anna wasn't all that excited to see her either.

Slowly awareness dawned that something had changed, beyond the appearance of the strange woman. At first she couldn't put a finger on what it was, and then it hit her. Soft lights were on all around her, bathing the lobby in a pale yellow glow that warmed the room. Where did they come from? A second ago the only light that cut through the darkness was from her flashlight. The other odd thing that struck her at the same time was the smell of smoke that filled the lobby, as if a wood fire was burning somewhere nearby. She was absolutely certain the smell hadn't been in the air a minute ago. Had someone lit a fire in a fireplace somewhere? A spark of encouragement surged through her. Maybe Sadie had been able to start a fire to keep warm. It wasn't exactly balmy in here. While the sudden appearance of lights made her nervous, the smell of a fire gave her a little hope.

"Where's Sadie?" She tried to match the strange woman's sharp, authoritative tone. *Get snippy with me, bitch, and I'll throw it right back at you.*

"We have no guests named Sadie. Now you must leave."

Guests? She made it sound like this was a hotel rather than what it really was. "Where's Sadie?" she insisted. She didn't believe the woman any farther than she could throw her. The freak knew more than she was telling.

The corners of the stranger's mouth turned up, and the sight sent ice into Anna's blood. It wasn't a smile. It was the visage of a shark poised to attack. "Perhaps you refer to Rose's young guest."

"I don't know a woman called Rose. I'm talking about Sadie, my wife. What have you done with her? I know she's here, so it's no use lying to me." She didn't know anyone named Rose, yet at the same time the name resonated in her subconscious. All of sudden, everything clicked into place. The necklace, Sadie, Rose—they were all connected.

"Why, I've done nothing with…what did you say her name is? Sadie? If she's here, she's safe because we're here to help. We've always been here to help the less fortunate. It's what we do so very well." The woman clasped her hands together in front of her tidy apron. Her back was straight and her eyes empty as she stared down at Anna.

Those quietly uttered words chilled Anna to the soul. Lorna had talked about the evil they encountered at her house on the west side, and of the serial killer who'd taken the life of her friend, and she'd really believed she'd been embellishing for the sake of a good story. All of a sudden she was rethinking her assessment. This woman had an air about her that screamed malevolence. It was the first time Anna had ever been around someone who made her feel as though she needed to get as far away as possible.

It also strengthened her resolve to find her wife as quickly as possible. "I'm getting Sadie." She shoved the car key in her pocket and rushed around the reception desk to the bottom of the stairs. The woman was standing in the middle of the staircase in what appeared to Anna to be an attempt to block her from coming up. She fully intended to simply barge past this odd and frightening woman. The advantage was hers because she was bigger, stronger, and more determined. No problem taking the bitch down. All she had to do was shove her out of the way and walk up the stairs one at a time. She didn't make it far. The moment she was within reach, the woman put her hand on Anna's arm, and her vision went completely dark.

❖

"Damn it, damn it, damn it," Lorna muttered when they pulled up beside Anna's car. Why Anna couldn't let them handle this search the right way was beyond her. Or not. When had Anna ever done things the way Lorna wished? Pretty much never was the most accurate answer. Looking back, Lorna could recall dozens of times when they had come at things like polar opposites. Interesting how at the time it had completely passed her by when they lived together, and yet now it was so incredibly clear. The fact they'd stayed together as long as they did seemed to be a little miracle.

Katie was already out of her car with a giant flashlight in her hand by the time Lorna put her own car in park. Before they could even get out, Katie had paused next to Anna's car and laid a hand on the hood. "It's still warm," she said. "She hasn't been here very long. That's good. Maybe we can stop her before she gets herself in trouble."

Without waiting for Lorna or Renee, Katie headed toward the entrance of the main building, her stride long and purposeful. From the looks of it, she was in full cop mode. That could be bad for Anna, depending on what she'd done already. If they found Sadie here, it would go down better for Anna. If not...well, that was going to be Anna's resolve.

"If she broke in, we could have a problem," Katie said as Lorna and Renee raced up the steps behind her. She amended her previous thought, afraid it would most probably be bad for Anna.

"I know," Lorna said, blowing out a long breath. "I was hoping we weren't this far behind and could stop her before she did something stupid. She's never been the impulsive type until now."

They all stopped in front of the massive entry door. On the ground was the pry bar that Lorna had to assume was the same one Anna had brought with her. Her gaze moved from the abandoned pry bar to the fully intact, ornate glass door. No shattered glass and no splintered wood around the door frame. No one had touched it, from what she could tell. That was a good thing from that standpoint of avoiding an encounter with law enforcement. It also left one big question looming: if Anna hadn't forced her way in, where was she?

Lorna tried the door handle, which was just as tightly locked as when they were here earlier. Anna hadn't gotten in through this door. "You have the keys, right?" Lorna looked up at Katie.

Katie shook her head. "No. I couldn't reach a soul at this time of night so we're going to have to wing it."

"This is weird," Renee said as she reached down and picked up the pry bar. "Why bring this if she didn't intend to use it? All it would take is one good swing to shatter the glass and open the door."

Lorna shook her head. She'd been thinking the same thing. It wasn't like Anna to abandon a plan once she had it in her head. The word stubborn came to mind. It would be hard to count the number of times she'd seen her dig her heels in and refuse to budge on something. "I don't understand what she's up to. I know she isn't about to leave without finding Sadie first. Once she gets something in her mind she sticks with it to the bitter end." She stepped to the railing and leaned out. Cupping her hands around her mouth, she yelled, "Anna!"

Her voice seemed to echo over and over on the quiet night air. When the sound finally settled down, she strained to listen for an answering call. When nothing came back to her, she was disappointed. Not even a tiny sound of movement like footsteps or doors opening. Where in the hell was the woman?

"She has to have gone inside. Maybe she found a door we missed earlier and it was open." It was the only thing that made sense to her at the moment. Except it didn't really make sense at all, considering Jeremy had checked all the doors, twice. When they left here, there was no way into the building.

"I don't get it," Katie said. "People routinely check state-owned property to make sure it's all secure. It's part of their job. The chance of finding an open door in any of these buildings is pretty slim, even without the padlocks and chains they placed on most of the doors. If she is inside, how did she get in?"

That was the million-dollar question. "No damn idea. Bolt cutters, maybe on one of the side doors?"

Katie tried the door just as Lorna had and then stepped back. "Well, it's pretty clear this door is still locked up tight. Where did she get in if not here?"

"Unless she locked it behind her," Renee said, and it was a logical thought. "Maybe she got in through this door, and that's why she didn't need the bar to force her way in."

The more she thought about it, the more she questioned Renee's train of logic. Lorna shook her head again. "No, why would she? She had to know we would follow her out here once I listened to her voice mail. If she didn't want us to follow, she never would have left the message." In fact, she had to assume, as dangerous as that was, that Anna was actually banking on the fact that Lorna would follow as soon as she listened to the voice mail.

None of this clicked into place for her, and the longer she stood here, the more uneasy she became. It wasn't the mystery of where Anna was as much as it was some indefinable feeling. Something subtle and chilly seemed to reach out fingers to touch her cheek. It sent shivers through her body, and she didn't like it. Not one little bit.

Following Katie's lead, she took hold of the door handle again, intending to wrench the damn thing open one way or the other. This time when her fingers wrapped around the cold metal, electricity raced up her arm. She screamed and tried to pull her hand away. Strangely, she couldn't. Her hand felt like it was glued to the door handle, and as she held on, her vision began to blur and her knees grew weak. Vaguely it occurred to her that she wasn't going to be able to stand much longer. She wasn't wrong. Pain shot up her thighs as her knees smacked into concrete.

"Come," said the pretty woman in the flowing white cotton nightgown. It was a plain garment with no embellishment and no style. The fabric was obviously cheap and thin as a cloud. It made her look ghostly. *"She is coming, and we do not have much time."*

"Are you speaking to me?" Lorna asked. She glanced around, surprised to discover that they were alone inside a big room. Or maybe she wasn't too surprised. Finding herself in strange places, strange times, and with strange people was becoming a routine part of her life. Her perception of reality had taken a huge shift over the last year so that seeing a ghost, and she was pretty certain it was a ghost, didn't much faze her.

The woman tilted her head and looked puzzled by her question. *"Of course I am speaking to you. Do you see another with us? I certainly do not."* She threw out her arms and did a full circle, coming back around to face Lorna once more.

"But this is a vision." Her rational mind told her it wasn't real and she was simply experiencing another of her psychic visions. What made this one a bit stranger than any of the others was that she didn't usually step inside them to participate. Well, not usually anyway. There was that Catherine moment when she had not only stepped inside the vision but also inside of Catherine herself.

"It is and it is not. I am here and so too are you. A vision perhaps, though a vision in which we must both participate. It is more important for you to understand."

"This is fucked up," Lorna said almost to herself. She liked the visions better when there was no interaction. Her one previous experience had nearly cost her life.

"I do not understand what you mean, but it is of no matter. Now please, I beg of you, hurry before she hears us and returns. You do not want her to come back and find us here. We must go."

Vision or no vision, Lorna wasn't getting the gist of what the *ghost was so worried about. Clearly, they were alone here in the shadowland. "Who is this 'she' you're so damned worried about? It seems clear to me that we're the only ones in this place."*

She held out a hand, motioning frantically toward Lorna. "No, we are not alone. Nurse Thompson is nearby. Please," she nearly cried.

"Nurse Thompson?" Who in the hell was Nurse Thompson? Whoever she was, this ghost obviously didn't like her, and the fear in her eyes was quite real. Still, the ghost's problem wasn't hers at the moment. Her problem was finding Anna and Sadie, and this wasn't very helpful. She needed to have a vision that would actually be a means to an end. From all appearances, her psychic powers were going a little wonky.

Lorna looked around and realized with a start that she was inside the Healing Waters Hospital, except it wasn't the one she'd come to tonight. The room surrounding her came into focus, and the reality was shocking. Not so much that she was inside instead of outside as she'd been when she touched the door handle. Rather, she was not in the same time period. This room looked brand-new and, more frightening, occupied. It was no longer the empty shell of a building in a compound of overgrown lawns and empty parking lots.

Looking around the ghost and down the hall, she could see the flicker of firelight through an open door. The crackle of burning wood and the scent of fragrant tamarack filled the air. Under other circumstances it would be pleasant. Here, it just felt creepy. She would wager the fireplaces in this old building hadn't seen a stick of wood in at least three decades, if not longer.

The reception desk that took up a great deal of the entryway was polished and shining, adorned by a large bouquet of daylilies. A four-legged dark oak chair with a padded leather seat was pushed next to the work surface that was cluttered with papers and several old-style pens and sharpened pencils. A wall-mounted pencil sharpener with a small turn handle was on the wall next to the desk. She was a little fascinated by the piece, realizing she'd never seen one like it before. It was rare to see a pencil these days, let alone a sharpener with a rotary handle.

Lorna pulled her attention away from her surroundings and back to the frantic nightgown-clad woman. "What's happening?" she asked. "Where are we? When are we?" If she could interact in this vision, it seemed only fair she could ask questions too.

"You have to help them," the woman said as she held out her hand. "Hurry. You must hurry." She motioned anxiously for Lorna to follow.

Maybe she could ask questions, but it appeared that getting answers to them was a completely different story.

"Help who?" She felt a little like a child who stomped her feet and held her ground until she got what she wanted.

"All of them."

Lorna amended her earlier thought. She might get her questions answered, only it appeared that the woman would respond just to the ones she wanted to answer. She gave serious consideration to just standing here until she could get answers that gave her at least a little direction. So far that wasn't happening. Before she could ask anything further, the ghost reached over and touched her.

The hand that grasped Lorna's was shocking because it felt so real. Warm and solid and real. This vision was getting downright freaky. Briefly she wondered if this was what happened when her powers grew stronger. It wasn't like she had a psychic mentor she could ask. Someone needed to write a psychic manual because she was sure confused.

The woman tugged her insistently toward the staircase, and Lorna decided the best thing to do was follow. It appeared this woman wasn't going to be deterred from whatever mission she was on, and holding her ground wasn't working very well either. If you can't fight 'em, join 'em. They were halfway up the long staircase when the woman stopped and put a hand to her mouth. Her eyes grew wide with fear.

"Oh dear. No, no, no." Her words were muffled against her hand. "We are too late. She is coming for us. I told you we needed to hurry. Now we are too late. She is going to find us."

She whirled and took Lorna's face between her hands. Again it hit her how real this woman of her vision felt, this ghost of someone who had long ago left this world. "You are the only one who can help now. She has them. She has all of us. Please, please, for the love of God, set us free."

"Lorna." Renee had her face between her hands and was almost yelling into her face. Her breath was hot on her skin as they both kneeled on the floor. She didn't remember dropping to the ground.

"What?" She blinked. *My knees hurt like a son of a bitch.*

"Are you back?" Renee's eyes searched her face, and her fingers soothed the hair back from her forehead.

She shook her head a little to clear the lingering cobwebs of the vision. "Yeah, I'm here. That was pretty fucking weird. How did I end up down here?" Rising to her feet, she held her hand out to help Renee up too.

"You should try being on our side," Katie said. "I've never seen someone's face go as white as yours, and then you just zoned out as you dropped to your knees. It was like you were in a different world."

"You should have been inside my little pea brain if you want to talk about different worlds."

"You had a vision, didn't you?" Renee still had her face in her hands. Katie had said she was pale, but looking at Renee, Lorna didn't think she had anything on her. There was no color in her face at all. She must have scared the crap of her, and that made her feel bad.

"You could call it that." She searched Renee's eyes and, despite her pale face, was satisfied by what she saw in the depths of her gaze. Her woman was tough and could handle the strangeness that came with loving a psychic.

"What do you mean?"

"It was one of those times you had to be there to grasp it."

"Try us," Katie said.

"You know I'll understand," Renee added.

She did know that, and it would do her good to talk it through. "Well, here's the deal. I just saw and talked to a ghost, and Houston, I'm pretty sure we have a problem."

Chapter Twelve

The Watcher's feet hit the sand with such force his entire body shook, head to toe. With lightning speed, he'd felt the change. She was in deep trouble. Dangerous trouble. So far he had been able to keep her safe and during each step along her journey had been successful in guiding her to a better place. Now everything he had worked so hard to put into place was in jeopardy.

Evil was pursuing her like a cougar stalking its prey, and he was not about to let the cougar take her life or what she was destined to bring to this world. Her powers had grown in the time since she had come here, and the good she had done with the gift God had given her stretched far beyond what he had hoped for. She was, in so many ways, his salvation. In all the years he had walked upon the earth he had never come across one who walked in his grace as she did. It was a miracle he did not discount in any way. He would never allow the darkness to take her. Never.

He no longer cared what his fate was to ultimately be. For so long all he had wanted to do was find a path back to heaven, to reclaim the wings he had lost through no one's fault but his own. He accepted that his way was the fallen way, and he no longer worried what would happen to him. All he wanted was to protect her, and whatever it took to do so, that is what he would do, even if that meant he would cease to be.

Storm clouds gathered in the sky above, and he turned his face toward the coming downpour. He had grown accustomed to weather that cried as often as it shined. As he expected, the rain began to fall, and his long black hair ran with water. Seeming to pick up on the mood of the sky, the ocean began to churn. Violent waves slammed against the beach, racing across the sand to swirl at his feet. Its cold spray struck his face, the taste of salt bitter on his tongue. It was no more bitter than the pain in his heart. Frustration at being bound to this place made him scream into the night. There had to be a way to go to her. She could not fail in this battle between dark and light because he was tethered to this place.

He turned his face to the sky, where in the eternal curtain of black velvet and sparkling stars, he put voice to this heart's desire. He had little to lose while she had everything to risk.

"I come to you now, oh Lord, a humble servant who fell from your grace. Hear my prayers. Release my feet from the grip of the sand that has held them captive for millennia after millennia. I beg of you, release me so that I may go to her, so that I may keep her safe. Hear my words, oh Lord, and set me free."

Sadie awoke to find herself once more in the darkened empty room. Or was she? Her heart was pounding like a drum as she pushed up from the floor and stared into the corner where not so long ago she'd gaped into the mirror as she'd stood side by side with the woman from her vision. It was empty now.

Understanding seemed to come slowly, and as it did, with it came more questions. The face, so much like her own, was from a past long since gone. A great-grandmother, a great-great-grandmother—she didn't really know where she fell in the branches of the family tree. All she did know was that they were of one blood and that something terrible had happened to her in this place. The truth of it crept along her skin.

Rose had tried to tell her, not in so many words, which would have been helpful, and Sadie simply hadn't been able to understand. Nice, clear communication had apparently been too much to ask for, because Rose had opted for cryptic.

Perhaps that wasn't being fair. She had seen her face, touched her hand, and what she'd picked up from the ghost of the woman who was her ancestor was that she'd been scared to death. Whatever had happened to her in this place, Rose had been terrified, and that terror had lasted beyond her own death. How messed up was that? Incredibly sad too. It wasn't right for any soul to be followed into death by that kind of emotion.

Even in the face of her overwhelming terror, Sadie couldn't shake the sense that Rose had a greater purpose in coming to her than just finding her own peace. Something more than her own salvation was at stake, and that's what Rose seemed to be trying so hard to get Sadie to understand.

Except she still didn't get it. Yes, she realized at this juncture that she was a direct descendant of this woman. She couldn't deny their uncanny resemblance. In different clothes and with different hairstyles, they could easily pass as sisters. That wasn't the critical piece of the puzzle. Something else was driving Rose, and Sadie struggled to figure out what it was. Seemed odd that she was wishing for a hallucination, but right at the moment, that's exactly what she was doing. She wanted to spend more time with Rose, to understand and help. If she could do that, then perhaps she could find a way out of the locked room.

She went still as a sound broke the silence in the once-more empty room she found herself in. Was that footsteps she was hearing? Oh, dear God, had Anna found her at last? All thoughts of Rose fled as hope surged in her chest. Going home had never sounded as wonderful as it did right now. It had taken a lifetime to discover the kind of love she shared with Anna, and she was far from ready to give it up. Not even this crazy situation she found herself in could shake her belief that Anna would come for her. She hoped that moment was now.

She jumped up and ran to the window, peering out between the bars. The grime of decades was thick, making everything appear dusty and distorted. Not enough, however, to block her view. Three cars were parked near the entrance to the building. Three glorious cars. She choked back a sob. They hadn't left her here; they'd returned.

Once more she raced to the door and grabbed the doorknob, shocked when it turned in her hand. She was so surprised that her hand fell away, and for a moment all she could do was simply stare at it. Tears started down her cheeks, and she didn't bother wiping them away. She was free after what seemed like an eternity of incarceration, and the reality of it left her a little stunned. Once more she grabbed the doorknob and, wrenching the door open, took three quick steps out into the hallway before abruptly coming to a stop. The hallway wasn't dark and it wasn't empty. Coming toward her with fear painted across her face was Anna.

"Oh, my God, Anna," she said on a sob. Anna shook her head ever so slightly, and it was only then she figured out why she hadn't rushed to her. Her heart sank.

Behind her was Nurse Thompson.

Without another word, she backed up until she was once more in the long room. As Anna and Nurse Thompson followed her inside, the room became as cold as a walk-in freezer. All her joy at seeing Anna's face turned to dread. This wasn't just a harmless vision. Whatever was happening here was centered on the nurse, and Sadie was convinced she meant them harm. It wasn't just her life in jeopardy now; it was Anna's as well.

"Now," Nurse Thompson said as soon as Anna and Sadie were standing side by side, their hands clasped together. The feel of Anna's flesh against hers was the only thing keeping her from charging the nurse. "You two can find a bed and make yourselves comfortable. You will be staying here a long time." As she talked, she'd backed up until she was once more at the door.

"You can't keep us in here," Sadie said defiantly. She was getting pretty sick of this bitch. Maybe taking her down wasn't such a bad idea, although she'd have to let go of Anna, and she didn't want to do that. Her bravado was much stronger when she was holding on to Anna.

"We will see about that, now will we not?" The snide tone to her voice made Sadie want to launch herself at the witch. Before she could, the nurse backed out of the door, and Sadie heard the dreadful click of the lock. That stupid, stupid lock. When they were alone, she immediately flung herself into Anna's arms and let all the emotion from the last few hours wash over her. She began to sob, as much for herself as for Anna. "You idiot," she cried. "You shouldn't have come back here for me, but I'm so glad you did."

Anna's arms were strong as they held her tight. She kissed her all over her face. How she loved the tenderness of her lips and the scent that was so uniquely hers. "I couldn't stand it anymore. I knew you were in this place somewhere, and I couldn't leave you here."

Words that made her heart soar at the same time they gave her pause. Sadie stepped back out of her embrace and looked at her. "Why did you leave earlier? I tried like a crazy woman to get your attention. I screamed and pounded on the windows. You should have been able to see and hear me, yet you never even looked up. You just left." She held out her bruised hands. "These are going to take weeks to heal."

Anna was shaking her head, and she took Sadie's damaged hands gently into her own. Her touch was tender as she stroked her thumbs over the bruises. "None of us saw you or heard a thing, and we checked everywhere. Every door, every window, and every building in this complex. Oh, Sadie, I'm so sorry you were hurt."

"I still don't understand why you didn't come inside to check for me. I was stuck in this room for so long, and I couldn't get out because the door was locked. I thought for sure you'd get inside and find me. Why didn't you come?"

Anna continued to stroke her bruised hands, and the warmth of the gesture touched her. "The entry door on the first level wasn't open. Locked up tight, I mean. We tried it a few times and couldn't get it to budge."

Sadie shook her head vehemently. "No, that's not possible. I had the key, and I wouldn't have locked it behind myself when I came in. There would have been no point since it usually only takes me maybe half an hour to scout a location. Besides, out here there's nobody around for miles. You should have been able to walk right in."

"Well, I'm telling you, darlin', the door was locked up tight. Most of the ground-level doors were not only locked; they were chained and padlocked as well. We tried and couldn't find a way in. Lorna was convinced you were here because she was getting some kind of weird psychic vibe, but we had to go call a police friend of hers before we could get access to the inside."

"So where's Lorna now? How did you get in without her friend? Or are they with you?"

Anna was shaking her head, her mouth turned down in a frown. "I went home, and it drove me crazy thinking you were out here. I finally decided it was stupid to wait for the keys. Lorna's cop friend Katie was trying to get them, but after about a million calls, she said it would be morning before she could get us in. I managed to hold it together for a couple of hours before I couldn't stand it any longer. I grabbed a pry bar and came back out. I had to get to you whether it was legal or not."

"You broke the door?" Sadie was shocked. This was so not like Anna, who did everything by the book. Actually, more than being shocked, she was a little impressed. The scofflaw version of Anna was pretty intriguing. She wanted to hug her tight and run right home with her.

Anna's expression grew puzzled at the question. It didn't seem like a particularly hard question to Sadie, but it appeared to come across that way to Anna. She'd said she came out with a pry bar and there were basically only two things to do with a tool like that: pry open a door or use it to smash a window. The only question was, which route did she go?

"Actually, no, and that's what's so odd about me getting in the building. I was going to smash the hell out of that pretty oval glass in the door, and then I decided to try the door handle one more time before I started to go postal on the glass. Strangest thing was, Sadie, it was unlocked. Three of us tried it earlier, and that door wouldn't budge a millimeter. You might have left it unlocked when you came in, but by the time we got here, it was bolted solid. Until a few minutes ago, that is. When I grabbed it this time, it swung open as though it was expecting me."

That sentiment gave Sadie the chills. Given everything that had happened since she woke up here, she suspected someone, or something, had indeed been waiting for Anna. "I hate to say it, but I think it probably was."

"It?"

She waved her arms. "This place. It's like we're caught in an episode of *The Twilight Zone* or a chapter of a Stephen King book. Something really creepy and really weird is going on around here."

"I actually sort of understand. I feel it too."

"You want to hear the strangest thing of all?"

"I don't know what can get much stranger than being held hostage by a ghost."

"I talked to my great-great-grandmother."

"Rose?"

Sadie's eyes snapped up to meet Anna's. "How did you know that?" Not even she knew of Rose's connection here until just a little bit ago. It was insane that Anna had just rolled her name off her tongue as though they were old friends. Her woman surprised her more and more every minute.

"The condensed version is that Lorna had a vision, or whatever it is she gets, when she touched the necklace I had made for you. When it did its woo-woo stuff, Lorna wanted to know the history of the stone. Apparently the vision she got wasn't about you, which is what I was hoping for. Instead it was Rose, and that's why Lorna wanted to know more of your family history. I tracked down your mother, which by the way was quite an accomplishment given she's hopping around Europe, and she was able to tell me where it came from. I guess that's why when Nurse Crazy grabbed me on the stairs, I wasn't totally surprised."

"I would have been."

"I probably would have too, except having Lorna here to open my eyes is most likely why I didn't freak out or find it a big shock when I saw the nurse. I was more concerned about you than being scared of her."

"Maybe not to you, but that bitch scares the bejesus out of me."

Anna wrapped her arms around her again. "I can't even begin to tell you how sorry I am I didn't get here sooner. I should never have left in the first place. As soon as Lorna said she believed you were here, I should have just broken that door right then and there. I'd never have forgiven myself if something had happened to you."

"Don't beat yourself up over that. I'm stuck in some bizarre nightmare that includes the ghost of my great-great-grandmother, but other than that, I'm okay. I've got to say I'm glad you're here. Though, baby, we still have a problem." Anna might not see it yet, but she certainly did.

"We're together now. There isn't a problem we can't solve together."

Sadie loved the sentiment and loved that Anna felt that way about the two of them together. Unfortunately, it really didn't solve their immediate dilemma. "We can't get out of this place. It's more than just the fact that crazy nurse locked us inside. It's like we're in a different dimension. Did you notice what she's wearing? It's got to be a least a hundred years since anyone wore a get-up like that. You know I notice things like that."

She did too. Her job working locations didn't mean she paid any less attention to the costume department. They often worked hand in hand to get the right look for a film or television show or whatever it was they were working on at the time. That woman's outfit screamed turn-of-the-twentieth-century, which also happened to coincide with the date the main building was constructed. Nothing too supernatural about that.

"You think the nurse is keeping us here, and that might be true. What I don't get is why. Even if your grandmother was admitted here, that crazy woman doesn't make sense. Would someone who isn't even related come back from the dead to trap you inside this place?"

Sadie had been pondering that issue as well. She'd decided the answer split fifty-fifty. "I think the simplest answer is yes and no. Nurse Thompson, or at least that's what she calls herself, definitely has an agenda that appears to factor me into it. I've been wondering about it since this nightmare began, and I've finally concluded that it had to have started way back when my grandmother was here. I also think there's more to it than just a relative who had something happen to her here. My grandmother keeps telling me I have to help them."

Anna held out her hands, palms up. "Who are them?"

She sure as hell wished she knew. It would sure make getting out of this mess a lot easier. "That's just it. I have no idea."

Renee didn't typically feel any of the vibes that Lorna or even Jeremy experienced when they came in contact with forces beyond the physical world. Her abilities didn't go that deep. At least they didn't until tonight anyway. Just like Lorna, she was picking up trouble, because it seemed to vibrate from the very brick of the building. Likewise, her body was buzzing as though she was holding on to a live electrical wire. It made her jumpy in a whole lot of ways. Something just wasn't right with this place. If it had an aura it would be dark.

In a new twist on her psychic gift, Lorna seemed to be tapping into the unseen and bringing life to it in a way that was drawing them all in. At the very least it was drawing Renee in. Her sense of urgency was rubbing off as well. Rather than reading auras, she was sensing despair and loneliness, as if souls cried out to her for help. Sadness wrapped around her like a thick wool blanket, and she wanted to throw it off to let in the air. Not that she didn't want to help if she could. It was just that the crushing weight of the emotion was exhausting.

"There's something not right about this place," she said as her eyes stayed on the door handle. An urge to grab it, pull the door open, and find out what was on the other side was strong. Her hands stayed at her sides, her fingers curled tight. "Really not right, if you know what I mean."

"No kidding," Lorna said. "I'm right there with you. I'm making an educated guess that some bad shit happened inside this building, and I get a very sick feeling that it's never stopped. Whatever it is, it's really fucked up."

Katie put a hand on Renee's shoulder, which made her jump. "Sorry, ladies, but I'm not in this loop. Would someone care to explain? You know, bring me into your psychic loop."

Renee patted the hand still resting on her shoulder. "Right, sorry, Katie. We've developed a bit of shorthand after a few of these psychic events. It's easy to forget that others aren't dialed in."

"I'm definitely not. Bring me up to speed if you would, please."

Renee nodded and put a hand on Lorna's shoulder. "We have the resident expert who can explain."

"A woman came to me," Lorna said. "She told me we had to save them. I'm pretty certain she meant Anna and Sadie, but I'm not sure she meant just Sadie and Anna, if you catch my drift."

Renee absolutely understood. The vibes rolling through her body were too intense to be coming from only a couple of souls. It felt more like an army of them. Apparently she was intimately dialed into whatever Lorna was sensing. "She didn't mean just the two of them. I'm certain of that. There's more at stake here than just Sadie and Anna."

"You saw them too?" There was a whisper of hope in Lorna's voice, as if she was pleased not to be alone in her touch on the other side. Renee felt bad she would have to let her down. Picking up on senses was one thing, but seeing visions was another. So far, visions were outside of her skill set.

Renee shook her head slightly and tried to clarify it for her. "No, it's nothing like that. Sorry, babe. I still don't see visions or hear voices like you do. In a way I wish I did. For me, it's more that I feel souls, lots of souls, waiting and hoping. I don't know why, but I think they're waiting for us to do something." It was the best she could do to try to make it clear.

Lorna ran her hands through her hair and for a moment closed her eyes. She opened them and said, "In your way, though, you're tapping into the same thing I am. You're feeling some of the vibes I am. It's important."

That was a fair assessment, although she believed it had more to do with her growing bond with Lorna than growing powers. The closer they became, the more she tuned into her. It was exciting and scary at the same time. "It would appear so, yes."

She met Renee's eyes, her face pale and tense. "Ah, crap, here we go again."

Yes, indeed, here they went again. She knew exactly what Lorna meant. It wasn't that she objected to the way the two of them were increasingly in tune. Rather it was what they were tuning into that was unsettling. Renee rubbed her hands over her eyes as she thought a few months back to the scene along the perimeter of a cemetery as law enforcement recovered the remains of a dozen young women who had died at the hands of a serial killer. Lorna had found them and Lorna had brought them home. She'd been there as support and, as she was beginning to believe, as a booster to Lorna's natural gift. They were an incredible team.

"As much as I hate to say it, yes, here we go again. I don't know what kind of insanity is happening here or went on before they closed the hospital down. But they need our help, and we're probably the ones who can help them. The only decent choice we can make is to stay here and figure out what they need from us. We can't leave until then."

Over the last months it had been becoming clearer and clearer that destiny had brought Renee and Lorna together for more reasons than simply to discover the love they'd both been missing. For some time now, Renee had come to deeply believe that she was destined to spend her life with Lorna, and she was pretty certain Lorna felt the same way.

Seeing Anna and Lorna together had shaken her a bit at first, and she couldn't deny it. Still, her belief that Lorna was the woman who would always have her soul remained strong. She held an equal belief that their love came with some very unique strings. They were not simply friends and lovers. Together they had the power to help the voiceless. It was a higher calling they'd never be able to escape. She didn't want to escape it.

Lorna laid her palm against Renee's cheek. The gesture chased away the chill, and the look in her eyes made her warm all over. She would never get tired of her touch or of staring into her deep, expressive eyes. "We'll do whatever we must to make this right. You and me together."

Renee covered Lorna's hand with her own. "Together."

"Always."

"Always," she echoed.

Katie looked from Lorna to Renee and back again before picking up the pry bar. "Okay, so we've settled that you two are a kick-ass, cohesive, crime-solving unit, and what I'm also hearing from both of you is that something inside this place is messed up and dangerous. Am I getting that right?"

Lorna's hand dropped away and she turned to look at Katie. "I would say that's a definite yes. Anna and Sadie are most certainly in danger. I believe terrible things happened to people who were housed in this place and somehow their being here is tied to whatever tragedies occurred."

It made Renee a little nauseous to even think about the sort of things that might have occurred within the walls of a turn-of-the-century mental hospital. The kinds of treatments that had started off with the best of intentions had too many times morphed into something far different. History books were full of stories that made her cringe. To think that just across the threshold in front of them such horrors may have occurred was heartbreaking.

"I agree with Lorna," Renee told Katie. "Bad things happened in this building, and if we don't hurry, I'm worried more bad things will. We've got to get inside."

Katie studied the heavy pry bar and then gave them a curt nod as she pulled her arms back and brought it up high in the air. Her eyes on the big door, she said to them, "What I call that is probable cause, so screw protocol and waiting for keys. Ladies, we are getting into this mausoleum right fucking now." She swung the pry bar, sending it crashing through the century-old glass of the front door.

CHAPTER THIRTEEN

Jeremy slid the armless gray chair next to Merry's bed and laid his head on his arms. His head felt so heavy, he couldn't keep it up any longer. Exhaustion and concern were kicking his ass. The room was bathed in shadows, and a constant murmur of activity floated through the door even though it was pulled most of the way shut. The faint unpleasant scent of cleaning solutions that seemed always present in hospitals filled his senses. Too tired to care about any of it, he closed his eyes.

He was grateful that Merry slept peacefully and that a blush of color was creeping back into her thin face. Loving someone as much as he loved her was harder than he'd ever imagined. In the past he'd always been so cavalier about fuzzy emotions like love and passion because, frankly, he didn't get it. Now at long last, he did. What he felt for Merry and their unborn child was so deep it was almost painful.

No, it wasn't almost painful; it did hurt. When she went into distress, his actions kicked into automatic and he moved quickly to do what had to be done in order to save her and the baby. On the outside he was calm and focused. On the inside he was a goddamn mess, fear and frustration warring silently inside him in equal measure. The very idea that he could lose one or both of them was a reality he refused to consider. Nothing was going to take either of them from him.

With his head resting on his folded arms, he smiled in the darkness, thinking of his mother. She used to tell him he was a boy in a man's clothing and that one day the little boy would grow up. He'd ignored her—as boys were prone to do—and went on his oblivious way acting like a typical guy with no sense of deep connection. Wouldn't Mom be surprised, and pleased, to see him now?

His smile faded as he thought of how much he wished she were here tonight. He wanted her to see that he'd left that boy behind and become the man she'd always believed he could be. He wanted her to know Merry and to be around to meet her granddaughter when she came into the world in a few months. She would be proud; he knew she would.

"I'm trying, Mom," he whispered into the darkness. "I'm really trying."

His head popped up as he jerked back in his chair and almost fell out of it. Jesus, what the hell was that? It felt like someone had stood right behind his chair and skimmed the back of his neck with their fingertips. Except that was impossible, given that he and his sleeping Merry were the only people in the room.

"Mom?" His voice shook. "Is that you?" It seemed a little too coincidental that he was wishing his mother could be here with him and then he felt a touch on the back of his neck. Just like he remembered her doing a hundred times when he was a kid. "Mom?" he asked again.

Nothing happened. No more butterfly whispers on the back of his neck. He wasn't psychic like Lorna, yet all of a sudden he was wondering if maybe this thing Lorna seemed to be channeling since moving to Aunt Bea's house was creating the ability to imagine the impossible in him as well. Things like sensing his mother standing beside him in one of his darkest hours. Or feeling her touch on the back of his neck in the moment when he needed comfort the most. Yeah, like that.

He smiled at the mere thought of his mother being here with him in spirit. Maybe it was true and maybe it wasn't. But it didn't really matter because he chose to believe it was his mother standing beside him and that she'd reached across the veil separating the living and the dead to let him know she understood. The comfort it gave him made his heart a whole lot lighter. No matter how old a guy got, he always needed his mother.

"What?" Merry murmured as her lashes fluttered and her eyes opened. "Is something wrong?" A note of fear crept into her voice, and her hand moved to her belly.

He leaned over and smiled, putting his hand on top of hers. Her eyes were only partially open, sleep still weighing heavy on her. He kissed her cheek and smoothed her hair back with his other hand. "No, baby, everything is really good. Go back to sleep. I'm right here with you."

She leaned into the hand he rested against her cheek. "You won't go?"

"No, I won't go. You're stuck with me whether you like it or not." She probably had no idea how stuck she was with him. He—and Mom—were here for the duration. That's what loved ones did at times like this.

A ghost of a smile crossed her lips. "Good. I like being stuck with you." Her eyes closed, and in less than a minute, her chest was once more rising and falling in the smooth rhythm of sleep. He leaned over and kissed her on the forehead before he laid his head back on his arms and closed his eyes again. The warmth of her body so close to him and the whisper of her easy breathing drew him toward slumber. Right at this moment and in this time and place, all was right with his world.

Thank you, God.

❖

Lorna felt it the second they walked over the threshold. Energy pulsed through the building as if it were coming from the walls, the floors, the ceiling. This place was alive with a vitality that was impressively powerful. Or would it be more accurate to describe it as frighteningly powerful? Everything she'd felt outside the building was magnified many times over now. It was a bit like walking into an obstacle course riddled with live electrical wires. Yes, it felt exactly like that.

"They're here," she whispered, feeling, without knowing why, that it was important not to make a lot of noise. An old familiar saying, the walls have ears, took on a brand-new, rather ominous meaning.

"Where?"

Lorna held up her hand as Katie's question echoed off the walls. While she'd uttered the word in a low, quiet voice, it nonetheless came across far too loud in the otherwise silent room. "Shhh. We don't want her to hear us." Instinct told her they had to come in undetected if at all possible.

"Her?" Renee, likewise, said the single word so softly Lorna almost didn't hear her. "Anna?"

She did hear her, though, and the question actually stopped Lorna. Her? She had indeed said *her*, and she had no clue where the word came from because she hadn't been referring to Anna or Sadie. It was pulled from somewhere deep inside and was as important as it was unexpected. It had the same feel to as it as when John McCafferty showed himself. She, whoever she was, was waiting and probably listening. Every sense in her body, physical and paranormal, was screaming danger. She was evil, and she would hurt them if she could.

The entryway where they stood seemed like a safe place, or should be anyway. It appeared they were the only three in the cold, dusty, empty building. But she sensed at a very deep level that they weren't alone, despite the quiet. In fact, when she thought about it, things were a little too quiet, as if someone— or something—was masking sounds and movement. Sadie was in here, she was absolutely certain of it, and judging by the car outside, she'd lay odds Anna was in here somewhere too.

"Okay," she said in a low voice as she swept her gaze over

the entryway. "You want to play sneaky? Yeah, well, we can do that."

"Who are you talking to?" Renee whispered in her ear, her hand gripping Lorna's arm.

A valid question to which she didn't have a very good answer. She narrowed her eyes and studied the room. *Where are you? I know you're here.*

"Don't know…yet, but she's going to show herself." It was the best answer she could come up with at the moment.

"There's the *she* again. Who is she?" Katie had her hand on her gun. Lorna suspected the uneasy ripple in the air had her feeling a little off too. It was somewhat comforting to know she wasn't the only one sensing something off. It was also comforting to have Katie, and her gun, at her back, though honestly, she wasn't sure in this instance the gun would do them any good at all. Was it possible to take out a spirit with a forty-five?

Chills crawled down her back. "I don't know. I just know she's here and she's an evil bitch."

Lights flickered at the top of the stairs, drawing Lorna's gaze upward. At the same time, quiet laughter cut through the silence. It wasn't a happy sound, and it made the hairs on the back of her neck stand up. Sometimes it really sucked not to be wrong. *She* was making her appearance and doing it in style. Shades of the egotistical John McCafferty all over again.

Lorna took one step toward the staircase, and just as she did, the touch of a hand on her shoulder stopped her cold because Renee and Katie weren't close enough to be able to reach her. Cool air whispered across her ear as a woman's urgent voice breathed "Run" into her ear.

She didn't stop to analyze, didn't second-guess the command. She whipped around, yelled "run" to the others, and took off at a sprint toward one of the hallway doors. Out of the corner of her eye she glimpsed Renee and Katie following her closely, and she silently thanked God that they'd done so without question.

The laughter coming from high up on the staircase grew louder. "You can run, my dears, but you cannot hide. This is my kingdom, and I know all and see all. There is no corner you can huddle in that I will not find you. No door I cannot open. No window I cannot lock. You are mine."

"Bet me, bitch," she said under her breath as she ran. "I'll catch you first."

❖

Anna hit the wood door hard. "Goddamn it," she sputtered as she kicked the solid and unmoving barricade. Sadie wasn't kidding when she said they were essentially prisoners in this room. The door was so firmly in place it was as if it had been welded to the frame. The windows were likewise a total bust, as the bars that covered them were welded in place and spaced too close together to allow either of them to slip through. Whoever built this place wanted to make very certain no one either got in or out other than through a few doors. The signs outside all read *hospital*, but Anna thought they probably should have read *prison*. It would have been a more appropriate designation.

"What the hell kind of place is this?" Anna spun to look at Sadie. "It's like some kind fortress guarded by a psycho."

Sadie shrugged. "The gatekeeper is most definitely a psycho. This whole thing is way outside my wheelhouse. I don't even exactly know how I ended up here."

"But?" Studying Sadie's face, she got an unsettling feeling. Sadie wasn't telling her something.

"But I think my great-great-grandmother drew me out here."

Weird as everything was right at the moment, it didn't explain the whole story. Something else had to be going on. "Sadie, she's been dead for a hundred years, so how on earth could she draw you here? And more importantly, why? What can you possibly do decades after her death?"

In the odd shifting light of her flashlight, she could see Sadie roll her eyes. Normally, that would have irritated the hell out of her. She hated that expression and usually took it personally. Right now, she loved it because it was such a Sadie reaction and it made this abnormal situation feel a little like day-to-day. The fear of not knowing where she was or if she was all right made everything just a tad more special—even sarcasm and eye-rolling. The joy of seeing Sadie and of being able to touch her made everything else unimportant. Except perhaps getting out of this room and away from the crazy lady who'd locked them in here.

"That, my darling, is a duh. Doesn't really matter which realm she's existing in, because my great-great-grandmother is here. Maybe she's always been here and what she needs is for me to set her free. I don't know what's going on in this place, only that I'm here for a reason, and I have to figure out what that reason is before something bad happens. The longer I'm stuck in this room, the more I feel a responsibility to put whatever it is right."

It sounded crazy yet not, all at the same time. If she were sitting in her living room she'd have called it bull. Standing here, locked inside a room of an abandoned building, it felt all too real to make that call. Sadie might very well be right. All of this had to be for a reason, or why would it happen in the first place? "So we're trapped inside a haunted insane asylum until we figure out why you're here and what you have to do. That's pretty much what you're saying, right?"

Sadie nodded. "In a manner of speaking...a rather politically incorrect manner of speaking."

Her eyes shifted to the rusted bars over the windows. "I didn't mean any disrespect to your grandmother or anyone else who got stuck in this hellhole. It's just what they would have called it back when it was built." It was true. Hospitals for the so-called insane were located all over the country, and it was a term that didn't apply to many of the people who found themselves committed to one. Still, history was history, and *insane asylum* was what people used to call places like this. Not to mention that what was happening right at the moment qualified for insane in her book.

Sadie took Anna's hand. The touch of her fingers as they held tight to her filled her with welcomed warmth. It was comforting to feel her touch in a situation that seemed totally out of control, and out of control was a nice way of putting what was happening to them.

Sadie rested her head gently against Anna's. Her hair was soft as tendrils fell against her cheek. The sensation brought tears to her eyes, and she blinked them back.

"I get what you're trying to say, and it's true. That's what they named this place, even if many of the people here were far from insane."

"Like your grandmother." She had a hard time believing anyone related to Sadie could be anything except healthy and sane. She was one of the most grounded and exciting people she knew. Sure, she had a pretty unique job that had her thinking outside the box on a regular basis. That didn't mean she was mentally unbalanced. On the contrary, it made Sadie that much more interesting. She had to believe her great-great-grandmother was just as sane.

Sadie stepped back and nodded. "If I had to guess, I'd say she probably had some issues, maybe depression or maybe she was bipolar. No way to really know for sure. The way they treated women back in the day, who could blame her if she was depressed. What I do feel in my heart is that she was not insane, not clinically or otherwise. She was trapped here just like we are now. She needed help, and all she got was a prison."

"She's not trapped anymore, and she could help us leave." Anna couldn't deny the feeling that this long-lost relative of Sadie's had lured them here for some reason only the mysterious ghost knew. It was all so crazy, and if she wasn't experiencing it, she wouldn't believe it. Ghosts or other paranormal anomalies were not something she put much faith in.

Well, she'd held that line hard, until today anyway. The truth was hard to accept and equally hard to ignore. She wanted to believe this was nothing unusual, just an unfortunate set of circumstances that had led them to be locked in an old room. Unfortunately, too many things weren't adding up, like Sadie's missing car, the locked and then unlocked front door, and creepiest of all, Nurse Thompson. The truth, as hard as it was for her to stomach, was that they were at the mercy of otherworldly spirits. God, she hoped Lorna would listen to her voice mail really soon and come back out here to save the day or, more accurately, the night. She wanted out of this place right now.

"She can't help us leave."

Sadie sounded so certain, and that certainty didn't fill her with warm fuzzies. "Why?"

This time Sadie shook her head. "I don't know exactly. I haven't been able to figure out that part yet. So far, I just know that she needs us to do something important before we can leave. I'm also pretty sure we need to do it before that bitch of a nurse does something to hurt us."

That didn't strike Anna as possible. How exactly could a spirit from the great beyond even touch them? Seeing ghosts was one thing, but physically interacting was another. "If this is what I think it is, she's a ghost, Sadie. That means she can't harm us."

Sadie put her hands on her hips and tilted her head. "Of course she can't. Just like she can't turn the lights on and off. Just like she can't keep us locked inside a room. Can't imagine why I didn't think of that."

Okay, so maybe she had a point.

CHAPTER FOURTEEN

L orna didn't have to tell her twice to haul ass. Renee took off at a run and headed toward the back of the big building. She figured she'd find plenty of places to hide there. As she rounded the corner of the reception desk, she smacked her hip on the edge. She winced at the pain and thought *that's gonna leave a mark* as she blazed by.

The first door she went through squeaked on hinges that hadn't been used in years. It squeaked again when she kicked it shut, which made her heart race. Would that awful woman be right behind her, drawn by the sound of the loud hinges? How would she know? She'd appeared out of nowhere without so much as a whisper of a footstep. Like a ghost.

She stopped as it hit her hard. Like a ghost. Holy crap. It was John McCafferty all over again. What was that story by Ray Bradbury? Oh yeah, "Something Wicked This Way Comes." Well, Ray, truth can be stranger than fiction, she said to herself. Something wicked was right on her heels.

A year ago, this would have been impossible for her to believe, and now, it was simply another night in her exciting life at Lorna's side. In the time after her divorce she'd hoped, though not truly believed, that she'd find love again. That she'd be able to make a comfortable life with someone who touched her heart. Her dream had come true, just not exactly as she'd imagined.

She'd found a greater love than she believed possible, and what came with it had turned her life into one big adventure.

Like right now as she stood with her back against the closed door inside a dark, musty room. The small flashlight she held wasn't a whole lot of help. It gave off only a small sliver of light to cut through the black interior of the room. It was like using a match in the depths of a giant cave. Didn't smell much better than a cave either. How she wished for something like the big light Katie had produced from her patrol car. Now that was a flashlight. It would fill the room like daylight. Wishing wasn't going to help much. There was no big light to be had, no daylight to banish the dark. She would have to make do.

Here in the rear of the building it was pitch-black and eerily quiet. It smelled of dust and disuse, like a place that hadn't felt the brush of fresh air in years. No sounds of running steps, no creepy ghosts in old-fashioned nurse uniforms. Only the sound of her own quick breathing broke up the silence. Slowly she moved away from the door and swept her little light back and forth, looking for what, she didn't really know. She just felt like she needed to do something.

In the apparent middle of the room, she stopped and stood still. Listening, she heard nothing. Not Lorna, Katie, or…or, what did she call her? A ghost? The devil? The silence let her know she was alone. Her pulse was racing and her heart pounding. Cold fear made her hands shake. Closing her eyes, she breathed in and out, forcing herself to embrace calm. Years of practicing yoga had distinct advantages. The calm she called forward flowed over her easily. Yes, it was exactly what she needed. Feeling better, she turned and retraced her steps to the door she'd come in through. She didn't see that she had a better option.

Cringing as the door squeaked again when she opened it, she peered out into the hallway. Empty. Yes! She stepped out and began to quietly walk in the opposite direction of the entryway. It seemed to her that the farther back in the building she moved, the more the presence of evil seemed to flow away.

Renee would like to say it felt safe here, but it didn't. Not that it felt precisely scary either. It was more unsettling than anything else she could put a name to. If a person was standing in front of her, she'd say they had a troubled aura. The building didn't have an aura she could read, though she felt it embodied a spirit, and its spirit was most decidedly troubled. Bottom line—something wasn't right here.

Why was the question that kept rolling around in her head. Most buildings were inert and gave off little in the way of energy. This one was completely different. It didn't take a big brain to figure out that tragedy had occurred between these brick walls. Tears had been wept in these rooms and hearts broken. It was the nature of the beast, and the way its patients had been treated was all a consequence of its time. Closing the doors and pretending it had never happened didn't change the facts or make amends. Most of the people who'd worked here more than likely had the best of intentions, even if their methods sometimes did more harm than good. Others, like the one who chased her now, had simply found an outlet for the darkness in their souls. It shouldn't be surprising that the darkness lived on. Some actions couldn't be ignored or forgotten and instead waited for the day when the scales would be balanced. She suspected that was the case here.

It wasn't just the reality of what this place had once been that made Renee look around now. Not that she could see a thing that helped. It was an empty shell that somehow wasn't that empty. It was just that she couldn't see what still filled this place to the brim. How she wished she had Lorna's psychic powers. Then maybe she could make sense of what she was feeling.

Then again, earlier she'd been able to feel a little of what was flowing through Lorna. Playing her light against one of the walls, she had a thought. It might work, and it might not do a thing. Then again, she didn't have anything to lose.

She turned the flashlight off and slid it into her pocket. Taking a deep breath, Renee laid her hands against the walls. Lord knows, she was no psychic, not even close. She was, however, sensitive, and it occurred to her that this place was trying in its own way to reach out to her just as it had already done to Lorna. Just as it had flowed into her when she'd held Lorna's hand. Secrets screamed out from the spirit of the building, begging to be brought into the daylight and old wrongs made right. She was absolutely convinced of it.

Her hands against the cool plaster walls, she closed her eyes and concentrated. It was her hope that something would come to her, some bit of guidance to show her the way. She wanted to experience the same sense of connection she'd had earlier with Lorna. Except nothing happened. There was no pulse of energy, no vision of what was or what was to be. Nothing but the rough feel of old plaster against her palms. Her hands fell away and she took a step back.

"Renee." A sharp whisper came from out of the darkness.

Her heart raced at the familiar voice. "Lorna?" she whispered back as she snatched the light out of her pocket and moved the beam in the direction of Lorna's voice. When her light fell on Lorna's face, she cried out and ran to her. She didn't think she'd ever been happier to see her.

Lorna wrapped her in her arms and placed a kiss on top of her head. "You okay? I just about killed myself without a flashlight. It's fucking dark in this mausoleum."

She laughed and hugged her back. How she loved her voice and the way she told it like she saw it. It didn't hurt that hugging her was also the best feeling on earth. It never failed to give her strength and courage. "I'm fine. Where's Katie? Is she all right? Did that thing get her?"

"Not sure where she is exactly. She took off the other direction. I don't know if you've noticed, but this place is huge. I'm surprised I found you, especially without a flashlight. My night vision isn't exactly special-forces ready. I guess I sensed you. It's like we're tuned into each other. Go figure."

She hugged her tighter. "We are so tuned into each other. It's awesome. And yes, you are totally special-forces ready. I've heard stories about the military using psychics for warfare. Baby, you'd kill it."

Lorna groaned. "Oh, good God, that's the last thing I need. It's bad enough doing this shit to help friends. I sure as hell am not going to go all army. I am definitely not military material."

That was her Lorna talking, and the normalcy of the conversation steadied her. Her strong, beautiful, and talented psychic woman was absolutely military ready, but that was a discussion for another time. They had closer and more pressing matters right in front of them. "Something here needs us," she told Lorna. "Needs you. It's very strange. I get the feeling we are meant to be here and we're not going to be able to leave until we can do whatever we're supposed to."

Lorna blew out a long breath and ran her hand over Renee's hair. "Yup, I feel it too. I'm beginning to think none of this is coincidence. We're all here for a reason. You, me, Sadie, Anna. Who would believe becoming a psychic would be so complicated?"

"You got this, baby," Renee said, then kissed her on the cheek. "And we all have your back."

"I might need you to cover my behind before this is all said and done. Some kind of new weirdness is going on here, and I'm not quite sure how to handle it. What am I saying? I never know how to handle this."

"You will," she told her and meant it. Lorna liked to sell herself short, but Renee knew better. When they walked out of here, and she did mean when, Lorna would have worked her very special brand of magic.

Lorna squeezed her hand. "Thanks for the vote of confidence. Now let's figure out where we go next. Preferably somewhere that crazy woman isn't."

Both of them jumped when a voice whispered, "Here."

A beautiful woman in a long white nightgown stood across the room, holding open a door. She was bathed in a dim otherworldly light that hadn't been there a moment before. "We must hurry," she whispered. "She is coming. You do not have much time. Please. Hurry."

Renee held on to Lorna's hand so tight she wouldn't be surprised if she broke her fingers. "You see her, right?"

❖

Jeremy's head jerked up, his eyes blinking, and a tiny line of drool hung suspended at the corner of his mouth. He wiped away the drool with the back of his hand and looked around the darkened hospital room. It appeared exactly as it had when he'd laid his head down earlier and went to sleep. He and Merry were all alone, the door slightly ajar just as it was when he first sat in the chair he'd pulled next to her bed. It let in a little light and a lot of the noise from the hallway but wasn't open nearly wide enough to allow someone to slip inside.

The initial shock of being abruptly awakened passed. He couldn't let go of the feeling of unease because he didn't imagine the strong grip on his shoulder. Someone had taken a firm hold and shook him awake. Yet no one was here. No one he could see, anyway. Funny how paradigms shifted once a ghost or two appeared. He used to be such a down-to-earth, logical guy. Now, he looked at everything in his world differently. Like shadows. Instead of being only plays on light and dark, these days they might be simply shadows or something else. Something that might be alive.

The shadows in Merry's hospital room didn't feel sinister or threatening. He studied the movement of light and dark and took nothing from it. Whatever, or whoever, thought he should be awake had accomplished its goal and moved on. He was certainly alert now, and an unsettling feeling was threading its way through his body. He'd had this feeling before, and it meant one thing, at least to his mind: Lorna needed him.

They'd always been close and had become even more so after their relocation to the west side of the state. That house of Aunt Bea's had transformed them both, and he still wasn't entirely sure if that was a good thing or a bad thing. He did lean more toward good, given how it had helped to bring so many lost souls home. It was weird, though, to be intimately wired into the world beyond, and there was no other way to explain what had constituted their altered reality. He and Lorna were tapping into a dimension he had previously thought of as the stuff of folklore.

Boy, had he called that one wrong. Even all this time later, he shuddered recalling how the spirit of that creep John McCafferty had hijacked his body and gone on to very nearly kill his sister. That man had been an asshole in life and, as it turned out, an even bigger asshole in death. They'd managed to stop him before he could kill again, and it was a better world because of it. Yeah, he guessed this power they had was a good thing.

Earlier he'd been sure it was his mother who came to him, and he still believed that. It wasn't Mom now who called to him; it was his sister. For a moment he considered what had happened in the last few hours. His mother whispering to him from heaven and now his sister's spirit drawing him from a deep sleep. Could it be possible this psychic thing that manifested in Lorna and that seemed to be leaching over into him as well was always within them both? Made him wonder, but not for long. It really didn't matter because it simply was what it was. What it told him tonight was that he was needed.

He pushed up from the chair and went over to the sink in the corner, where he splashed water on his face and then dried it with a couple of the rough paper towels from the dispenser on the wall. As he stretched, his back popped. Sleeping bent over in a chair probably wasn't the best in terms of spinal health, and his body felt it. As he rolled his shoulders he figured all in all he wasn't in too bad a shape, and a couple hours of sleep had done him good. He walked back over to the bed, bent down, and placed a gentle kiss on the top of Merry's sleeping head. Briefly he rested his hand against her midsection, picturing their tiny daughter who someday would be as beautiful as her mother. He smiled, taking great comfort in the touch and knowing both were in good hands for the rest of the night.

As much as he hated to leave Merry's side, he didn't feel that he had much in the way of choices. Lorna was in trouble. He felt it all the way to his toes. If he stayed here, she might be okay and she might not. The only way to be certain was to do what they seemed to do best these days: tackle evil head-on as a united team. It was like adding a second battery.

The same went for Renee. She didn't seem to have any psychic powers at all, just an ability to read auras. It was pretty cool, actually, and he liked hearing her assessments of people. He could have used her help a couple of times when he did business with people that down the road he wished he'd never met. Even though she wasn't psychic, she too was like an extra battery for Lorna. He wasn't sure if it was because of her aura-reading powers or because she loved his sister so deeply. Either way, it worked and he was happy for it.

Even Merry, who didn't seem to possess even a drop of paranormal anything, added to the mix. For whatever reason, the universe had seen fit to bring them all together, and their little cadre worked. A little miracle that had no rational explanation. Tonight, however, they would have to do this as a trio.

Now, it was time to render aid. Lorna needed him, and just as she was always there for him, he was damned straight going to be there for her, even if this was about helping Anna. Of course he was pretty damned motivated to get this done as quickly as possible and get right back here to his family. His goal was to get Anna, and hopefully Sadie, home safely so he could get back to Merry's side before she awakened. He didn't want her to wake up and find him gone.

Once he made it out into the hospital waiting area, he pulled out his cell phone and punched in Lorna's number. The call went straight to voice mail. He didn't like that at all. She should be picking up. He wanted to talk to her right now and find out what the hell was going on out at Healing Waters before he got there.

He stuffed the phone back into his pocket and hurried down the empty hallway. Not much activity in the hospital this time of night. That was good, he liked the quiet. Made it easier for Merry to rest.

It didn't hit him until he was all the way outside that he had a rather significant logistical problem. He didn't have a car. Lorna had driven them to the hospital in the Yukon and had taken their vehicle with her out to Healing Waters. He was on foot, and it was at least twenty-five miles or more from the hospital to Miracle Lake. He wasn't up for a marathon.

"Son of a bitch," he muttered. "What the hell do I do now?" It was too late to get a rental, too far to run even for a seasoned runner like him. This was the wrong time to be without wheels. Then he smacked himself in the forehead as the obvious solution dawned on him. There was at least one advantage to being back in his hometown: good friends with great cars. No time like the present to call in chips. Lord knows he'd helped everybody else out at least once, if not two or three times. He started with his best friend, Ryan. He owed Jeremy big-time, having hauled his drunken butt home on numerous occasions. It was a bingo on the first call.

Ryan pulled up in front of the hospital in his shiny new car twenty minutes after Jeremy woke him up. His short blond hair was standing up in all directions, and he was dressed in mismatched sweats. Jeremy got in, turned to his friend, and said, "Looking pretty sweet, my friend. I take it you were sleeping alone?"

Leaning sideways to glance at himself in the rearview mirror, Ryan shrugged and told him, "It was an off night."

"Sure, off night. I'm buying that, dude. You haven't shaved in at least two days. Takes the five o'clock-shadow look a little far."

"Fuck you, Dutton."

"Love you too, man."

Ryan laughed. "Okay, so what's the deal? Why did you tear

me out of bed in the middle of the night? What's so important you couldn't call at a decent hour? You're messing up my beauty sleep."

"Sorry about that, 'cause it's obvious you need a lot of beauty sleep."

"Again, fuck you."

Jeremy slapped him on the shoulder. "Seriously, I appreciate this. I need to get out to Miracle Lake and Healing Waters Hospital like right now."

"Are you fucking kidding me? Why would you want to go out there in the middle of the night? There's nothing there anymore."

"It's important, man, or I wouldn't ask. I can't really explain more, and you wouldn't believe me even if I did."

"I think you're getting too much rain over there on the coast. It's making your brain soft."

It was definitely doing something to his brain, though going soft wasn't it. Far from it. He didn't have the time or the energy to explain to Ryan. "It's like this. You have two choices. Drive me out to Miracle Lake or loan me your car."

"You know, you've gotten pretty weird since you became a west sider. You oughta consider moving back to this side of the state, where we're nice and normal and don't go racing out to creepy old hospitals in the middle of the night."

"I don't know how to break it to you, but you, my friend, haven't been normal since the second grade."

"You come to school dressed like a teddy bear one time, and you never live it down."

"Not a chance, dude. That was hands down the funniest day ever. I even have the pictures to prove it."

"Yeah, whatever. We'll go back to my crib, I'll go back to bed, and you can drive wherever the fuck you want. Don't wreck my car, and don't park it anywhere it'll get door dings. Oh, and fill it up with gas before you bring it back. Capisce?"

"And if I don't, will the teddy bear kick my butt?"

"With one big, fat claw."

"Seriously, Ryan. Thanks." They might sound like they were fighting, but it was far from it. Their banter was born of a lifetime of friendship. He'd known Ryan would be there for him just as he would be there for him. That's what friends did for each other. A few hundred miles between them couldn't change that.

"No problem." Ryan's gaze shifted from the road to Jeremy's face, and a small smile crossed his face. "Yeah, no problem at all, my friend. This just means you now owe me. I kinda like it. No, I totally like it."

After Ryan vacated the driver's seat and walked back into his house, Jeremy got behind the wheel and made his way to the I90 West on-ramp. He flew down the freeway, intent on getting to the Healing Waters exit as soon as possible. Right now he was operating on pure instinct, and he hoped to God it was the right instinct. If for some reason Lorna wasn't back out at Healing Waters, he'd be screwed. She'd told him before leaving the hospital that's where she was going. He assumed that's where they still were. She was up against something dangerous—he could feel it in his bones—and he had to find her fast.

After pulling off the freeway and onto the highway, he took one of the curves too fast and nearly put Ryan's car in the ditch. They might have been friends since grade school, but somehow he didn't think that fact would save him if he wrecked his new car. Fortunately, he got back on the straightway immediately and quickly pushed the accelerator again. Fields went zipping by with nothing to see but open spaces lit by weak moonlight. Finally the lights of the small community surrounding Miracle Lake broke through the darkness. He breathed a little easier.

A few more minutes and he would be at the old mental hospital. Driving out here, especially when he was in a hurry, he could understand why they decided to build the asylum this far out. It was distant enough from the city that people could bring the ones they wanted to forget about out here and never have to see them again. Its isolated location meant there were no reminders of what they'd done to those they supposedly loved as they themselves went about their day-to-day lives. It made him sad to think about the broken souls that had withered away inside those walls. No one deserved to be forgotten simply because of emotional or mental illness. It wasn't right then, and it wasn't right now.

As he pulled up into the parking lot, he let out a deep breath. Damn, how long had he been holding it? The band around his chest eased, and his breathing was no longer painful. He felt like a drowning man who'd just made it to the water's surface. Three cars—the Yukon, one he presumed to be Anna's, and one he hadn't seen for a bit, Katie's—were parked side by side. The relief he experienced at seeing the familiar dark sedan was huge. He and Lorna might have a talent for seeing on the other side of reality and using it to help, but Katie had a firm grip on the here and now. That was something they all could use and appreciate and, depending on what they found inside, critical.

His appreciation at seeing Katie's car and his relief at realizing everyone was, indeed, here at Healing Waters didn't last long. The air almost crackled and not in a good way. It was more in the way of making the hair stand up on his arms. Whatever was going down here was going down, as Lorna would say, right fucking now. How he hoped he wasn't too late. There were no lights on inside, or at least none that he could see from where he stood.

After digging through the glove box and coming up with a flashlight—it actually surprised him to realize Ryan would think to put one in the car—Jeremy jumped out and raced for the front of the main building. No time to waste. He needed to get inside and help.

He put one foot on the first step leading up to the building entrance before he stopped. This time the hair on the back of his neck stood up. He brought his head up slowly, moving his eyes from a pair of shiny plain-toe black-leather oxfords to the pale face of the unsmiling man blocking his entrance to the building. He wore black pants and a crystal-white shirt topped by an elegant black cape. Jeremy did a double take on that one. Yeah, it was definitely a cape. He didn't even realize anybody wore those things outside of Batman or maybe the Phantom of the Opera. This one was taking strangeness to new heights.

The odd man wasn't wearing a hat, though it appeared his cape might have a hood. His hair was like his cape and his pants: jet black and very long. He didn't often, or ever, for that matter, run into a guy with hair either that thick or that long. It wasn't the most unique thing about him, however. No, what struck Ryan silent was the fact that the man had to be over seven feet tall.

Sadie was holding Anna's hand, and together they were still trying to brainstorm a way out of the locked room when the door swung open to smash against the wall with a bang. She immediately thought about how it was going to leave a hole in the wall. Like it mattered.

Then her second thought was, oh, crap. Nurse Thompson filled the open doorway, her face smug and a nasty smile turning up the corners of her mouth. Her body language and her expression made Sadie's blood run cold. This woman, or whatever she was, wore trouble like a bad perfume.

"Your friends"—she said the word like it was something dirty and unspeakable—"have arrived."

The only friends Sadie could think of were those who'd been with Anna earlier. She hoped it was them because she wanted to get out of here in the worst way. "Lorna?" she whispered into Anna's ear.

Anna nodded slightly and squeezed her hand. To the apparition in the doorway she said defiantly, "Good. They'll have us out of here in no time. You won't be able to lock us in here any longer. Lorna's powers are strong enough to take this spirit out for good."

Nurse Thompson's laugh was icy, and her eyes narrowed to slits. "You think that, do you? You are both foolish women, just like our dear Rose. She actually believed that bringing you here would change things. As I said, foolish. None of you can change one little thing. I alone control what happens in my hospital."

That pissed Sadie off. She didn't like this woman as a ghost, and she was positive she'd have hated her in the flesh. She was nasty and evil, and only God knew what she'd done to her great-great-grandmother. "Look, bitch, I'm pretty well at the end of my patience with you. Time for you to return to the hell you came from."

Again the woman laughed. "Do you believe I am threatened by you in any way? You are as stupid as you are foolish."

Sadie still held on to Anna's hand. When she'd married Anna, she'd done so because she loved her. In her mind it was simple. Love and marriage went hand in hand. During the hours she'd been held captive here, she'd reached a deeper understanding of what her vows meant to her. Anna was beautiful and smart and complicated. She could be shallow one day and deep as the ocean the next. The waves of personality that were so Anna weren't uncomfortable or difficult. She loved them because they made her all the more interesting. Anna truly was her heart and always would be. It wasn't just love they shared; it was destiny. This thing in front of them wasn't going to change that.

Sadie didn't give an inch to the defiant spirit before them. "You should be threatened. I don't know what you did to the people you were supposed to take care of here, but I know whatever it was, it was wrong. You're going to pay. I'll see to it." With each word her determination grew. She felt much more confident and stronger with Anna by her side.

"She's right," Anna said. "We'll both see to it. You're not real, and you can't hurt us. We, on the other hand, can make sure everyone knows what you did here. We'll figure it out, and we'll expose you and this place."

She loved the way Anna's mind was working. This situation they found themselves in reeked of something from one of the paranormal movies she'd worked on. Taking a cue from one of those scripts, Anna hit on the one bit of power they could wield. Exposure of the truth. How they could hurt a ghost or a spirit was anybody's guess. Probably no way to do it. Bringing hidden wrongs to light was real and doable and perhaps exactly what her grandmother brought her here to do. It was the one weapon they had at their disposal.

"This is my hospital, my responsibility, and I have taken care of it since the day it was built. I have always decided what is right and wrong, and that, my dear ladies, will not change. You are most deluded if you believe I cannot hurt you, for I can and I will."

"Try it, bitch," Sadie bit out. Her patience had finally reached its end. She was past ready to kick the crap out of this woman, ghost or not. There had to be a way to wipe her out, and she was determined to figure out what it was.

All of a sudden Nurse Thompson's body went rigid and her head turned toward the staircase leading to the lower levels. "NO!" she screamed as her hands balled into fists. "I will not have it!"

Sadie thought the expression on Nurse's Thompson face was something beyond fury. She hadn't heard a thing coming from outside their temporary prison, yet the nurse whirled in the doorway, screaming and running toward the staircase. In an instant it was as if she'd forgotten all about her and Anna. One second they were her whole focus, and the next she no longer cared. It was a break she greatly appreciated. She didn't like anything about that woman, if she could even be called a woman.

For a moment Sadie simply stared at the empty space where Nurse Thompson had been standing a moment before. It took a few seconds before what she was seeing hit home. When it did, she turned and stared wide-eyed at Anna. It was one of those moments when she felt like God was smiling on them.

"The door," Sadie whispered and couldn't keep the hope out of her voice. "The door is open."

Anna nodded, smiled, and pulled on her hand. "It's now or never, babe."

Sadie squeezed her hand back. She didn't have to think about it. She'd been waiting for this opportunity since the second she woke up here. "Run!"

They had nearly reached the open door when it started to close as if an unseen hand was pushing it closed. "No, no, no," Anna cried and threw herself in between the door and the frame. Her face was a mask of concentration as she said, "Get something to put in the door. I'm not going to be able to hold it long. We've got to block it open somehow."

Easier said than done. Sadie turned and took in the room in a quick glance. The stupid place was essentially empty, just as it had been since she came to in here. Nothing of much bulk beyond the bed frames was available. They appeared to be all she had to work with. Using every bit of effort she could summon, she kicked the nearest bed. Either she was stronger than she thought or the century-old frame was simply too fragile to resist the impact of her foot. It broke apart on the first try. She grabbed the bed rail that looked like it might be the strongest and ran back to Anna.

Maneuvering around Anna, Sadie was able to jam the rail into the rapidly closing space between the door and the frame. With a wave of relief, she was pleased to see that the bed rail was keeping the door from latching. *Take that, you creepy old nurse. We're not locked in here anymore.* Anna stepped aside and rubbed her shoulder.

"Thanks, babe. I'm not sure how much longer I'd have been able to keep the door from closing and locking." Anna rubbed her arms and rolled her head. "I don't know what that bitch is or why she's so intent on keeping us in here, but I've got news for her. She picked the wrong two women to screw with."

Once again, they were perfectly synced. As the minutes passed, her determination to not only get out of there but figure out what her great-great-grandmother needed grew stronger. That nurse had an ugly spirit, and she figured into this whole mess in some way. Sadie intended to learn how and why, then send her on a one-way ticket back to hell.

She looked around the room and in her mind's eyes went back to the visions she'd experienced earlier. Focusing on the nurse was the logical thing to do in a situation that was illogical, yet it didn't feel right. Fingers of unease stroked her mind. She was missing something, and then it hit her. "It's not the nurse so much as it is my grandmother." As the words left her mouth, they grew in gravity and importance. She was on to something.

"What do you mean? That lunatic is out to get us."

"That's true. She is one evil force, and I'm convinced she enjoyed hurting people. Just the same, I think we're mere fun and games for that weirdo. She's getting off on the control she has over us right now. Let her OD on it because it's my grandmother who needs something important from us. I'm sure of it. She's been trying to lead me to what she needs, and so far I've done a poor job of understanding. I have to work harder and figure it out."

"What could she possibly want?" Anna waved her arms. "Look at this place. It's nothing but the shell of an old building. A great set for your television show, but that's about it. There doesn't seem to be anything around here that could help someone who died decades ago. You can't do anything important for her now. That bus pulled out of the station a long time ago."

Sadie was adamant in her conviction she was here for a reason. There was something more in this hospital, and her grandmother was hell-bent on getting Sadie to find it. Now that Anna was here with her, she felt less alone, less scared, and definitely braver. Anna's presence helped make her bold and strengthened her resolve not to leave until she figured out why her grandmother had brought her here in the first place. The mystery was intriguing and the sense of responsibility pressing.

"There's only one way to know. Let's get this door open enough to wiggle out of this room, and then we can go find out what she wants. After that, we can call it a night and go home." It sounded easy when she said it, and Sadie knew deep down it wasn't going to be even close to easy. It didn't matter. She had to discover the truth behind her grandmother's appearance. People like her didn't have ghosts appearing in their lives out of the blue. Since she couldn't deny what she was seeing—and hearing—she had to believe there was a really important reason it was happening now. Time to figure it all out.

Anna ran a hand down her cheek. "You're crazy, you know? I think we should get out of this hell house and go home, where things are nice and normal. As in no ghosts and definitely no locked rooms. We need to go back to our very great lives together."

She loved what Anna said. They were great together, and she'd never felt it more than right at this moment. Sadie kissed her and said, "Soon, my love, soon. Now push, and let's get this door open once and for all and get the hell out of here." Together, they put their shoulders against the blocked open door and shoved.

CHAPTER FIFTEEN

L orna wasn't entirely convinced she wanted to follow the woman through the door, or anywhere for that matter. Mainly because she wasn't really a woman, not in the flesh-and-blood sense anyway. She had been once upon a time, but she wasn't any longer. How good an idea it was to blindly follow a ghost was up for debate.

Not just the fact that she was a spirit bothered Lorna. She'd seen enough of them by this point to not find them distressing. No, it had more to do with what she was asking them to do. The door she wanted them to follow her through led to a lower level, and at least to her mind, the basement of a building a hundred plus years old didn't seem like a good place to be. Dark, dank, and empty or maybe not so empty, given this place had the ghost thing going on. Nope, she didn't want to go there at all. Then again, some little tickle at the back of her mind was urging her forward. She was almost drawn toward that door, as if on the other side something important waited for them. As if there was a hand on her back, right between the shoulder blades, pushing her in the direction of the lower level. Ignoring these feelings or the visions or anything else odd that had happened to her since moving to the house on the ocean hadn't worked out so well. Regardless of what she felt or what she wanted to do, it all happened anyway. It could be different here. But probably not.

She grabbed the door, yanked it open, and started down the stairs after the flowing vision of white who preceded her.

The smell hit her hard by the second step. It was what? Old clothes, dirt, and mildew came to mind. She wrinkled her nose a little more with each step. The beam of her flashlight played across the steps and the cobwebs that clung to the edges. The undisturbed dust flew up into the air with each step she took. No one had been down these stairs in a long time. The smell was strong and bitter, and she wondered how much had been left here to rot that even after all these years the scent lingered. It was a sobering thought.

"You okay?" she asked Renee.

Behind her Renee said, "I'm all right if you don't count gagging on enough dust to take down even the wimpiest asthmatic. Smells like this place has been closed up tight for decades. You'd think somebody would come through once in a while and air it out. I doubt there's any mice. They'd choke to death on dust and the putrid odor."

"Probably has been locked up for a few decades. Besides, who in their right mind would want to come down here? And if it was cleaned out when they closed this place down, there's probably no reason for anyone to journey into the bowels. There'd be nothing down here to look at."

"You hit that nail on the head, and I don't think either of us is in our right mind to come down here now. I'm getting a really bad feeling about this, and it's not just because of the smell."

"Lorna!"

Her head snapped upward at the sound of Katie's voice coming from the door, and she squeezed her eyes shut. Behind her lids, stars sparked. When they stopped, she shaded her eyes with her hand and opened them again. Lorna and Renee were ablaze in the glow of Katie's mega flashlight. She gestured toward the dark abyss below. "Hey, Katie, we gotta see what's down here. The force is pulling me this way, if you catch my drift."

Katie did not sound impressed. In fact, she sounded downright irritated. "You need to wait for me, force or no force. You can't go barging into dark basements without me."

"I know you're a big, bad cop and all, but trust me. I'm pretty sure what we're dealing with here requires my special brand of force. I don't think your gun's gonna do jack." It was understandable that the cop in the room would want to run point. It's what she did for living. Lorna didn't think this was a situation that called for a cop. It wasn't her area of expertise. Not that Lorna considered herself an expert by any stretch. She hadn't been doing this long enough to be one.

Katie caught up with them on the stairs. "I don't know what you're talking about, and you don't go barging into dark rooms by yourself. Are you trying to get yourself in trouble?"

Like Lorna, Renee had a hand at her forehead to keep Katie's big light from blinding her. "Just watch her work," Renee said. "She has a way with the preternatural beings. It's the ghosts and goblins that need to be wary. She'll kick their butts."

The irritation in Katie's voice didn't lighten up at all. "I don't care. I'm trained for this kind of thing, and you two aren't. This is not the time to be stupid."

Lorna shook her head and continued down the stairs. She didn't take offense at Katie's words. They weren't personal and she got that. Katie was operating in cop mode just as she was operating in psychic mode. Thing was, she was pretty sure psychic mode trumped. "So the police academy has a course in Ghosts 101?"

"Not funny, Lorna." She lowered the light so it wasn't blinding them any longer.

"Not trying to be." And she wasn't. Even after what they'd experienced together finding the victims of the serial killer, who just happened to be one of Katie's fellow officers, she still didn't totally get it. She'd seen what Lorna could do firsthand and yet continued to try to explain it in rational terms. What Lorna could do wasn't exactly what she'd describe as rational. There was no real-world explanation. She'd come to understand it because she had no choice. It wasn't going away and in fact was growing stronger. She was what she was, and she could do what she could do. That was the only explanation needed. Right now, Lorna had a hunch that whatever was at the bottom of these stairs just might be the catalyst it was going to take for Katie to truly understand at last. She turned and continued down the stairs.

"Damn it, Lorna," Katie muttered from directly behind her, having gone around Renee to catch up with her. "Just wait the hell up."

That wasn't going to happen. "Keep up, girlfriend."

Katie stopped as suddenly as she'd raced down the stairs to catch Lorna. "What on earth?"

Lorna kept going. Truth was, she wasn't too surprised by what she saw. "You see her, don't you?"

"Is that…?" A whisper of awe was in Katie's voice.

"You got it."

"The ghost is real?"

That was a tricky one. The vision in front of her looked solid and real enough, yet she wasn't. At least not in the sense of belonging in their world. Her time had come and gone, and the vision before them was a temporary visitor.

"As real as a ghost gets," she shot back.

"It smells awful," Katie said as she put a hand over her nose. "Is it her?"

"I don't think so."

"We should probably go upstairs and wait for backup."

"No." It wasn't up for discussion. Despite the horrid smell, they had to go down.

"It could be dangerous. Who knows what the fumes are."

Lorna glanced back at her. "We're not going down these stairs for our health."

"Why can I see her?" The awe in Katie's voice was hard to

miss. Katie had obviously given up on the practical arguments and turned her attention back to the apparition.

"I don't know." And she didn't. Until now she'd believed the vision thing was hers alone. More change, just what she needed to deal with. Well, if she'd learned anything over the last few months, it was to be adaptable.

"First one for me too," Renee said. "Apparently we're all in on this one. Lorna doesn't get to have visions all to herself this time around."

Oddly, it was comforting to have them in on this, especially Renee. For a change she wasn't heading into the unknown by herself. Lorna had just put her foot on the floor at the bottom of the stairs when the slam of the door at the top of the stairs made her whirl. The click of the lock was like a gunshot going off in a cavern. Talk about the unexpected. She'd thought the only danger waiting for them was at the bottom of the stairs.

Behind Katie and Renee was nothing but blackness. Someone, or something, had just locked them in. This locked-door thing was starting to get really annoying. A slight cold breeze whispered across the back of her neck as she gazed upward. "Uh-oh, ladies. I don't think we're alone anymore."

The Watcher stood looking down at the young man, grateful beyond words he had taken heed back at the hospital in the city where he'd been sleeping at the bedside of his beloved and followed the lead he had tried to impart. His powers were limited beyond the touch he had been able to place on his shoulder. He had come out of his slumber and, thank the heavens, seemed to instinctively understand what was needed of him. This one, while not as sensitive as his sister, still had the ability to tap into a world beyond his own.

Standing on these steps and staring into the sensitive eyes

of someone who by rights should never be able to see him was a miracle. That he was across the mountains and far from the sands that had held him captive for centuries was yet another. It spoke to the gravity of the deeds that had occurred within the walls of this place and of the work that awaited them inside.

He was most grateful for the man's sensitivity, for he knew they would need it before this night was out. The woman who had never left this place had grown incredibly strong over the years. The evil that had lived in her heart during her mortal years had bloomed in the time since she had crossed over into the shadow realm. Her touch upon the world had not diminished in any way, and she tried now to do harm to those who attempted to set things right. Her heart was as black as her deeds.

His prayers had been answered, and for the first time since his fall, he felt the hand of God upon his own shoulder. It released his feet and freed his soul. Did it mean redemption was finally within his grasp? He did not know the answer and he did not care. His entire focus and his whole reason for coming to this place was to help her. Something evil walked these halls, and it was well past time for it to be sent to hell. He had to protect her above all else.

If it was the last thing he ever did, he would help. This was an important mission, though the reason for it was not yet clear to him. He sensed deep in his heart that he needed to be here and he needed to join whatever power he had to hers. Combined with her brother and the one with the light around her body, they could and would defeat the evil one. By doing so, the secret that was held deep within the walls of the building would once more be brought into the light of day.

It was the only thing that mattered.

He stared into the stunned eyes of the young man, who was clearly trying to make sense of the giant who stood above him. How long had it been since any mortal had gazed upon him? Once those gaping looks of astonishment had amused him. Now, sadness filled his heart. Though it was a futile wish, he longed to experience such feelings again and again. His kind had been wiped from the earth, and no one even remembered a time when the Watchers and their towering height were a common sight.

No more. Now they were simply legends buried within the pages of a holy book, their very existence a debate amongst scholars. Some said their mention was but a fictional reference intended as a warning. Others, few others, argued that the Watchers were a race of fallen angels long since vanished from the planet.

The latter thinkers were almost correct. He and his kind did exist, and they were most certainly fallen angels. But they had not, as those scholars declared, vanished. Or rather, he had not vanished. As one by one the Watchers had fallen to time, despair, and banishment, he had felt each and every loss until no more remained to fall. Grief had brought tears to his eyes and a bend to his shoulders on the day he knew he was alone. He was the last of his kind, and every single day, he prayed to return home.

At this moment, it no longer mattered that he was the last or if he ever earned his way back to heaven. He finally understood his purpose, and the fact that he was here only proved it. For the first time in his very long existence, he was released from the chains that had kept him bound to the sands on the edge of the great ocean. He was here for one reason only, to protect her from the evil that sought to destroy her.

And he would fulfill his destiny.

❖

The rush of relief that washed over Anna the second their feet hit the hallway was swept away by the sight that greeted them. Would a simple break be too much to ask for? By the looks of things, the answer would be yes.

"What on earth…" she mumbled.

"Oh, damn it." Sadie grabbed her hand. "Here we go again."

"I don't get it." She didn't either. They should have been

able to jet down the hallway and out the front door the same way she'd come in not that long ago. But oh no, it couldn't be that easy.

"She makes it happen."

It took her a second to figure out who she was, and then it hit her. "You mean the nurse?"

Sadie waved a hand toward the top of the stairway. "That would be my theory. You know I've worked on a lot of shows, and some of them were of the paranormal variety. There have been ghosts and vampires and all sorts of things I thought couldn't possibly exist. It was all fun and games until I ended up here. I've reached the conclusion that perhaps some, if not all, of those stories had a basis in truth."

"Are you saying you think this is paranormal?"

With everything Anna had seen since this craziness had started, it surprised Sadie that she would even ask the question. It did seem about as obvious as a powered-up neon sign. Except it was just incredibly hard to wrap her head around it. It was so outside the norm. She turned her face so they were looking at each other, eye to eye. Sadie's face was serious without so much as a hint of doubt. "I don't think. I know," Sadie told her.

Anna turned and stared at the end of the hallway. Her brain might be saying no way, but her heart and her eyes were saying hell yes. The orderlies standing guard at the top of the staircase blocked any avenue of escape. They weren't real, yet they were as solid as Anna and Sadie. It was a crap shoot whether they'd be able to get past them. Paranormal was the only explanation, and that was pretty damned bizarre.

The two brawny orderlies were trouble, that much was clear, and how they would get past them was their next challenge. And it wasn't her only concern. Just as problematic in her mind was a bigger question: where was that awful nurse? Whatever was happening in this place, she was the key. She'd most likely been the catalyst for the whole thing right from the beginning. Jesus, she'd always known evil existed in the world, but this was beyond anything she'd ever imagined. They'd stepped outside the world she'd always believed was the only one that existed and were now trapped in some dimension she would never be able to fully describe. It was real and unreal at the same. Most of all, it was frightening. God, how she hoped Lorna could break them all free.

She was mulling over what to do when Sadie leaned into her and whispered, "Do we try rushing them? I mean, they're not real, right?"

The men were big, dressed in all white, and watching them intently as if they could read their thoughts. Given how weird everything was at the moment, she wasn't so sure they couldn't tell what was going in in their heads. Since Sadie had gone missing, her world had taken a huge reality shift.

She narrowed her eyes as she studied their position. In plain speak, it sucked. Rows of doors lined the hallway, and she had no way of knowing what was on the other side of any of them. The last thing she wanted to do was race into one of them only to find themselves locked in another room. The way things were going, the odds of that happening were pretty high. So, scratch that option.

She studied the burly men, who did, in fact, appear to be very real, and then turned her gaze down the length of the hallway behind them once more. She turned up the corners of her mouth in a slow smile. She'd missed it when she looked before. Now it seemed to glow like the beacon of a lighthouse. A really incredible beacon. Maybe God was smiling down on them and this escape might work out after all. Take that, Nurse Thompson.

She leaned close to Sadie's ear as if she were going to kiss her. Instead, she grabbed her hand and whispered, "Run!"

CHAPTER SIXTEEN

R enee was only a step behind Lorna when she felt a powerful hand push her. Given Katie and Lorna were both in front of her, logically it couldn't happen. But she wasn't imagining the hand in the middle of her back that shoved, making her stumble and roll down the remaining few steps. Pain knifed through her shoulder at the same time she heard a loud pop, after which pain lasered through her body. Irrationally she thought, I don't have any herbs strong enough for this one.

As she'd tumbled down the stairs, she'd bumped Katie and clipped Lorna in the legs. Through her pain-filled haze she was grateful to see she hadn't knocked either of them down. Katie put a hand on the wall to steady herself, and Lorna stumbled but had been close enough to the bottom to keep herself from going all the way down. Katie was the first one to reach Renee where she landed at the bottom of the stairs in an awkward heap and now kneeled beside her.

"What happened? Did you trip on something?" Her hands swept across her head, across her shoulders, and then down her arms. A good cop doing a quick injury inventory. Obviously her first-aid card was current.

Renee blinked and ran her question quickly through her mind. It was hard to think when her body was screaming. She did know that nobody had been behind her on the stairs, and there was nothing on any of the steps to trip on. The shove was intentional and the power behind it filled with fury. "I was pushed," she said simply as she wondered if the pain was going to back off at any point.

Katie gasped and turned her head up the way they'd come. "No one was there before, and no one is there now."

Trying to breathe through the throbbing pain that didn't seem to be fading, she put a hand on Katie's arm. "I'm aware of that, but I was pushed just the same." She didn't imagine it; she knew what she'd felt.

Lorna now kneeled on the other side of her, gingerly assessing the damage. Her touch was gentle, yet the pressure brought tears of pain to Renee's eyes just the same. This was not a good situation in one that was already bad. "I think you've dislocated your shoulder."

That wasn't hard to believe, given the way she felt. It was like someone had shoved a hot poker through her shoulder. "I believe you're right. Feels horrible."

"It was her, wasn't it?" Lorna was staring into her eyes, a mixture of concern and fury in them. "She pushed you."

She nodded even as Katie protested, a look of horror on her face. "I didn't touch her."

Lorna reached across Renee and put a hand on Katie's shoulder. "Not you, *her*." She inclined her head toward the far wall.

Renee hadn't seen her before, but now she did. Tall, angry, and with her back ramrod straight, she stood against the wall with her hands in the pockets of her crisp pressed apron. As it had been the last time she made an appearance, the previously dark room was now bathed in light. The empty room was no longer empty, and the musty smell of disuse was gone, replaced by an odor she couldn't quite define. It was sharp, astringent, and made her want to cover her nose.

"Who?" Katie asked as her head turned to survey the room.

"You don't see her?" Renee was surprised because she was as real as the three of them. "Do you see the lights, the furniture?"

Katie was shaking her head as she rose to her feet, her gun now out in one hand and her flashlight back in the other. "Where? Where is she?"

"Your friend does not believe yet," the nurse said. "She has to believe to see."

"You pushed me, you bitch," Renee bit out, surprised by her own vehemence. Her normally forgiving nature was nowhere to be found when it came to that woman. Even Renee could be pushed too far, and in this case that was a literal statement.

The nurse's eyes were dark and angry. "You are interfering. You needed to be taught a lesson. I do not tolerate those who stick their noses in where they do not belong."

"Oh, I'll teach you a lesson." Big words from a woman lying on a concrete floor with a dislocated shoulder. She meant every one of them nonetheless. At this point she didn't figure she had much to lose.

Lorna leaned down and whispered in her ear, "I got this, baby."

"Who are you talking to?" Katie was still unable to see the evil apparition. She still didn't believe quite enough.

Renee was staring at the nurse and disliking her more every second. "She says you don't believe and that's why you're not seeing her."

"Give believing a shot," Lorna said.

"Sounds crazy but what the hell." Katie rose to her feet, closed her eyes, and took a deep breath. When she opened them again, her head turned in the direction of their unwanted guest. "Well, I'll be damned."

Brittle laughter bounced off the walls, and the sound of it filled Renee with such dread, all of a sudden she forgot the pain in her shoulder.

❖

Jeremy finally found his voice, even though he was still stunned by the man towering over him. "Who are you?"

The giant on the stairs didn't answer. Instead, he waved his hand, and the door to the mental hospital swung open. Bending down to enter through the opening far too low to accommodate his massive height, he stepped through and disappeared into the shadows.

Okay, so the guy obviously wasn't the talkative type. This wasn't exactly the time for chitchat anyway. Taking the steps two at a time, he was up and across the entry seconds behind him. After he'd stepped inside, he saw with dismay that the tall man was already halfway up the stairs. Jeremy raced after him, unable to catch up to a guy with a stride three times as long as his. Once more he ascended the stairs two at time. It was the only way to stay even close to the caped crusader.

At the top of the stairs, two things struck him at the same time: the giant was nowhere in sight, and the place was lit with gas lamps that gave off a low hiss and golden glow. For a moment he became fixated on those lights. It seemed wrong somehow. Shouldn't the lights be electric? The building had been in use well into the twentieth century, yet these were straight out of the nineteenth century. It didn't make sense they wouldn't have been upgraded somewhere along the line.

The other thing about the lights that bugged him? When he drove up and parked, the building had been dark. Not a single flicker of light in any window he could see from the parking lot. The way it was lit up now, he should have been able to see something. Granted he'd been frantic on the way out, but not frantic enough he wouldn't notice lights in the windows.

He almost laughed at the troubling inconsistencies. After everything they'd been through recently, not much should strike him as odd. Not mute giants, not old-fashioned gas lamps, not anything. If John McCafferty's spirit could take over his body, then it sure wasn't impossible for lights to go on and off without a reason.

"Okay," he said quietly. "Think." A better idea was to listen. Now that he was inside, he was less concerned about the tall man and more focused on finding his crew. They had to be in here somewhere, and he wanted to meet up with them first thing. Stop, be still, and listen. That's what he needed to do. He closed his eyes, shut out the hiss of the lamps, and concentrated.

"Help me out here, Lorna."

As if she heard him, he felt a pull and caught the whisper of sound coming from the rear of the building. It was the sign he was hoping for, and it was enough.

"Thanks, sister." He opened his eyes and raced in the direction of the whisper. He didn't bother to try to hide the sound of big, pounding feet as he ran down the stairs and toward the back of the building. What would be the point? One thing he'd come to understand over the last year: they were no longer just dealing with the world of the seen. The unseen, the unacknowledged had become an integral part of their existence. It should bother him and yet it didn't. It was the new normal.

Funny how a life could change so quickly. He'd spent all of his, until the day he moved across state, in the very real, very conventional day-to-day world. He did what was expected of him and never even thought about what might exist beyond the norm. Nothing seemed out of the ordinary and nothing felt out of sync.

Except that wasn't exactly the way it all went down, now was it? He'd sensed the changes long before he sold his share of the business to his partner. What had come to him back then wasn't as blatant as the visions that assailed Lorna. It was more an unsettling disquiet he couldn't shake, no matter what he did. It was what had driven him across the mountains, jobless and without any prospects for starting a new life. It was what had put into motion everything that had happened since that drive.

It had brought him here now as he stood before a closed door, the distinct sound of movement and voices on the other side, an unknown danger waiting to get its claws in him. He pulled at the handle, dismayed at its refusal to open. Did this place have any doors that weren't locked up tight? The apparent answer to that was no.

He needed something to force it open, and if he wasn't mistaken, he'd spotted just such a pry bar outside the front door. All he had to do was run back out and grab it. At this point he wasn't above smashing a door to smithereens.

The sound of pounding feet made him spin and go into a defensive posture, the flashlight he still held his only weapon. It wasn't an ideal defensive tool, but hey; he would work with whatever he had. When the beam fell on Anna and the woman he assumed had to be Sadie, he lowered his arm back to his side. He was relieved to see them. One less problem to worry about. Now all he needed was to find Lorna.

"Hurry," Anna said with icy fear in her voice. "They're going to be right behind us."

He flashed his light behind them. "Who?" Nobody was following them that he could see. Maybe it was the giant and his big black cape. Though their interaction was brief, Ryan didn't think he was much of a threat. He sensed the big guy was here to help.

"The orderlies and they're big."

Okay, he wasn't expecting that, and he still didn't see anyone, orderly or otherwise. "No orderlies, Anna, big or small."

Anna and Sadie both turned to look back the way they'd come. Then they stared at each other with questioning expressions on their faces. "They were right behind us," Anna explained, holding Sadie's hand. "I'm not joking, Jeremy. Two big, mean-looking guys."

"Not a big man in a cape?"

Anna and Sadie looked at each other again. "No," Anna said. "Definitely nobody in a cape. These guys were huge and dressed all in white."

He shrugged and knew it could very well have been. The unexplained was at every turn. The orderlies might have been following Anna and Sadie, and by now they could also have faded back into the shadows they'd come from.

"Well, they're not there now, and I've got bigger things to worry about. I've got to get this door open." He waved his hand toward the door at this back. "Lorna and the others are down there."

"Ah, Jeremy." Anna's voice was trembling this time.

"What?" he snapped, ready to go into a full-on yell. He needed them to help and stop screwing around. As he spun away from them and back toward the door, the words died on his lips. Standing beside the now-open door was the giant.

Lorna took a chance. If ever there was a time to call on her powers to kick into high gear, this was it. Granted, that bitch had stepped out of her paranormal realm and into Lorna's reality, so there wasn't a question what they were up against. It was most assuredly going to get physical. But she needed to know why the change had happened.

The angel of death staring at her right now held all the cards when it came to what this was about, and that pissed her off. If she wanted to play hardball, well, she'd chosen the right team, and Lorna was ready to bat. She would figure this out, and she would take her down.

Quickly she scanned the room and settled her gaze on an old steel gurney, covered with dust and sitting in the middle of the room. If anything could show her what she needed to know to fight, she was pretty confident that piece of equipment could do it. Concentrating, she prayed as she hurried over to it and grabbed hold of the cold metal. This had to work.

The room was well lit and humming with activity. Two men were wheeling in a gurney, the figure lying prone on top struggling against the leather restraints that held her arms and legs secure. The woman's face looked vaguely familiar, and then she realized why. The scared and struggling woman resembled the photograph of Anna's wife. This had to be the great-great-grandmother who once owned the beautiful reset diamond.

Lorna was standing at the bottom of the stairwell, an unseen spectator in the drama unfolding in front of her eyes. The men rolled the gurney beneath a bright light suspended by a long black cord from the ceiling. It flickered when one of the men hit it, and it began to swing back and forth. The woman started to scream and to beg.

"Please, I can pay you. Please do not do this." Tears streamed down her face and she struggled against the restraints. Her hair was a tangled mess, her gown rumpled.

The nurse, the same one who'd pushed Renee down the stairs and laughed about it, ran her hand over the woman's hair, smoothing it back from her pale face. Her eyes were big and dark. "Oh, my dear girl, you really do not understand, do you? It must be your troubled mind. That is why your husband has already paid us well to ease your troubles. You will never have another disturbed thought once we finish with you. I promise, dear one. Your life will be transformed."

"I do not want to die," she cried. "I have children. I have money."

"And your husband will raise them well, I have no doubt. He is a good man, and his payment was generous. No, there is no need for you to worry about family or money. Rest easy. It will be over in a moment, and you will not feel a thing. All your troubles will be gone."

The nurse picked up something that looked like an old-fashioned hand drill. As Lorna watched in horror, the two men who had rolled the woman in put their hands on her head to keep her still. The nurse laid the tool against her skull and began to turn the handle. Blood started to dribble from the woman's head, picking up in intensity as the handle was turned. Her screams ratcheted up louder and louder. Then they began to trail off until they finally stopped altogether. Her body stilled as the nurse continued to turn the handle, and the only sounds in the room were the hum of the light and the squeak of the drill. The sound was like fingernails on a blackboard.

After what seemed like forever, the nurse stopped turning the handle and stared down at the unmoving woman. What she was looking for, Lorna couldn't tell. A few minutes of intense study seemed to satisfy her, and she reversed the direction of the drill until she could lift the tool away. As if on command, the orderlies dropped their hands from the woman's head and stepped away. She didn't so much as twitch.

All three stood staring down at the woman. Her chest was no longer rising and falling. The flow of blood from the hole in her skull had slowed until it was little more a mere trickle. Her skin was turning even paler than it already was. Her lips were beginning to turn a light, unnatural blue.

"Well, I believe we have accomplished the family's wishes," the nurse said as she picked up a towel from the small table where the bloody drill now lay and wiped her hands, studying her nails and her palms as if looking for the tiniest speck of blood. When she appeared satisfied her hands were clean, she dropped the towel, now streaked with blood, back on the table.

One of the orderlies looked down at the woman and then took one finger and poked her in the cheek. He looked up and over at the other one, who shrugged.

The one who'd done the poking said, "Nurse Thompson, I think she's dead."

Nurse Thompson pursed her lips before taking hold of the woman's chin and twisting her head back and forth. When she looked up, a small smile crossed her face. "My, my, perhaps you are right. Well, sometimes it works and sometimes it does not. You boys know what to do. You will find an urn already waiting."

She turned her back and left the room without another glance.

The two orderlies pushed the gurney out of the room, and

Lorna followed. They continued down a dark hallway and through two swinging doors. Inside the big room, they opened a heavy iron furnace door. Picking the body up, they slid it inside and shut the door. Their movements were so smooth Lorna knew this wasn't the first time they'd done this. Or the second. With sickening clarity she understood this was routine business, and they'd probably done it a hundred times.

One of them walked over to a table holding a line of copper urns and slid one closer to the edge. Lorna walked over and peered at the shiny receptacles. On the one closest to the furnace, the one the orderly had moved, was already engraved, ROSE HALBREN, 1882–1903.

CHAPTER SEVENTEEN

On any other day Anna would have freaked out at the sight of the huge man with flowing black hair who held open the door to the lower level, his size so out of proportion to the building it looked as though he held the door to a playhouse open. This was definitely not any other day, and she was not freaking out. She'd experienced one crazy thing after another, so one more was no big deal.

Rather than scream, which under normal circumstances would have been very appropriate, she grabbed Sadie's arm and pulled her in the opposite direction. "We have to get out of this hellhole. I am done with all the insanity." Just across the room, a wide door with windows revealed the night sky. She wanted to see that sky, up close and personal. She wanted fresh air and no ghosts. Repeat: no ghosts.

Sadie shook her head and pulled away. Jeremy had disappeared through the open doorway as soon as the giant man opened it, and Sadie was following him. "We have to help." Her words were confident.

Anna didn't agree. "No, we have to get out of here." The last thing she intended to do was go through any door that didn't lead directly outside. She liked to think of herself as strong and capable, but right now, she sounded like a terrified ten-year-old. Damn it. Sadie had been through enough, and she'd been captive in this place way too long. The time to leave was yesterday, not after traipsing down some dark and creepy stairs. Besides, Jeremy was perfectly capable of helping Lorna. They didn't need either her or Sadie.

"Anna," Sadie said sharply as she stopped at the top of the stairs and stared at her. "They came to help me, and they don't even know me. They came because you called. We are not leaving them down there. They could have told you to go to hell when you called and asked for help, but they didn't. No way am I walking away from this fight, and neither are you. We aren't the kind of people who turn their back on their friends."

Guilt hit her hard, and she was pretty sure that's exactly what Sadie intended. She was right too. Anna had called out of the blue and pleaded with Lorna to come help her. Lorna had every reason to hate her and turn her back on Anna, yet she'd done exactly the opposite. Despite all the ugliness that rested squarely on Anna's shoulders, Lorna had taken the high road and was here tonight to help. No bitterness, no recriminations, no nothing. She simply came because Anna asked. What kind of cowardly bitch would she be if she walked away from Lorna now?

She sighed. There were times to walk away and times to do the right thing. This was one of the latter. "You're right. We have to go after him."

Sadie gave her a quick kiss on the cheek, the touch of her lips warm and comforting. "That's the woman I married. Come on. Let's go help kick some ghost butt."

Kicking ghost butt didn't hold much appeal to her. Nonetheless, she followed Sadie closely down the stairs and into the unknown darkness that lay below. The squeaks of every step on the hundred-year-old staircase made her incredibly nervous. Nothing like announcing their arrival to the devil. She didn't know what they were going to find at the bottom of the long staircase, but she had a strong feeling it wasn't going to be anything good. Nothing good had happened since she'd stepped foot inside this old hospital except for finding Sadie.

She wasn't wrong either. As her foot hit the concrete floor below, everything seemed to be a blur of motion. Renee, moaning in what she could only describe as pain, was sliding across the floor as if unseen hands were dragging her. Her legs were kicking, though she never seemed to be able to make purchase. A door opened and she was tossed through it. Unseen hands slammed it shut, followed by the sounds of locks turning. It all happened so fast she wouldn't have been able to help even if she'd taken off at a dead run.

As if seeing Renee manhandled by nothing wasn't bad enough, Anna watched Katie's gun fly from her hand and bounce against a far wall. It hit the floor with a loud bang, and for a second she thought it had gone off. With relief she realized it was only the sound of metal meeting concrete. Just as with Renee, Katie was pulled across the room by unseen hands with her heels dragging and her legs kicking. A second door opened and she was thrown in. Once more Anna heard the door close, and the sound of a lock engaging was crystal clear. Only Lorna remained standing, her unflinching eyes locked on Nurse Thompson.

"Fuck you, bitch," Lorna said in a low, venomous voice. "I know what you did." She'd heard Lorna before when she was angry or unhappy. This was very different. The tone of her voice now was something she'd never heard before, and it sent shivers up her spine.

Nurse Thompson's laugh chilled Anna to the marrow of her bones. So did the sound of the door at the top of the stairs slamming shut. Damn doors around here refused to stay open. She thought vaguely if she ever saw another locked door, it would be too soon.

The nurse stood tall, her back straight, her posture arrogant as if nothing they could say or do would touch her. Judging by what she'd seen so far, Anna was afraid she might be right. She sure hoped Lorna had some magic up her sleeve.

"Don't you understand? Don't any of you understand? It doesn't matter what you know." Her eyes drifted past Lorna, past them all until they landed on Sadie. Her smile made Anna's stomach turn. "You have come back to me, and you have brought your friends. Very thoughtful of you, and it is fortunate that we have plenty of room for everyone. Oh, I have waited a very long time for you. I always knew you would return."

Sadie's gaze was on hers. There was no fear in her eyes. Like Lorna, there was something hard and unforgiving in them. "You were crazy in life, and you're crazy now."

The nurse's gaze shifted back to Lorna, and her hands remained folded in front of her apron. She was as calm as if this was a conversation she had every day. "I simply do what has to be done. I keep everyone safe and always have. Each of us has a job in life, and this one is mine. I do it well. Better than anyone if you must know."

"What is she talking about?" Anna whispered. "I mean, she's a real nutcase and all, but she does seem to have an agenda."

Nurse Thompson's head whipped around. "You." She held out a bony finger in Anna's direction. "You are a meddling fool, and I will make certain you do not destroy what I have so carefully built and guarded. I have a very special plan for you."

Making good on her word, Nurse Thompson swung her arm around, and the blow felt as hard to Anna as if someone had struck her in the head with a baseball bat. Her head whipped to the side and her vision began to fade to black as she lost her footing and began to tumble hard across the concrete floor.

❖

Lorna had been waiting for exactly this kind of opening. She lunged at the nurse and took her to the floor in a move worthy of a Saturday-night wrestling match. It was really weird and a new one on her. She was getting accustomed to dealing with spirits and visions, the kind that happened in some shadowy world between the living and the dead where much was seen and nothing was touched. Not the case here at all. The woman was solid and, damn it, warm. It was like she was flesh and blood, but that, her rational mind screamed, was totally impossible.

It was also totally unfair. Lorna had nothing to fight her with except her psychic powers, and given her opponent's solid form, she wasn't exactly sure how they would help. She needed something more substantial, like maybe a cross or holy water or magical spells. Anything tangible that might shake this thing up and give her the edge she so desperately needed.

As she rolled across the floor fighting with the devil, her feeling of powerlessness grew. The nurse pulled her hair and scratched her face. Somewhere along the line, this crazy woman had done her fair share of street fighting, and she fought dirty. Never in her life was Lorna as grateful for her Ironman training as at this moment. She was as strong as she'd ever been, and she needed every ounce to subdue the insane woman…ghost…who fought with unnatural power. Big surprise there. Supernatural power from a supernatural being. It was bad enough dealing with spirits in visions; this was a twist she could honestly say she was not too fond of. She preferred her spirits more spirit-like. One who actually drew blood was, well, a bitch.

"Jeremy," she yelled when she had the fighting tiger pinned. "I need you now." The woman was twisting and spitting, her legs kicking as she tried to free herself. Her jaws snapped as she attempted to bite Lorna. Talk about street fighting.

"What do we do?" He kneeled beside her, holding the woman's legs while waiting to hear her idea on what else to do with the devil she was sitting on.

She wished she knew. How could she make this thing disappear forever? She couldn't even begin to comprehend how the nurse had managed to morph from ghost to flesh-and-blood, let alone how to send her back to hell. Seriously, there should be a manual for this kind of crap. "I don't know," she said, breathless after the rigorous cat fight.

"We gotta do something with her. She isn't giving up."

He was right too. The nurse didn't seemed fazed in the least.

She still struggled with an amazing amount of power, though fortunately for them, she wasn't able to free herself. There was power in numbers in all realms.

"Duh. Give me a sec." Her mind was whirling as she felt something on the top of her head. For a second she wasn't sure what she was feeling, and then she realized what it was. Someone had laid their hand on her head, and it wasn't Jeremy.

Silence swept over the room, though it was more as if her ears went deaf, because the woman beneath her continued to struggle and scream as she fought to free herself from her captors. Lorna heard none of it and barely felt the twisting of the woman she sat on. She turned her head and looked up. Beside her stood a man, a giant of a man, dressed all in black and with long, flowing black hair. The hair would have made her stop even if he hadn't been wearing a black cape. Shades of Dracula was the first thing that jumped into her mind. If she hadn't been seeing it, she wouldn't have believed that this night had just become even stranger.

She pulled her gaze away and glanced around, astonished to see that no one else seemed surprised by his appearance. How could they not be? The man was NBA tall and looked quite out of place in his tidy, though Gothic, attire. Someday, she was going to write a book. They'd call it fiction because nobody in their right mind would believe it. She barely believed it, and she was the one currently sitting on top of a ghost and looking up at what had to be the giant from "Jack and the Beanstalk."

As she gazed up into his pale face, peace flowed over her body like a fine spring rain. He, simply by standing next to her, made her feel safe and at ease. Then he held out one of his massive hands toward her, and suddenly she knew. She understood it all as if they'd spent an hour together talking, and yet not a single word had passed between them.

Standing up, she released her grip on the squirming madwoman. She took his offered hand, her small one dwarfed by his. With her free hand, she took hold of Jeremy's because he too had released his grip on the woman's legs. When she wrapped her fingers around Jeremy's, she could hear again, and Nurse Thompson's wild screams once more filled the air. She gave new meaning to the term screech.

Jeremy's voice was full of with panic as he squeezed her hand a little too tight. "What in the world are you doing? We shouldn't let her go." He said the words, though he didn't move to try to restrain the woman again, and she wasn't surprised. Instead, he kept hold of Lorna's hand. It reminded her a bit of when they were children and were frightened by scary movies or bad thunderstorms. They were always there for each other, in good times and in bad.

"Encircle her," she told him as she turned to look into his eyes. "We can destroy her, but it's going to take us all to do it. Sadie."

Understanding came into his face and he nodded. "I think I get it," he said and held her hand firmer. "Good plan, sister. Let's take this monster out."

She looked up at the stairs toward Sadie. This wasn't a job just for her and Jeremy. In fact, Sadie was a critical piece of this puzzle. Anna was out cold on the floor, which was too bad because she'd use her too if she was conscious. As it was, the four of them would have to be enough. "Hurry, we need you."

Sadie ran to the other side of Jeremy and took his free hand. With her other, she reached out to the tall man. The circle was complete: Lorna, Jeremy, Sadie, and the tall stranger. When they surrounded Nurse Thompson, holding their hands tightly together, she rose cursing to her feet. She pushed against them all one by one as she tried to break free of the healing circle.

"You cannot hurt me," she screamed, her face turning crimson. She wasn't an attractive woman to begin with, and the fury that infused her had turned her face into the mask of a monster. "I am immortal. I will stand guard over my special ones for eternity. I am special."

Lorna looked at her wild eyes and listened to her insane protests. She was no longer frightened by this soul who belonged in the past, for the man had brought her the wisdom to send the deranged woman back. He was strange and unexpected and exactly what she needed at this critical moment. The words Lorna knew she needed came without effort, as if she'd known them for years.

"Our Father, descend upon us and purify us. Lord, mold us, fill us, use us. Banish all the forces of evil from this place, destroy them, vanquish them, and cleanse this place for all eternity. Banish from this building all spells, black magic, diabolic infestations, oppressions, possessions: all that is evil and sinful. Burn all these evils in hell, that they may never again touch any in this place or any other creature in the entire world. By the power of almighty God, in the name of Jesus Christ our Savior, leave forever, and be consigned into the everlasting hell."

A blast of cold air hit her so hard she flew back, losing her hold on the giant and on Jeremy. She landed on the floor, and her head hit the concrete with such violence, her vision went black.

❖

To Renee it sounded as though a tornado was happening outside the door. Screams filled the air, and things hit the door with enough force she thought it would at least splinter the wood, allowing her to go free. It didn't, and she remained locked inside a room with no light. To make things worse, it smelled as though a thousand dead bodies had decomposed inside here. It was all she could do not to gag and vomit. But she wouldn't give that bitch the satisfaction. She was going to get out of here, and she was going to help Lorna.

Her hands hurt as she pounded against the door, screaming and kicking. It wouldn't move and the doorknob refused to turn. How often had she heard the refrain, "They don't build things like they used to," and this was a testament to that sentiment. A hundred years later and the door was still tight and solid.

Tears flowed down her cheeks, and all she could think of

was getting to Lorna. This couldn't be the end; she refused to let it be. She intended to marry Lorna and spend the rest of her life with her. After everything that had happened to her, she'd finally found the pot of gold at the end of the rainbow, and now it was being ripped from her hands. By a damn ghost. It wasn't fair. It wasn't going to happen.

"Let me out!" she screamed. "Let me out of this goddamn room!" The horrible odor inside brought tears to her eyes and made her cough as she screamed over and over. Someone had to open the door for her. She had to get to Lorna.

The sound of an explosion made her step back from the door, and her screams faded. Her heart constricted as the implications of what it might be shook her to the core. "Please, God," she prayed. "Let her be all right." God couldn't be this cruel. Not to her and not to Lorna. Not after everything Lorna had done to protect her family and friends, and even strangers. Not after she'd swallowed her pride to help the one who broke her heart. No, God couldn't be that cruel.

She had started back to the door, intending to beat it down if she had to, when it suddenly popped open, and a crack of light filtered in. She wanted to run to it, rip it open, and race out. But fear made her more cautious, and once more she backed up a few steps. With her fingertips, she reached over and pulled it open enough to see outside. The light illuminated the interior of the room enough for her to get a picture of where she was being held. For a moment, what she was seeing didn't fully register. When it did, she pushed the door all the way open, the light of the big open room spilling inside her cell to reveal its grisly secrets.

She gasped and slapped her hand to her mouth. Mother of God, what kind of place was this? All around her were stains, dark ugly stains that must have been there for years. They covered the floor and the walls, and the realization of their origins turned her cold. Instruments of torture hung from big hooks, and like the floor and the walls, they were covered with the unmistakable evidence of the room's purpose.

Renee stifled a sob and hurled herself out of her temporary prison. After what she'd just seen, she could barely process what awaited her outside. Her gaze took in the scene playing out in the big room, though making sense of it was nearly impossible. She didn't try because she saw the one thing that made her heart nearly stop. Lorna lay unconscious on the floor, her face as white as snow. Maybe God could be that cruel.

She ran to her side and pulled her into her arms. The movement made her shoulder scream in pain, but she ignored it. Her pain didn't matter. Only Lorna mattered. She pressed her face against Lorna's hair and whispered urgently, "Don't you dare die on me, do you hear me, Lorna Dutton. You promised to love me forever, and I'm holding you to that."

Her body shook so hard she was surprised she could still hold on to Lorna. She wasn't about to let her go, despite the burning in her shoulder. Some stupid-ass ghost was not going to take the woman who'd captured her heart away from her now. She'd waited too long to find love to lose it because of a psycho spirit. "Please," she cried, and her tears fell from her cheeks to land on Lorna's hair. To lose her like this couldn't be right in any realm of existence. "Please don't leave me, baby girl, please. I need you."

Lorna's eyes fluttered open and she blinked several times. "Not going anywhere, beautiful."

Chapter Eighteen

Renee bent and kissed Lorna hard before she helped her up to a sitting position. Lorna thought it was the sweetest kiss she'd ever experienced, and all she really wanted to do was stay wrapped up in Renee's arms and forget about everything else. When she came to and was staring into Renee's watery eyes, it was like waking up in heaven. Not too bad after getting her ass kicked by a spirit.

"Are you okay?" Renee's voice was tense. "Are you really okay?"

Lorna smiled and stared into the eyes she loved so much. "I'm fine. I'm probably going to have a killer headache, but nothing's broken. Are you all right? Your shoulder." If she was being honest with Renee she'd tell her that not only did her head hurt like a son of a bitch, but her body felt like she'd been through a prize fight. It could be just the tussle with the nurse, but she didn't think that was all of it. The unseen forces had taken their pound of flesh as well, or at least that's what she suspected. Kind of hard to quantify a fight like the one they'd just gone through.

Renee sighed and leaned back against the wall. It seemed that once she realized Lorna was fine, the pain in her shoulder kicked up. Her tears vanished but her face was pale and drawn. "Hurts like Hades," she admitted. "But I'll make it through."

Lorna kissed her. "Always knew you would. You're a tough one, if you don't already know it."

Renee's head turned toward the room she'd been held in. "I don't know how tough I am. I may never get the sight of that room out of my head."

Lorna wasn't sure what she'd seen, only that it wasn't good. Didn't surprise her much, considering everything else around here and given what she'd seen Nurse Thompson do to Sadie's great-great-grandmother. But that was a discussion for another day.

Lorna kissed her and said, "I'll make it go away."

"I'll hold you to that."

Lorna looked around, trying to get her bearings back. Not that she was planning to tell Renee, but that little smack on the head really had rung her bell. She was going to have a big fat headache in the morning. More like now, actually. "Is she gone?" Despite the pounding in her head, it appeared the only ones still in the room were of the human variety.

Jeremy came over, reached down a hand, and helped her to her feet. "Yeah. I'm pretty sure we sent Nurse Crazy back to hell, where she belongs."

Once standing, she had to give herself a second to let the dizziness pass. Definitely a bell ringer. With Jeremy at her side, they turned to Renee. It took both of them to help her up, and she winced when Lorna took the arm with the injured shoulder. She was trying to be as gentle as she could, but it wasn't enough. Cradling her arm to keep the weight off her shoulder, Renee leaned against the wall. That shoulder was going to need the attention of a doctor right away. A second trip to the ER was in order.

Satisfied that Renee was okay for the moment, Lorna looked around the room again. "The big guy?" she asked. Something about that man seemed familiar, as if she'd seen him before. Surely she'd have remembered. After all, he had to be close to seven feet tall. And how about that hair? How many guys had two or three feet of shiny black hair? None that she could think of. So yeah, she'd have remembered meeting that fellow.

It was perplexing how close she felt to him, as if they had some kind of special connection, and maybe they did. It would make sense, given their nearly telepathic communication earlier. Good grief, like she needed another little gift. Being psychic was plenty. No need to add telepathy with giants on top of it too.

Renee put a finger under Lorna's chin and turned her face toward the far wall. There he was, standing next to the woman she'd seen Nurse Thompson murder in her vision. She was pale and smiling as she held the giant's hand. Oddly, she looked healthy and alive. Or alive in the ghostly way. She no longer had angry red wounds in her head, and that made Lorna feel good. What that wicked nurse had done to her was so terribly wrong, and Lorna was glad to see her restored to the beauty she'd been before the brutal attack.

The two of them stood together, the tall dark man and the tiny beauty. A ghostly version of the Beauty and the Beast. Though calling him a beast didn't seem right. Freaky tall and a little on the Gothic side, but he was far from a beast. Goodness radiated from him, and she'd bet Renee would say he had a beautiful aura.

Seeing them gave Lorna pause. Again things here weren't quite following the pattern she'd come to expect. They'd banished the evil woman who'd stolen her life, yet she was still here. If her psychic skills were holding true to form, the woman should be on her way to heaven. That she wasn't, Lorna reasoned, meant one thing: their work was not yet done. Crap.

Lorna's eyes were still on the duo as she asked, "Do you guys see what I see?" She was really hoping this wasn't another vision that she had to figure out by herself.

Katie, like Renee, had been freed from the confines of her locked room and now stood with her reclaimed gun in her hand. She had a note of awe in her voice as she answered, "Copy that. I see two that I shouldn't be seeing, and to tell you the truth, I'm having a little trouble processing the sight. They don't teach this in the academy."

"Welcome to my world," Lorna muttered as she moved toward the two figures standing together, one tall, one tiny. Both sets of eyes gazed at her intently as she drew closer.

"My great-great-grandmother," Sadie said as she too walked toward the duo. "Rose."

Yeah, she'd already figured that one out all by herself. After all, the diminutive woman and Sadie were almost twins. No denying the family connection even though one was alive and one was long dead. "Do you know what she wants?" Lorna turned to look at Sadie, who stood a few steps behind her, arm in arm with Anna.

Sadie shook her head and pursed her lips. "Not exactly. I wish I did. She's told me several times to help them, but I can't for the life of me figure out what she means."

Lorna had to agree. Her cryptic words were impossible to reason out. An odd game of Scrabble that she was losing. As far as she was concerned, she'd helped Rose, so what more was there to do? This wasn't working out at all like anything she'd encountered thus far in her psychic journey. She stopped very close to them, and it occurred to her that while they seemed solid and real, there was something equally unreal about them. Perhaps the fact that, if they could speak, they didn't. Or the fact that even standing this close there was none of the warmth she would expect from another living being. The weirdness just kept rolling along.

"I don't understand," she said to them both. "What do you need me to do?"

Neither one said a word or even moved their lips, for that matter. She was about to throw her hands up in frustration when the tall man inclined his head. She got the distinct impression he wanted her to follow them. Okay, since she had little else to go on, that's what she did. Sort of. They walked through what appeared to be a solid wall. For a long moment, she simply stared at the spot where they'd been standing and wondered what she was supposed to do next. Her abilities didn't include walking through solid walls. There were other rooms on the perimeter walls, only not in the spot where the two disappeared. So where did they go?

Then something occurred to her, and she starting mulling over the possibility. Could it be? No, it was the kind of thing a person saw in a movie but that didn't really happen in real life. Or did it? At this point she had nothing to lose and everything to gain.

She walked over to the wall and began to run her fingers along the seams in the concrete. It didn't appear to be anything uncommon, just a regular concrete wall in an old basement. At first she felt nothing unusual, and then she hit pay dirt. Sure as the world, when she touched an upper corner on the left side, she was greeted with a tiny click. This wall wasn't a wall at all; it was a cleverly disguised hidden panel. On creaky hinges, it slid open, and as it did, a light came on automatically. Son. Of. A. Bitch.

"You all need to come take a look at this. I'm seeing it, but I'm sure as hell not believing it."

Behind her Renee, Katie, Anna, and Sadie gathered. Each let out a little gasp when they peered through the opened panel.

"What in the world?" Renee whispered, as if she was afraid of disturbing something or someone.

"Yeah, my thoughts exactly," Lorna said as she grabbed Renee's hand.

"This is messed up," Katie muttered as she took her cell phone from the clip on her belt. "I need to call this in."

"Probably be a good idea."

Sadie put a hand on Lorna's shoulder and squeezed. "It all makes sense now. Thank you."

"Who would ever guess?" She'd seen some pretty bizarre things since her gift was imparted on her, but this was a sight that would stay with her forever.

Lorna guessed the room to be about six feet deep and maybe twenty feet long, give or take a few feet either way. Wooden shelves, sturdy though plain, lined each wall, floor to ceiling.

Functional was the word that came to mind. Not a room that was designed for beauty. Unlike the rest of the building that had been cleared out, this room was still in use.

Side by side, in perfect alignment on every shelf, sat rows of copper cans or, more accurately, copper urns. Like the room and the shelves, the urns were not ornate. Rather, they were simple and uniform in size. Hundreds of small urns with names and dates engraved on each lid.

Lorna stepped inside and picked up an urn that caught her eye. Unlike all its counterparts, this one was slightly askew, creating a break in the otherwise perfect lineup of containers. It was as if someone had recently moved it and failed to put it back as it had been. Someone like the ghost of a murdered woman, the same one who'd drawn her here. As with most of the other urns lined up on the shelves in the room, green oxidation dripped down its sides, giving it an almost art-like appearance. It was hauntingly beautiful and sad at the same time. Lorna took the flashlight from her pocket and turned the beam to the words and numbers graved on the lid. Despite the oxidation she could still read what had been carved there a time long past: ROSE HALBREN, 1882–1903.

The Watcher faded into the shadows as the door slid open to bring into the light those souls whose lives were stolen and then forgotten so long ago. Here they'd been hidden away and denied the path to the hereafter they so righteously deserved. One thousand two hundred and thirty-eight souls had waited in this room, some for more than ten decades.

He smiled as he saw the light touch the copper prisons where their ashes were confined to darkness, her evil intent to hold them captive forever. In these souls he finally discovered the true nature of his destiny and, at long last, understood why God had kept his feet grounded on this earth. It was his mission to bring these souls home, and he could not have accomplished that goal without her light.

He watched her now as she gently caressed the urn of the one who had marshaled the courage to fight the evil Nurse Thompson. His own journey to enlightenment had been a lonely one, yet he now understood that in the end, he could not have made it alone. He needed all of them. Lorna. Jeremy. Renee. Sadie. Most of all he needed Rose. He stepped from the shadows and held out his hand one more time. Rose smiled as she put her delicate hand in his. The touch, denied to him for many years, brought tears to his eyes. To experience the joy of this moment was worth the eternity of isolation. This was good and right.

As he stood holding her soft hand in his, he felt his essence fading, and when he turned, he instinctively understood that this time only one was still able to see him. She was indeed a special person, and he would keep her in his prayers for all time. Without her, he would still be lost. With her, he had found his salvation. She had taught him of selflessness and forgiveness. She had brought him into the light and given him back the wings lost so long ago. With one hand, he still held on to Rose, knowing that she would be with him forever. A beautiful, gentle soul who needed him as much as he needed her.

He laid the other hand on his heart as he nodded at Lorna. She, too, would always have a piece of his heart, for she was special beyond measure. She smiled and nodded back, laying her own hand over her heart.

He tipped his head upward, and for the first time since he'd fallen from grace, he smiled. The expression felt odd, and he brought his free hand up to lay a finger against his lips. His smile grew as the warmth surrounding him spread. With his head still tilted up, he greeted the light he'd waited millennia to see. A gentle wind whirled around them, catching his hair and lifting it up. His cape flapped and the warm breeze kissed his skin. His heart swelled, and he gently squeezed Rose's hand as the light washed over and around them both.

Then they were gone.

❖

Sadie stood next to Anna, and tears streamed down her face. "This is it," she said. "This is what she wanted us to find. She's been here all these years, and no one knew. No one cared."

Anna was still dumbfounded by what she was seeing: row upon row of urns, each bearing the names, birth dates, and dates of death of what looked to be hundreds if not a thousand or more souls. She ran a finger along the names, and her heart hurt. So many people, so many lives lost, and no one knew they were here. She'd hated that nurse before but now, what she felt toward her was even stronger. "What an evil bitch. How could she do this to people? Why would she do this?"

Sadie took the urn that held the ashes of her great-great-grandmother from Lorna and stared down at it. "Why didn't anyone come looking for her? How could my great-great-grandfather just leave her here? What kind of bastard would do that?" Her tears fell against the urn, sliding down the sides and making the copper glisten.

Lorna gave Sadie a little hug. "I'm so terribly sorry, Sadie. I'm sorry for what happened to your grandmother. We haven't really met yet, but I'm Lorna."

Sadie turned and put her arms around Lorna. She hugged her tight and then kissed her cheek. "Thank you," she said. "For everything. You have no idea what this means to me."

At first Anna thought Lorna was going to jump away from the bear hug that Sadie was giving her, and then she was surprised when Lorna just smiled. It was a real smile that made Lorna's eyes come alive. It was a look that Anna hadn't seen in a very long time, and it warmed her heart to see it now.

"You're very welcome," Lorna said and returned the hug.

Sadie looked down and touched the urn again. "I really don't understand why no one came for her." There was a sob in her voice.

"I think I do," Lorna said as she studied the rows and rows of urns. "I'm not trying to dis your grandfather, but I'm making an educated guess that the guy put her here because he didn't want her to ever leave."

Sadie hugged the urn to her chest as she turned her intense gaze onto Lorna. "Do you think she was mentally ill?"

Anna's heart ached at the sorrow that filled Sadie's words. From Anna's point of view, it seemed that during the time Sadie had been kept here, she'd become very attached to Rose. She didn't blame her; it was heartbreaking to think of anyone being stuck here under the control of Nurse Thompson. It had to have been hell. Then to have them appear as ghosts and draw Sadie into the drama that had played out here a hundred years ago made it all even worse.

"No, I don't," Lorna said, and Anna could tell by the look in her eyes that she was being honest with Sadie. She wasn't just telling her what she thought she wanted to hear, and Anna really appreciated her honesty. "I think she may have been depressed or something along those lines, but mentally ill, never. I don't believe she could be something in death that she wasn't in life. The woman we saw was not ill, mental or otherwise."

Sadie held the urn tighter to her chest and smiled. The smile chased away most of the shadows. "Well, she's not alone anymore. None of these people are, thanks to you."

Lorna was shaking her head. "I didn't do anything. Rose did."

Anna wasn't buying that argument, or at least not all of it. Without Lorna it was entirely possible Sadie would still be a captive here and these lost souls would still be hidden in darkness behind the unknown panel. "You brought them home, Lorna. You all brought them home,"

Anna said, "Lorna, Sadie, Jeremy, and Katie. None of this

would have been possible if you hadn't come when I called. I can't ever thank you enough."

"We're kind of like the twenty-first-century ghostbusters," Jeremy said from the doorway. He'd been standing there taking it all in, the same look of disbelief on his face that Anna was pretty sure had been on all of their faces.

His words made everyone laugh, and all the tension that had been hanging over them since the moment they first came to this place lifted. In fact, Anna decided that even the air in the place seemed lighter all of a sudden, as if banishing Nurse Thompson once and for all had lifted a cloud that had been hanging over the building since it first opened its doors.

Anna turned and took one of Lorna's hands. "I will never be able to thank you enough. You had every right to tell me to go to hell. You still have every right. You're one fine woman, and anytime you need anything, I'm here for you."

Sadie stepped next to her and put an arm around her waist. She looked up into Anna's eyes and winked, which made Anna want to cry. "We're here for you."

Tonight was full of miracles of a kind she could never have imagined. Finding Sadie was first and foremost, and she would never, ever take her for granted again. The thought of losing her had shaken Anna to her core. Life simply wasn't fine without her in it. Right now she felt as though she was being given a second chance with Sadie, and she planned to make it a chance that counted. Loving her was the most incredible thing in the world, and she planned to cherish every minute they had together.

"Yes," Anna said. "*We* are."

Lorna smiled, and Anna's heart melted a little more. She hadn't seen that smile in several years, and it telegraphed the one thing she didn't deserve and never thought she'd receive: forgiveness.

"Hey," Katie said from the bottom of the stairs, one foot on the first step, her hand on the banister. "You guys might want to hang out in this mausoleum, but I've had enough of this place to last a lifetime. Can we get the hell out of here? I've got backup coming, and we'll let them sort out that mystery." She waved a hand toward the hidden storeroom.

Anna looked around and then inclined her head in Katie's direction. "I think that's a great idea. I say we all head home." Home...what a beautiful word. She was going home, with Sadie. With her wife. She squeezed Sadie's hand and started toward the stairs.

"I second that," Renee said as she leaned into Lorna while cradling her arm. "This shoulder is killing me."

EPILOGUE

L orna hadn't been able to sleep. After all her months of training, all the pains, the pulled muscles, and finding a way to overcome the fear, the day was finally here. Today she was going to be an Ironman. Or fall flat on her face. It could go either way.

When she'd started this journey, it had been her whole focus. It was the thing that had saved her from diving wholeheartedly into deep despair when she'd first broken up with Anna. It was a pretty good plan, even if she did say so. It kept her busy and focused, not to mention pretty darned healthy.

Then everything else had happened.

The house on the ocean.

The psychic abilities.

Renee.

Everything had crashed together to create a life she'd never imagined. Thinking back on it now, she recalled how it had been one crazy-ass ride that she wouldn't trade for the world. Rather than wake up her wife...the word still made her smile...she got up.

Three days ago, their wedding had been a double affair. Standing with the ocean as their backdrop, Renee and Lorna, and Jeremy and Merry, had shared their wedding vows with friends and family. What a day that had been. Merry, after her scare in Spokane, had looked healthy and radiant. In a flowing gown, she'd been an absolute vision, and Lorna wasn't the only one who thought so. The look on Jeremy's face when he saw her come walking down between the rows of white folding chairs was something Lorna would never forget. Her only regret was that Mom wasn't there to see him. She'd have been so proud of her little boy and the man he'd become.

Renee, her beautiful bride, had been stunning in a pale-golden dress. Her hair was flowing and shiny, flowers tucked into the curls. She was pretty sure she'd had the same expression on her face as Jeremy had had on his. She'd never realized until now how it was possible to love someone this much.

The day couldn't have been more beautiful. The weather was lovely, all their friends had showed up, and that included Anna and Sadie. She'd learned some important lessons during the trip to Spokane. When they'd raced to the hospital with Merry, she'd realized how life could change in a moment. It holds no guarantees, no assurances, and no warning, so it was important to cherish those of the heart. Even those who broke hearts.

She also had realized that holding on to bitterness was a waste of time and energy. Every second that she had resented Anna was a second lost. What had happened between them hadn't torn either of them down. It hadn't broken them. No, it was simply part of the journey that had brought them to where they needed to be. Anna with Sadie and Lorna with Renee. The universe had a way of working its own brand of magic.

Standing in that hidden room with the rows upon rows of urns holding the remains of so many forgotten souls was a lesson in itself. She didn't want to hold on to destructive emotions and risk becoming even close to what they'd seen in Nurse Thompson. She'd destroyed untold lives in the name of control and power. She'd embraced darkness, and it had damned her own soul. Life was too short and far too precious.

Lorna had returned home from Spokane a changed woman as well as a formally engaged woman. After everything that had happened while they were there, no way in hell was she going to risk losing Renee. She'd found a fabulous ruby ring before they packed up and had it on Renee's finger before they ever left the Spokane city limits. Their wedding day had made her feel like the luckiest woman alive.

Now she felt like the most nervous woman alive. She sure hoped this reaction was normal. Friends who had already competed in the endurance test told her it was the way everyone felt before their first race. It was hard to envision how anyone could get through the race when they felt like throwing up. She looked up at the clock and sighed. Still two hours to go before she made the drive to Coeur d'Alene, put on her wetsuit, and started the longest race of her life.

Twelve hours later, Lorna was hurting like crazy and smiling just as crazy. People were screaming and clapping as she trotted toward the massive finish line. She'd completed her two-plus mile swim, ridden her bike one hundred and twelve miles, and was now less than twenty feet away from completing a full marathon.

As she crossed the finish line and heard them call out her name, tears flowed down her cheeks. Everyone more than likely believed she was crying because she'd made it through the grueling race, but they'd be wrong. It wasn't the medal they hung around her neck or the pats on her back that made her feel alive and special. It was the woman standing at the end of the finishers' chute, her face glowing and a golden band on her left hand, that made those tears flow.

About the Author

Sheri Lewis Wohl grew up in northeast Washington State, and though she always thought she'd move away, never has. Despite traveling throughout the United States, Sheri always finds her way back home. And so she lives, plays, and writes amidst mountains, evergreens, and abundant wildlife.

When not working the day job in federal finance, she writes stories that typically include a bit of the strange and unusual and always a touch of romance. She works to carve out time to run, swim, and bike so she can participate in local triathlons, her latest addiction.

Sheri can be contacted at darkdreams@comcast.net.

Books Available From Bold Strokes Books

Basic Training of the Heart by Jaycie Morrison. In 1944, socialite Elizabeth Carlton joins the Women's Army Corps to escape family expectations and love's disappointments. Can Sergeant Gale Rains get her through Basic Training with their hearts intact? (978-1-62639-818-4)

Believing in Blue by Maggie Morton. Growing up gay in a small town has been hard, but it can't compare to the next challenge Wren—with her new, sky-blue wings—faces: saving two entire worlds. (978-1-62639-691-3)

Coils by Barbara Ann Wright. A modern young woman follows her aunt into the Greek Underworld and makes a pact with Medusa to win her freedom by killing a hero of legend. (978-1-62639-598-5)

Courting the Countess by Jenny Frame. When relationship-phobic Lady Henrietta Knight starts to care about housekeeper Annie Brannigan and her daughter, can she overcome her fears and promise Annie the forever that she demands? (978-1-62639-785-9)

Dapper by Jenny Frame. Amelia Honey meets the mysterious Byron De Brek and is faced with her darkest fantasies, but will her strict moral upbringing stop her from exploring what she truly wants? (978-1-62639-898-6)

Delayed Gratification: The Honeymoon by Meghan O'Brien. A dream European honeymoon turns into a winter storm nightmare involving a delayed flight, a ditched rental car, and eventually, a surprisingly happy ending. (978-1-62639-766-8)

For Money or Love by Heather Blackmore. Jessica Spaulding must choose between ignoring the truth to keep everything she has, and doing the right thing only to lose it all—including the woman she loves. (978-1-62639-756-9)

Hooked by Jaime Maddox. With the help of sexy Detective Mac Calabrese, Dr. Jessica Benson is working hard to overcome her past, but they may not be enough to stop a murderer. (978-1-62639-689-0)

Lands End by Jackie D. Public relations superstar Amy Kline is dealing with a media nightmare, and the last thing she expects is for restaurateur Lena Michaels to change everything, but she will. (978-1-62639-739-2)

Twisted Screams by Sheri Lewis Wohl. Reluctant psychic Lorna Dutton doesn't want to forgive, but if she doesn't do just that, an innocent woman will die. (978-1-62639-647-0)

A Class Act by Tammy Hayes. Buttoned-up college professor Dr. Margaret Parks doesn't know what she's getting herself into when she agrees to one date with her student Rory Morgan, who is fifteen years her junior. (978-1-62639-701-9)

Bitter Root by Laydin Michaels. Small town chef Adi Bergeron is hiding something, and Griffith McNaulty is going to find out what it is even if it gets her killed. (978-1-62639-656-2)

Capturing Forever by Erin Dutton. When family pulls Jacqueline and Casey back together, will the lessons learned in eight years apart be enough to mend the mistakes of the past? (978-1-62639-631-9)

Deception by VK Powell. DEA Agent Colby Vincent and Attorney Adena Weber are embroiled in a drug investigation involving homeless veterans and an attraction that could destroy them both. (978-1-62639-596-1)

Dyre: A Knight of Spirit and Shadows by Rachel E. Bailey. With the abduction of her queen, werewolf-bodyguard Des must follow the kidnappers' trail to Europe, where her queen—and a battle unlike any Des has ever waged—awaits her. (978-1-62639-664-7)

First Position by Melissa Brayden. Love and rivalry take center stage for Anastasia Mikhelson and Natalie Frederico in one of the most prestigious ballet companies in the nation. (978-1-62639-602-9)

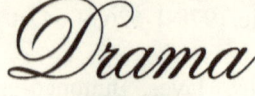

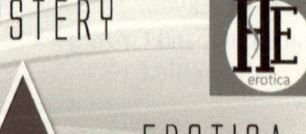
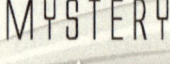

www.ingramcontent.com/pod-product-compliance
Lightning Source LLC
Chambersburg PA
CBHW030512020726
47494CB00004B/1064